FALL
FOR YOU
FELICE STEVENS

DEDICATION
To my family, for now and always.

ACKNOWLEDGMENTS

As always, thanks to my editor, Keren Reed for her unfailing patience with me. Thank you to Hope and Jess from Flat Earth Editing—sorry but you're stuck with me. Thank you to Dianne from Lyrical Lines—the Yankees could use someone like you for all the catches you make. And to Reese, thank you isn't enough for everything.

To all my readers, you are the reason I keep writing the stories inside my head. Thank you for allowing me to bring you love stories from my heart to yours.

CHAPTER ONE

Carson

"Good morning, Mr. Ballard. Your usual booth?"

"Yes, Peter, thanks," I responded carelessly, my gaze intent on the email I had open, still in disbelief at what I'd read.

Effective immediately, I quit.
Thomas Rollins
Executive Assistant to Carson Ballard
Ballard and Melbourne, Esq.

"He's got to be fucking kidding me," I growled and slid into the booth Peter brought me to. I hit Thomas's number on Speed Dial.

"I'm sorry, but Thomas can't come to the phone now. He's doing the happy dance of freedom. Leave your name at the tone."

The *beep* sounded, and I struggled to keep my voice to a whisper. "What the hell is going on? Is this some kind of sick fucking joke? When I get to the office, I'd better see your ass in your chair." I ended the call and glanced up to see a man standing in my view. "What?"

"Uh, hi. I'm your server? Davis? Do you know what you'd like?"

I considered him, narrowing my eyes. "What the hell happened to Demetri?"

Davis gave me a bright, perky smile I was too angry to appreciate, although I did admire how nicely he filled out the black slacks required of Peter's employees. Coupled with a stunning face and gorgeous eyes…no one should look that good so early in the morning.

"Demetri's sick. I'm filling in."

"Scrambled eggs, rye toast, dry, and coffee." I returned to the email on my phone, and it took a moment to realize the waiter hadn't yet departed. "Is something wrong?"

"I wasn't sure you were finished, since most people say thank you after they place an order with their server."

Astonished, I gaped at him. "Are you…schooling me in etiquette?" Under a swoop of dark hair, twinkling green-gold eyes met mine, and his lips curved in a grin that held little regret for his rudeness.

"If the shoe fits." With a shrug, he gave me his back before I could demand an apology. But I had little time to waste on some waiter with an attitude when I had to figure out what fresh hell my assistant had decided to rain down on me. I called him again. It rang four times until he finally picked up.

"I wasn't going to answer, but Norman said I should."

"Bully for Norman," I grumbled. "Do you mind telling me what the actual fuck is going on? You're joking, right?"

"Nope." He popped out the simple word and laughed with such abandon, my heart sank. "I'm done. Done-zo. Outta there."

"Why? Do you want more money? Is that it?" I had enough crap to deal with at the moment, and I paid him damn well to handle what I couldn't.

"You think throwing money at everything is the way to solve your problems."

"It doesn't hurt," I snapped. "You didn't mind your nice salary."

"And I earned every damn penny of it. Look, Carson. Unlike you, I want a life outside of the business, which for me means marriage and kids. Norman says—"

"Spare me your husband's golden words of wisdom. I've heard it all." I rolled my eyes. Norman was a psychologist, and in the few months Thomas had worked for me, Norman kept spouting theories on why I remained single.

He huffed in my ear, clearly exasperated. "This is exactly why I have to leave. You don't believe in anything besides work. All you think about is the business."

"Are you finished?" Stung by his harsh words, I dialed back the torrent of anger I wanted to unleash on him. He and I had spent every day trying to dig my family's law firm out of the hole my father and brother left it in when they died. I should've known Thomas would eventually screw me over and leave. Everyone did. "I know you love lists, Thomas, but spare me the A to Z of my failings."

"I'm telling you this so maybe you'll pull your head out of your ass. You're not responsible for your family's mistakes. You have nothing to prove to anyone."

My heart raced, and a fine sheen of sweat broke out over my face. I reached for a napkin to wipe myself. "Mistakes? That's what you call it? I don't have time for this shit. Have a fabulous life, and thanks for the pep talk." Without waiting for his response, I ended the call.

"Where the hell is my food, dammit? I don't have all morning," I muttered.

My waiter—whatever his name was, I couldn't remember—stood by the cashier with a smile, no doubt chatting up Louisa, the owner's daughter, hoping for a date, when he should have been getting me my breakfast. For Christ's sake, he hadn't even poured me a lousy cup of coffee. I raised my hand to get his attention, but he either ignored me or didn't see my hand motions.

"This is ridiculous." I flagged down a passing waiter. "Can you manage to pull Romeo over there away from Louisa and ask him to get me my coffee and see where my breakfast is?"

"Sure, sure. Lemme get him."

I watched as my waiter was informed of my displeasure, after which, with a nonchalant shrug, he picked up a coffeepot and strolled toward me.

"Sorry," he pretended to apologize as he poured. "I'll go check on your food."

"I would hope so. And don't bother Louisa. She's got a jealous boyfriend who's six three and lives in the gym. He could make mincemeat out of you."

He screwed up his face. "What? Who? Me?" He snorted with laughter. "She's not my type." Still cackling like a fool, he filled other diners' coffee cups and disappeared into the kitchen.

"Idiot," I mumbled and propped my chin in one hand as I scrolled through my calendar. With Thomas gone, I had to make sure I knew what the hell I had waiting for me today.

"Hello, sweetheart. Sorry I'm late." My mother air-kissed me, the scent of her Chanel perfume filling my nose.

"Not a problem. I've been here almost fifteen minutes and just got my first cup of coffee. Our waiter isn't the best."

"Demetri? He's never been a problem."

For years, my mother and I had been meeting for breakfast at this diner. As busy and public as it was, I could say anything here, unlike at home, where I'd never felt comfortable. I'd come out to her over this very table, my stomach tight with terror, hoping she'd still love me.

My mother was the only person in my immediate family

to accept me. My brother had refused to acknowledge it and used to keep trying to set me up with "the right women," while my father hadn't been able to stomach being in the same room with me. It was why I'd left soon after graduation from law school and lived abroad, in London, working in the estates and trust division of an international firm, handling issues for American clients living overseas. When Dale and my father died, I came home to help my mother manage her grief and to sift through the wreckage of the once proud firm of Ballard and Melbourne.

"No, it's not Demetri. Someone who doesn't give a damn."

"Oh, dear." Her eyes twinkled. "Someone's Mr. Grumpypuss today."

"I have reason to be annoyed." I scowled into my black coffee. "Thomas quit."

Her dark brows rose. "Why?"

I rolled my eyes. "Said he wants a family and kids and all that nonsense. But I know it's Norman making him give it up." My waiter came out holding three plates—one in each hand and the third on his arm. "One of those better be mine. I've been here over twenty minutes. I don't have all day."

He served the customers several seats away from us—people I knew had sat down after me—then came toward me with a plate of pancakes.

"That's not mine. I ordered eggs."

"I know. I never said it was yours. I wanted to know what the lovely lady would like."

Obviously this guy knew who to play up for the big tip. My mother always was a soft- touch.

"You're so sweet. I'll have the yogurt and fruit, please. And a cup of tea with lemon."

"Coming right up." His smile at my mother held all the warmth missing when he met my eyes with disdain. "Yours is ready. I'll get it for you in a second." He walked to the table behind us, and I called out after him.

"Good. I almost forgot what I ordered, it's been so long."

"Carson, be nice," my mother admonished. "He's trying his best, I'm sure."

"Sometimes your best isn't good enough. Thank God he doesn't work for me. He'd be gone in a day."

"Getting back to Thomas. What are you going to do? Did you have any idea this would happen?"

"He's been saying for some time that he didn't want to work the long hours, but I didn't pay attention. I figured it was being a newlywed." I finished my coffee and sighed with frustration, knowing that with the lousy service, it would be a while before I received any more.

"You're such a romantic, darling."

My lip curled with scorn. "I had great role models, didn't I? A father who hated me because I'm gay. A brother who made fun of me once I came out and said it was a choice, something he could change if I'd let him set me up with a woman. That I was destroying the sanctity of marriage, yet he was too busy running around with strippers and models to settle down himself."

"Your brother was troubled. He was always searching for something. I think that's why he drank so much." She fumbled for a tissue, and for the first time that morning, I regretted my words. For all that Dale and I didn't get along, he was her child too. My father was another story—he and my mother were divorced years ago but had remained cordial.

I waited for her to finish wiping her eyes, then reached for her hand. "I'm sorry, Mom. I didn't mean to upset you."

Shiny-eyed, she attempted a smile. "You didn't. I wish you and your brother could've made amends before..." Her lips trembled.

For her sake, I spoke the words she needed to hear. "I forgave him. I'd like to think eventually we could've worked it out." Because I loved my mother, I kept secret the true extent of my brother's hateful words and actions. There would've been no reconciliation. Ever.

"Right now, I have to figure out what the hell I'm going to do. I have deadlines Thomas and I were working on. Important meetings in the month ahead that I counted on having his help to prepare for." I drummed my fingers on the table. "Where *is* the food? For God's sake, I've never had to wait this long. It's not Jean-Georges; it's some stupid eggs."

"When are they going to stop harassing the firm?" my mother asked, unperturbed by my outburst. "Don't they realize how hard you're working to make things right?" Her smooth brow wrinkled.

"They don't care. And frankly, they shouldn't. Dad and Dale were treating the assets like their own personal piggy bank." Had they lived, my father—the esteemed Lawrence Ballard—and his first and favored son, Dale Ballard, would've most likely been disbarred and maybe even jailed. The waiter approached us with our plates. "Oh, thank God. Finally."

"Here we are." The waiter—Davis, I now remembered—set my mother's food gently in front of her, in direct contrast to how he plunked mine on the table. "I'll get your tea."

"And I need more coffee."

"You sure do."

My eyes narrowed. Was he making a joke at my expense? I picked up my fork and took a bite of eggs. "You've got to be kidding me."

"What's wrong?" My mother took a spoonful of yogurt.

Davis reappeared, and I beckoned him over and pushed the plate toward him. "These are inedible. I guarantee these eggs must've been sitting around for a while. They're cold. Plus, the toast has butter on it, and I said dry."

"I guess the kitchen forgot. Do you want a replacement?"

"Yes, I'm lactose intolerant."

"That explains a lot," he muttered under his breath and walked away, but I heard him and called out.

"What the hell is that supposed to mean?"

Slowly, he turned. "It's obvious why you're not happy—and who could blame you? No ice cream, grilled-cheese sandwiches, or pizza? What do you put on your bagels?" He shuddered. "I don't know if I could deal with it."

"I'd like my eggs hot, not a diatribe on my dietary restrictions." I gritted my teeth. "Plain rye toast and more coffee."

"Yes, sir." He snatched the offending plate and marched away, returning a moment later with my hot coffee. Lips twitching, he poured. "I can see if there's any nondairy creamer for your coffee."

I made a face. "No, that crap tastes like poison. I'll take it black."

"I should've known."

The man was too cocky for his own good.

He sauntered away, giving me a nice view of his ass in those tight black trousers—the only positive in this whole lousy morning.

"I can't tell if he's serious or making fun of me."

"Oh, leave the poor man alone. He's trying. It's not as if you're the easiest person." Eyes bright with laughter, my mother sipped her tea. "How was he supposed to know you don't eat dairy?"

"I don't know, okay? Anyway, I have more important things to think about than some smartass waiter. I have to figure out what I'm going to do…calls I have to make. It doesn't help that I have so few ties to the legal community here. I can't even call in favors." When I moved abroad, I didn't bother to keep up with any classmates from law school. Not that I'd made close friends there—I wasn't a fan of the cutthroat environment it fostered, so I kept to myself.

The laughter faded from my mother's eyes. She reached

out and placed her hand over mine. "I hate that this is such a burden on you. Maybe the best thing would be to close the firm, pay all the fines, and…" She sniffled.

My mother's family was as intricately tied to the firm as my father's. Her great-grandfather, Darius Melbourne, was a founding partner. My paternal grandfather joined the firm at the turn of the last century, and though my mother was the only living Melbourne relation, she had no desire to practice law. My father met her at a family function. They'd later married and joined the two names.

Shocking tears burned my eyes, and I allowed her touch for a moment, then slid my hand away. I refused to give in and admit defeat. I could almost hear the snickers from my father and brother. Failure was exactly what they would have expected and why no matter how long and hard I'd have to work, I would rebuild the firm—from the ashes if need be.

"It's fine. I can do it. I just need to get to the office, see if there's any possibility of persuading Thomas to come back, and if not, hire a new assistant." My stomach hurt at the thought of breaking in a new person. "Where the hell is my food? This is ridiculous."

"Carson, please calm yourself. You're worked up over nothing."

Nothing? My assistant up and leaving me wasn't a blip on the screen. But I wouldn't let my mother see how devastated it left me. That would be weak, and I'd learned early on, when I'd been called half a man, that I had to be twice as strong as everyone else.

Seething, I waited another minute. Seeing more orders come out and I still hadn't received my food, I rose to my feet. "This is outrageous. I'm leaving."

"Carson, don't—" Alarmed, my mother put out her hand, but I had zero patience left.

"No. I have to run."

"Watch out—" she cried.

Multiple plates smacked into me, and the cold, slimy residue of leftover food and condiments splashed over my face. All of it slithered down my neck onto my shirt and tie. Dripping wet, I stared into Davis's horrified eyes.

"I-I'm really sorry. I didn't see you standing there." He reached out and peeled a piece of soaking wet toast off my cheek. I batted his fingers away.

"Don't touch me, you damn fool." I brushed at my ruined suit, trying to rid myself of the mess of eggs, bacon, and coffee.

"Here, Carson." My mother handed me a paper napkin, and I almost laughed but took the tiny square anyway.

"Mr. Ballard, I'm so sorry." Peter rushed over, apologies tumbling from his lips. "Of course we'll pay for the dry cleaning."

"Which isn't going to help me now, Peter. Why is this guy even a waiter? He has no idea what the hell he's doing." Catching sight of Davis's pale, strained face, I almost felt bad for the man. Then a sticky piece of sausage fell off the top of my head to land on my shiny Ferragamo loafers.

"I know, I know. I'm sorry. He's not the best."

"Obviously. I don't want him to ever serve me again. God knows why he works here in the first place. Almost half an hour sitting here, and all I had was a single cup of coffee, which I had to ask for. Now I don't have any more time to waste. I have to go home, shower, change, and make it to the office within the hour. Not a problem, right?" I sneered.

I brushed past Davis, who had the audacity to put a hand on my arm. "I really am sorry. I didn't mean it."

We were the same height, and I gazed into his miserable face, refusing to notice how his long, damp lashes framed shiny hazel eyes. "I don't have time to listen to excuses."

I wrenched free and strode away, ignoring my mother calling my name.

CHAPTER TWO

Davis

I stared after the jerk's retreating back, feeling as though I'd been sucker-punched. At a tap on my shoulder, my heart sank at the sight of Peter's furious face.

"I was just—" But he put a hand up, and I snapped my mouth shut.

"Don't bother. It's the third time this week you screwed up, but this goes beyond giving someone the wrong sandwich or forgetting a side dish. Three strikes and you're out. I told you one more fuckup would be your last."

"I know, but I didn't see him. He appeared out of nowhere."

"Save it. The Ballards are valued customers and have been coming here for years. I can't afford to lose them, but I can get another waiter in a second. Pick up your check next week. You're done."

Giving me no time to respond, he walked away. All around me, I heard the whispers and murmurs of conversation. And even though I was technically fired, I kneeled to pick up the scattered dishes. I placed them in the bin for the busboys.

When I rose to my feet, the woman who'd been sitting with the man who got me fired touched my arm.

"I'm so sorry. Please. Sit with me for a moment."

Is she kidding?

"Ma'am, I can't. I've been fired. I have to leave. You heard what Peter said."

"Well, he didn't say that to me, and I'm a paying customer who can sit with whomever she wants. Now come." The firm tone was in direct contrast to her tiny stature and sweet expression. She pointed to the opposite side of the booth, and I had no idea why, but I listened to her. I slid inside and could still feel the warmth of the seat cushion as I settled into place. An unexpected tingle ran through me at the forbidden thought of my body being where his had been. He might be a jerk, but he was gorgeous—icy-blue eyes, a hard jaw, and a frowning mouth I'd bet was a dream to kiss.

"What's your name?"

"Davis. Davis Turner." I clasped my hands.

"I'm Patricia Ballard. First, let me apologize for my son's behavior."

"Please don't. He's a grown man, and I'm sure he is fully capable of understanding how to speak to people nicely." I allowed a smile. "After all, you're his mother, and here we are, being civil."

"Yes, well…Carson, for all the privilege he's grown up with, hasn't had it as easy as people might think."

I tried to remain impassive, but my mother used to say my biggest failing was the inability to hide my true feelings in my facial expressions. Today was no exception.

"I see you don't believe me." She raised a well-groomed brow.

"Ma'am, no disrespect, but I've seen his type my whole

life. And that's not to say everyone who has money is rude or…"

I hesitated. I wanted to say, *or is a jerk, like your son,* but refrained. She didn't deserve to bear the brunt of my annoyance. Plus, I had to admit, I was equally at fault. I sucked as a waiter.

"Davis, I'm not trying to excuse his behavior. But to be fair, he wasn't all in the wrong, was he?"

I squirmed under her kind but stern gaze. "No, ma'am. I wasn't exactly the best waiter."

"Still, the fact remains that you're out of work, and I feel badly. The least I can do is try and help."

"Thank you for your concern, but it's not the first time I've messed up." I rose from my seat and gave her a slight nod. "And now I really do have to leave."

"I understand, and I'm truly sorry. I wish there was something I could do."

I shrugged. "I'll be fine. Have a nice day."

I left her seated and strode through the restaurant and kitchen to the little room in the back where the employees changed. Despite my brave words to Patricia Ballard, I was scared to death to be out of work in a city like New York. As frugal as I was, my expenses were still out of control. It was the reason my parents wanted me to stay upstate, but with my ex breathing down my neck everywhere I turned, I'd known I had to leave.

And where better to run and lick your wounds than the anonymity of New York City? I wasn't a kid with stars in his eyes. I was a thirty-one-year-old man who might not have street smarts but had already learned enough about life and its letdowns.

I took off the vest and shirt and put on the polo I'd worn this morning. I folded the pants, placing them on top of the shirt and vest, then slipped into my jeans and shoved my feet into my sneakers. Finished with my wardrobe change, instead of leaving, I sat on the bench and rubbed my face.

What the hell was I going to do now?

Well, whatever it is, it's not going to be here. I cast a final, rueful glance at my work clothes, and with my head held high, retraced my steps, giving a wave to the guys in the kitchen. Pedro, the line cook, his face red and sweaty from standing in front of the grill, called out.

"Sucks, man. Peter's a damn fool."

A barely there smile tugged at my lips. "Yeah, well, it is what it is. See ya around."

"Good luck."

I'm gonna need it...

I found Patricia Ballard waiting for me by the front register. At my approach, she placed her small self in front of me, blocking my exit. I was surprised by her forceful nature, although considering her son's disposition, it made sense. She put up a hand.

"Please let me speak."

"Why?" My brow furrowed. "I don't mean to be rude, but I'm not sure what you want from me."

"Please sit with me. There's a quiet booth in the corner where we can talk."

"Uh, Mrs. Ballard, you heard Peter tell me to leave and—"

"And he knows better than to interfere with me," she smoothly interrupted, a twinkle in her cornflower-blue eyes. "My family and I have been coming to his diner for over thirty years."

Bemused and bewildered, I trailed behind her to the booth tucked into the corner and sat across from her. "Look, I'm not the best waiter. I'm not even a good one. If I didn't get fired today, it would've happened soon enough. I'll find another job." My words sounded brave, but I didn't fool her.

"I do want you to understand something."

I laced my fingers on the tabletop. "If you're going to

apologize again—"

"I'm not. As I said, being under tremendous stress isn't an excuse for Carson's bad behavior. My son might've given up everything to come home and take over the firm, but he shouldn't take his problems out on you. That, coupled with his assistant quitting today without notice…" Her sizable diamond ring slipped sideways, and she played with it, staring at the Formica tabletop, unable to meet my eyes. "It's a lot on his shoulders," she whispered. "He's worried."

Dammit. I knew I shouldn't ask, but I couldn't stop myself. "What does he have to worry about?"

Ignoring my question, she posed one of her own. "What did you do before working as a waiter?"

"I, uh, worked for the mayor's office where I lived, upstate. It's a small town."

"And politics can be as bad as law."

"It can be exciting but a den of vipers as well. Both inside and out." My lips thinned. "I learned to watch my back."

"Our firm has suffered since the death of my son and ex-husband."

"I'm very sorry for your loss."

She took a napkin from the table and dabbed at her eyes. "Thank you. Carson is doing his best to work through it all, but I can't help him, except to offer encouragement."

"What kind of law?"

"Trusts and estates, some corporate. Ballard and Melbourne has been in the city for over a hundred years. My great-grandfather founded it, and Carson's grandfather joined sometime later."

Why was I not surprised? Carson Ballard had the trust-fund-baby look, and even more, the attitude of someone who'd grown up with every wish and whim catered to. I'd seen and had enough personal experience of that kind of behavior with Brian, who came from money as well. Back then I was young, dumb, and in love. Not any longer.

"Thank you for explaining it all, but now I really have to go. If there's one thing I've learned living in the city, it's that you can't afford to live here if you don't have a job. So if you'll excuse me…" I rose, but she grabbed my hand in a strong grip.

"Please? Just another second."

"I don't understand what you want from me."

A cunning light brightened her eyes. "I can fix your problem."

"My problem? You mean you know where I can get another job right away?" A smile curved her lips, and a dangerous, truly awful thought hit me. "Oh…no. Wait a minute. If you're thinking what I think you're thinking…"

"It makes perfect sense. Carson needs an assistant, and you've worked in a fast-paced environment. I'm sure you know how to schedule appointments, answer phones… everything an assistant needs to do."

"You want me to work for him? The man can't stand me. That's ridiculous."

Could this day get any weirder?

"Why ridiculous? Do you have anything better in the works?" she questioned in a no-nonsense manner.

"Well, no, but all this just happened in the past hour." I played with the folded napkin on the table. "Besides, what makes you think your son will want to hire me?"

Her laughter rose around us. "Carson is so frazzled, he'd take anyone who walked through the door."

"Not exactly how I like to be hired. Desperation."

"But we need you."

"We?" I asked, a bit baffled. "I thought it was your son who needed a new assistant. And let's be real. I doubt he'd want to hire me."

"True." Those sharp eyes met mine. "But while my son might be desperate, one thing he's not is stupid. He needs help." She reached into her purse, which I knew cost close to one month's rent on my tiny studio sublet, and took out a Chanel card holder and a pen. She scribbled a phone number, then slid the engraved ivory rectangle across the table. "Here's my card and my personal cell."

Because it would be rude not to, I took it and shoved it into my pocket.

This was all too bizarre.

"I'm sorry, Mrs. Ballard. I appreciate it, but I can't accept your very generous offer."

This time when I rose to leave, she let me go.

* * *

I went home, took a shower, and stared at the computer, browsing job listings. There were tons of jobs for assistants, but they'd need references, and I refused to give them Brian's name. The moment they contacted him, he'd use his considerable charm to find out where I lived, and I'd never be free. For almost two years, I'd successfully avoided him, and I wasn't about to give myself away now.

My phone rang, and seeing it was my father, I put a smile on my face and hit the screen. Another person I couldn't reveal the truth to—but for a completely different reason.

"Hey, Dad. How's it going? How's the weather down there?" My parents had retired and moved to a fifty-five-plus community in Florida where they made a whole new life for themselves. I visited them for all the holidays, and though I was glad they were happy with their circle of friends, I missed them.

"Great as usual. Eighty and sunny. Your mother's at the pool with her girlfriends."

"And you're with the guys?"

"Yeah. We just finished a game of cards, and we're waiting for the pool table to be free. I played a round of golf early this morning.”

"Rough life,” I joked.

"How's it going up there?”

"It's going great,” I answered, maybe a little too heartily.

"You sure about that? You sound funny.”

My parents and I were very close, and I never lied to them, although for the first time, I contemplated it. The last thing I wanted was to worry them about my jobless situation. My mother's heart attack five years ago had shaken me. I'd never considered my parents' mortality before sitting by her bedside in ICU. When she recovered, I'd urged them to close the small general store they ran and move. They didn't need to deal with twelve-hour days of standing on their feet, nor with battling upstate winter weather.

"Yeah, Dad, I'm good.”

"Brian hasn't been around, has he?”

"No. Of course not.” I rubbed my eyes. I couldn't keep up the pretense. "Uh, I don't want you telling Mom, but I got fired today.”

Dad sighed long and loud. "Why? What happened? I thought things were going okay, although I still can't understand why you're wasting your time as a waiter when you could get a computer job. Companies are always looking for qualified people like you.”

"Things were going fine, more or less. Until this morning.” I replayed my unfortunate breakfast service.

"Ouch. Dumping dirty plates onto a joker like that must've pissed him off.”

"Well…I'm not exactly innocent. If I'm honest, I'm a terrible waiter and I was sort of on my last legs there. I can't blame the guy entirely.”

"Hmph. Peter's still an idiot. He should've docked your pay or something instead of firing you.”

"Peter didn't owe me anything. You're only saying that because you're my father.”

"So what're you gonna do now?"

"I'm already on the hunt. Hopefully I'll have something soon." I mustered a laugh. "Want to hear something crazy?"

"Sure."

In the background, I heard a shout. "Hey, Greg. C'mon. We got the table."

"I'll be there in a minute," he yelled in return. "Go ahead," he urged.

"The guy who got me fired was having breakfast with his mother. She was nice—I swear you'd never know they were related. Anyway, he left, but she stayed afterward to talk to me, and get this: She offered me a job. To work for him as his personal assistant."

"You're kidding." His disbelief came through loud and clear.

"No. I thought it was a joke, but she was dead serious."

"What did you say?"

"What do you think?" I chuckled. "I told her thanks but no thanks. I have no patience for snobby rich guys. Can you imagine working for someone like him? He hates me, I'm sure. The last thing he'd want is to see me every day and be reminded of all those plates dumped on him."

"All true. But it *would* solve your problem. You do need a job, and it probably pays a whole lot better than slinging hash. Waiting tables was never supposed to be a permanent thing, and yet you've been doing it since you moved to the city."

"I tried retail, but I couldn't get enough hours to make it worthwhile." I hated when my father made sense. "I guess I'll have to see. I'll spend the day making calls and sending out my résumé. I'm sure something will turn up."

"I gotta go, but don't take too long. Job offers don't come on trees, you know."

"Yeah, I get it. I'll talk to you soon, Dad. Say hi to Mom."

"I will. Keep me posted. Bye."

The conversation concluded, I set the phone aside and redoubled my efforts to find another job, but the positions I was qualified for wanted the references I wasn't prepared to give.

I lived paycheck to paycheck, and I'd sublet the apartment from a Craigslist posting. I didn't know anyone in the city I could crash with, and I refused to let my best friend, Tommy, know I was in a bind. He'd tell me to come home, which wasn't an option. It was my problem to solve.

Over my parents' objections, I'd signed on as guarantor of their medical bills for what Medicare didn't cover, and I made payments for them if needed to prevent a default. As a waiter, I wasn't bringing in enough money, so I'd take the occasional online coding job for start-up companies. Of course, I wasn't the only one in the city with a side hustle, and the jobs weren't all that plentiful. I sent my parents what I could, but I refused to let them know how badly I struggled. Again, my foolishness had caused this situation, and I'd get out of it. Eventually.

None of this would be happening if I'd listened to my gut and not given in to Brian's sweet-talking ways. Chalk it up to being young and dumb, the thrill overtaking common sense. I knew sleeping with your boss was wrong, but sleeping with your boss who was in the closet? Never good. Oh yeah, and who was also the mayor of our town. Can't forget that brilliant fact. It didn't get much stupider on my part. I should've done my job and kept him at a distance.

"I'll find something," I said heartily to the empty room.

Three days later found me with an aching back, numb fingers, and burning eyes from too many hours spent staring at the computer screen, counting my rejections. Shadows crept around the walls of my studio as the daylight hours melted into evening.

"You are so screwed," I muttered to myself as I heated

up a frozen burrito from Trader Joe's. Rent was due in a week, and the other bills were coming in fast and furious.

I sat on the lumpy couch, pulled the card out of my wallet, and stared at it before turning it over to read the neatly printed phone number.

I can't do this...

My phone dinged with a notification from the bank that my overdraft had been activated. Which meant I had less than 250 dollars in my account.

"God help me, I hope I don't end up regretting this." I entered the number and listened to it ring.

"Hello?"

"Hello? Mrs. Ballard? This is Davis Turner…the waiter who was fired…" I gulped. "I'd like to talk."

CHAPTER THREE

Carson

"I'm sorry, what?"

My brows drew together as I listened to Edward, my new assistant.

"I said I quit." He stuffed his phone into his suit pocket and snatched his wallet from the desk drawer, as if he were afraid I might steal it.

"You've been here two days."

Edward drew himself up to his long, skinny height. "That's a day longer than Anthony, the man I replaced, isn't it?"

"What the hell is that supposed to mean?"

For someone who couldn't remember I didn't take milk in my coffee, he sure was feisty with me.

"It means you're impossible to work for. You don't need an assistant. You need a punching bag."

"I spent half the morning in the bathroom because I thought the bagel you got me had tofu cream cheese and my milk had nondairy creamer." I touched my stomach—it was still tender and gurgled under my fingertips.

"It was an honest mistake." A malicious grin tipped up his lips. "My bad."

I knew it wasn't a mistake.

"You mixed up names from phone calls, forgot to give me my messages…is there anything you did do right?"

"Yes. Quitting." He pushed past me to the elevator, leaving me staring after him.

"Son of a bitch," I whispered to myself as the phone lines lit up. I snatched the receiver. "Ballard and Melbourne, please hold." I pressed the appropriate button. "Ballard and Melbourne, please hold." Placing the second caller on hold, I returned to the first. "Hello, may I help you?"

"This is Lionel Hastings with First National Bank, is Mr. Ballard available?"

"Yes, Mr. Hastings. This is him speaking."

"We need to reschedule our meeting today for next week."

Startled, I glanced at the computer screen in front of me that showed my monthly appointments, and blinked. It was blank. I rubbed my eyes and stared at it harder as if to conjure up what I needed to see. Still empty, terrifyingly so, as I knew I had appointments for the entire month, and now they'd simply disappeared.

Like my sanity.

"C-certainly. When would you like to meet?" I flailed and grabbed a pad and pen. The front door to the office suite opened, and my mother walked in with a man several steps behind her.

"Next Tuesday at ten. Does that work for you?"

I wanted to yell, *I have no fucking clue*, but I needed to remain on his good side, as I had to set up new business accounts for the firm. Ballard and Melbourne's legal issues were no secret, and I could only hope Hastings was in a forgiving mood and would understand that I wasn't the responsible party who'd led the firm down its destructive path.

I was the sucker left to pick up the pieces.

But at the moment I had another problem to deal with. My jaw dropped, and I only half listened to Hastings. What the hell was the waiter from Peter's restaurant doing in my office? And in a suit, no less.

"Mr. Ballard?" Hastings's sharp tone snapped me to reality.

"Yes, yes sir, I'll see you then." I ended the call.

"Carson, we need to talk."

"We sure as hell do, Mother, but I have another call waiting, and Edward just quit on me, so…" Overwhelmed, I held up my hands.

Without a word, the waiter—*What was his name?*—reached over and answered the phone. "Ballard and Melbourne, how may I help you?"

"What *the hell* is going on here?" I asked my mother, who, with a self-satisfied smile on her lips, took my elbow and pulled me aside, ignoring my protests. "Wait. Stop. What is he doing? He can't answer the phones—"

"Will you please be quiet for a second?" Normally cool, it had been years since I'd seen her ire raised. "Yes, he can." She paused. "I hired Davis. To be your assistant."

I barked out a laugh. "You're kidding."

Really, I had to pride myself on my restraint because that was a PG version of what I really wanted to say, which was, *Are you out of your fucking mind?*

My mother's diminutive stature had fooled many into thinking she was merely a pretty confection, but woe to those who made that assumption. She held an English literature degree from Barnard and had worked as an editor for several major magazines. She sat on the board of MOMA, the New York Public Library, and several other major corporations.

Once she made a decision, she rarely wavered. Like now. She fixed me with a steely-eyed gaze.

"It's the obvious choice. Davis, poor man, still hasn't found a job. Three days he's been looking, with no success. Maybe you don't know how hard it is to live in this city because you've been lucky enough never to have to worry, but Davis does. His rent is due, and he'll be on the street if he doesn't find a job soon." The glare intensified, and I shifted, unable to meet her eyes.

Damn. I hated getting called out by my mother. It made me feel five instead of almost thirty-five. And she was correct. I'd acted like a total asshole that morning at Peter's, taking out my problems on Davis for no other reason than frustration and fear. The following day, I'd returned for breakfast and Peter had been all too happy to inform me he'd fired the clumsy waiter. I'd had a heaping serving of guilt along with my eggs and toast.

"But...my assistant? Why? You know enough people who could probably help him."

"Because he's not the only one who needs help. You have a problem keeping people—two now in three days, it looks like?" She raised a well-manicured brow, and my face heated. "Give him a chance."

I peered over my shoulder to see him sitting at the desk, fielding calls as if he'd been doing it for years. He must've felt the weight of my stare, as his eyes met mine and immediately darted away.

"I-I don't know."

"Well, I do," my mother said briskly, as if the matter had already been settled, and gathered her purse. "You need an assistant. I hired him, and he's staying."

Who was I kidding? I recognized that look—I'd been seeing it since I was a child, anytime I refused to eat my vegetables, or when I was a teenager and had been caught sneaking in past curfew. I was stuck.

I sighed. "I'll give it a shot, but if he proves to be as adept at answering phones as he was at waiting tables, he's not going to last."

"You'd be better off concentrating on what *you* have to do rather than Davis's ability to answer your phone." Her expression softened. "I know coming home has been a rough road, and you've had to deal with the brunt of problems that weren't your doing. It's more than any one person should have to bear."

My spine stiffened. "I'm fine. It's being dealt with."

"Of course it is. But at what cost? I hate seeing how it's changed you."

"It hasn't," I replied, my lips thin and numb. "This is who I am. Now I have to figure out what the hell Edward did to the calendar that erased all my appointments."

"I'm sure Davis will be able to help." The phone rang, and Davis answered it, as professionally as before. "See? He'll be perfect for you."

With a kiss, she left, and my stomach churned with frustration and fear as I kept an eye on the man sitting in front of me. He finished the conversation, and eyes lowered, clasped his hands on the desk. Waiting.

"Well." I cleared my throat. "This is slightly awkward."

"Just slightly?" he responded with a hint of a smile.

"First of all, thank you for jumping in and taking the phone calls."

"You're welcome. I'm sorry if that was pushy, but you looked a little overwhelmed."

"A little? I think you're being too nice."

He raised his gaze to meet mine, and a punch of lust hit me in the stomach. Which I immediately quashed. Davis might have eyes like stained-glass windows and a sweet smile, but I was less concerned with my dick at the moment than how to extricate the firm from the mess I was floundering in.

"Maybe so, considering the circumstances." Again that quiet smile.

"Yeah, well…" God, this was painful. And annoying as hell. I hated being on the defensive and at a disadvantage. I should be able to say I was sorry for getting him fired and move on. Like a fucking adult. Apparently, today was not going to be that day.

"Maybe you can help me. My assistant quit, and all the appointments on my calendar are gone. I have no idea what I have waiting for me the rest of the week. Or month, for that matter."

"Funny, isn't it, how sometimes things happen even to the best of us that are out of our control? I guess it's all in the way we learn to deal with it." He blinked, his smile growing wider.

"I don't need to be schooled," I snapped, my temper rising as I watched his brow quirk. "Maybe this isn't going to work. I know my mother hired you because she felt sorry for you, but if you have no idea—"

"But I do. I worked in an office for years before coming to New York. I can answer phones, set up a calendar, and keep your office running. I'm an excellent personal assistant."

"Better than carrying dirty dishes, I hope?" I smirked.

His jaw hardened. "And yes. Your mother did feel sorry for me, and I never would've reached out to her if my situation wasn't getting dire. All that aside, like I said, I can help you." He squared his shoulders and met my eyes. "I'm not lying."

"I never said you were." Our gazes clashed, and the phone rang. He made no move to answer it, and my toes curled in my loafers. One thing I prided myself on was my immediate attention to clients, and hearing the phone ringing, unanswered, drove me up the fucking wall.

"Okay. Go ahead and take the call. I'll wait."

Without breaking eye contact, Davis picked up the

receiver. "Ballard and Melbourne, how may I help you?"

The smoothness of his greeting led me to believe he was telling the truth, but I'd hold off on a final decision until I heard the entire conversation.

"Yes. Judge Landon's chambers at eleven thirty?" Brows raised, Davis looked to me, and I nodded. "He'll be there. Thank you for confirming."

I'd been preparing for the meeting and ready to beg, borrow, and plead to the judge not to let the sins of the father—and older brother—be visited on the younger child.

Me.

I sent him a thumbs-up, left him at the desk, and entered my office. I clicked on the file to bring up my notes…and nothing. Frantic, I clicked and clicked, my panic rising with each second ticking by. I tried the most recent, the trash, and nothing.

Zero. Zip. Nada.

"No, no, no," I muttered, the panic rising to choke me. "What the actual fuck?" I ran my hands over my sweating face. "Okay. Calm down. Maybe it's a glitch. Turn it off and on. That always works."

I pushed the button, watched the screen go black, then turned the computer on again. "Please, please, please." I sent up a prayer to anyone and anything that might be listening. I opened the file.

Empty.

"Ahhhh. No!" I screamed, and my door slammed open and Davis skidded through, the panic on his face mirroring what I knew to be on my own.

"What's wrong?" He came to a stop in front of me.

"It's—they're gone. Everything. All the notes I prepared for the meeting." I pointed at the worthless computer. "That *bastard*. He knew he was quitting, so he deleted everything just to fuck me up. I'll-I'll ruin him."

As I ranted, Davis circled the desk to stand behind me.

"Do you mind if I try something?"

"No, have at it, please. I looked everywhere. It was supposed to be backing up every minute, but I can't find anything. I never can. I hate these fucking machines."

He leaned over my shoulder, and I inched away. I was in full-fledged freak-out mode, but that didn't stop me from noticing how good he smelled. How warm his skin felt when it brushed mine.

Get a grip.

It must have been my fragile emotional state brought on by my teetering on the brink of potential disaster. I watched Davis's large, capable hands move over my keyboard and heard him muttering to himself.

"Come on. Here we go. Keychain access…aha!" A big smile lit up his face. "Is this what you're looking for?"

He highlighted something, opened it, and pages popped up. All my notes. Pages and pages.

"Oh, my God. That's it." Disbelieving, I scrolled through the first set. "The formatting is funky, but I don't give a shit."

"If you give me a little time, I can redo it for you, put it on Google Drive, and also set up Dropbox as an extra backup so you never have to worry. You can share the file with whomever you want, and it'll be accessible from any computer."

His words sounded like gobbledygook to me, but I didn't care. I had the notes I needed, and my heart returned to its normal rhythm. "I…thank you. I never would've been able to find these. I have no idea what you did, but I owe you. Big-time."

He stepped away from me. "No, you don't owe me anything. When I work for someone, this is how I roll. I give my best every day."

Funny enough, even though I knew little to nothing about Davis, I believed him. Frankly, he was the better person, because I didn't know if I would've jumped in so quickly to help someone who'd fucked me over.

Still, I couldn't resist teasing him a bit. "Except when you're carrying dirty plates."

He blushed, but those gorgeous eyes sparkled back at me. "I can always try that too. You have any around here you need me to clear?"

It was a crazy turn of events, but then again, my whole life had been flipped upside down over the past months. I'd barely gotten my feet under me, working endless days and nights, digging out from under the mess left to clean up. At the first whiff of a scandal, my father's and Dale's secretaries had both fled the firm and never returned my calls. I was alone, swimming in a sea of sharks. What had almost happened today would've been a disaster.

If not for Davis.

"No, but I think there's an empty desk out front waiting for you. Better get to work. See if you can do the same magic for my calendar like you just did for my files."

He grinned and saluted me. "Yes, *Boss*."

He made it to the doorway before I stopped him.

"Hey, Davis."

Midstride, he peered over his shoulder. "Yeah?"

"Thank you. And welcome to the firm."

CHAPTER FOUR

Davis

"It's after six, Davis. Go home," Carson called out from behind his computer screen.

"Actually, it's almost seven. And when you leave, I leave."

"Damn, is it really?" Hearing his surprise, I swiveled around and found him rubbing his eyes. "I guess I lost track of time."

Carson had spent the entire time since I'd started the job, locked in his office. I'd sat at my desk, the phone mostly silent, which I knew was not a good sign. Occasionally, a call from a client would come in, asking to have their files sent to another firm, and when Carson found out, I swore he died a little inside. I had enough work to keep me busy, having done a deep dive into his computer system to clean up his former assistant's amateurish attempt at destroying his files.

The work was massively time-consuming—the filing

system was a mess and was going to take weeks to sort out, while I still needed to keep Carson on track with his calendar, which I'd decided to print. I hesitated before tapping on the open door.

"Come on in." His smile was weary, and dark circles rimmed his bright-blue eyes. "You don't need to knock."

"I always want to respect your privacy. Here." I offered him the paper. "This is your calendar for the rest of this week and the next. For some odd reason, I have a feeling you prefer paper to computers."

He took it and laughed. "You do, huh? Well, you're right. I like something tangible. Something I can hold in my hand. After almost losing all my work, I'll never again rely on a computer to keep track of my records."

"I'll make sure to have them for you every Friday for the upcoming week."

Frowning, Carson focused his attention on the screen. "Damn. Lacy Johnson's sister just emailed."

My brows rose. "Lacy Johnson, the Broadway singer?"

"Yeah. We're trustees of her estate. Due to all the bad publicity surrounding the firm, her family wants to remove us and go with another firm." He dropped his head in his hands. "It would be a huge loss. Not only monetarily, but publicity-wise. I'm trying to stop the bleeding of our client list so we don't go totally bankrupt, but I'm beginning to wonder if it's a losing battle."

It was hard to reconcile the coldly arrogant man who'd belittled me at the restaurant with this broken man. What had happened? I suspected his mother had only touched the tip of the iceberg when she told me the firm had encountered problems after the deaths of Carson's father and brother.

"Is there anything I can do to help?"

Carson raised his gaze, eyes blazing fire and his mouth set in a hard line. "I don't normally dump on people. Forget it. It'll be fine. You should go home."

"One thing you'll find out about me? I don't always do what I should." I crossed my arms. "So that's not happening."

He smirked. "Already giving me a hassle and it's only the first week."

My lips twitched. "What can I say? I'm a rebel." I spotted several candy wrappers on his desk. "Did you even eat lunch today?"

He shrugged. "No time." He swept up the wrappers and crumpled them in his hand. "And sorry. I ate all my candy. I have nothing left to share."

"That's not real food. It's dinnertime."

"That's why it's time to leave and go have something to eat." He chewed his lip, his eyes returning to the computer screen. "I still have things to catch up on here. Besides, I have plans for dinner."

"A date?" At his raised brow, I grew hot and shrugged. "Okay. Fine. I'll see you tomorrow."

I walked away and made a pit stop in the restroom before picking up my things at my desk, which was how I heard him on the phone.

Eavesdropping wasn't a good look, but I never said I was perfect. I should leave, really. But like I told Carson, I never did the things I should, and so I stayed, listening.

"Babe, it's Carson. How the hell are you? Miss me?" Carson's laugh sent a funny pang of pity through me. "How about dinner? Haven't seen you since last summer in the Med. That was a wild night, hmm?"

I strained to hear the conversation.

"Oh, you are? That's great…Yeah, yeah, I understand. I wouldn't want my boyfriend meeting a hookup either… No problem. Bye." Carson grunted. "Dammit."

Knowing how much he'd hate it if he knew I'd overheard his failure, I hustled out of the office and down the elevator. I left the building but stayed outside, my thoughts still on Carson and his attempt to find a date. Funny how an opinion can change in a hot second. I'd gone from anger toward a selfish, spoiled man-child who didn't get his way, to my having my heartstrings tugged.

My decision was based on nothing more than sympathy, and I returned to the lobby and waited. Foolish, for sure, because Carson could remain upstairs for hours, now that he had no one to meet. But I didn't think he would and was proved correct when a little over half an hour later, Carson's tall, broad form exited the elevator.

I fell into step beside him. "So where's dinner?"

He stopped dead. "I thought you left."

"I did, but I had no desire to go home yet."

God, he was attractive. What I'd first seen as arrogance, I'd now describe as confidence, both in the set of his shoulders and the hint of the devil on his lips. The only thing saving me was the fact that he was straight. I could suffer my man-crush knowing I was safe.

He gazed at me thoughtfully. "How about I be the nice boss and take you to dinner to celebrate your first week—do you like sushi?"

Taken off guard, a horrendous rush of embarrassment flooded me. I hadn't acted the least bit professional, starting with the eavesdropping on his conversation and now waiting around for him.

"You-you don't have to do this. I'm going home."

Confusion clouded his eyes. "What's wrong? I thought you were hungry."

"Yeah, but you're my boss. It wouldn't look right."

"To whom? This is New York City. No one gives a shit." A charming smile curved his lips. "Now come on. I'm starving."

Less than ten minutes later, I found myself seated across from Carson at a small table in the corner of a bustling Japanese restaurant. The server came by to take our drink order.

Carson said, "I'll have a dry martini. What about you?"

"Do you have lychee martinis?"

"Yes, sir."

"I'll have one of those."

Eyes dancing, Carson laughed. "I see you're not from the club of hard drinkers."

"Hey," I protested. "Don't knock 'em till you try 'em. They're delicious." A little place Brian used to take me for dinner had introduced them to me, and I'd been hooked ever since.

"If you say so." Expecting that awkward time where we'd basically run out of things to say, I was surprised when Carson turned chatty. "Since you weren't hired in the conventional way…" He smirked, and my face heated. "Tell me about yourself. Other than knowing you're a whiz and lifesaver when it comes to computers, I don't know anything about you."

A good thing, in my opinion, as I could reinvent who I was. Carson Ballard didn't seem like the type who mixed business with pleasure.

"Not much to tell. I grew up in a small town upstate, pretty rural. My parents ran the local general store, and I stayed put. I went to college nearby, and after graduation, came home to help them. My degree was in political science and information technology."

"Poli-sci? You wanted to be a lawyer?"

The server brought our drinks and asked what we'd like to order.

"Should we do a bunch of things and share?" Carson looked to me. "Or do you want your own?"

If we hadn't started out with that awful encounter in the restaurant, I could actually like Carson. But we had, and I'd seen how angry he could get in a flash. I refused to let my guard down.

"I'm fine with sharing. I like everything."

He ordered a few different rolls, a plate of sashimi, spring rolls, and vegetable gyozas. "Remind me not to make a habit of skipping lunch. They always tell you not to go to the supermarket hungry, but the same could be said about a restaurant." He sipped his drink. "You didn't answer. Did you want to be a lawyer? Is that why you chose poli-sci?"

I took a sip of my martini and licked my lips from the sweetness. "I don't know…I never really thought about it—and I sure as hell couldn't afford law school anyway. I was interested in politics. How laws come to pass and the entire system of constitutionality. But I ended up using my degree in IT more."

"And thank God for that," Carson quipped and raised his glass. "Thank you again for saving my ass. I can't begin to tell you how devastating the loss of all my notes would've been." An angry flush darkened his face. "I'm going to fucking destroy Edward."

Whoa. Okay. There was the man I'd seen and disliked.

"Why bother?" My lychee martini tasted delicious, and the liquor loosened my tongue. "He's gone, and your problem is solved."

Carson's brows drew together. "Because he fucked me over. He shouldn't be allowed to get away with it. He's probably sitting somewhere laughing about it." Carson stared into his glass. "No one screws me and gets to walk away without consequences."

Our appetizers arrived, and I took a spring roll and one gyoza. When I noticed him not eating, I motioned to the rest. "Have at it. I know you're starving."

He dipped the spring roll, then crunched it but kept talking. "You couldn't have had much time for lunch yourself this week. Not with all the work you did."

Carson didn't need to know I subsisted on peanut-butter sandwiches and whatever was cheapest and on sale at the supermarket that was easy to heat and eat. At the restaurant,

Peter had given us meals during our shifts, and I missed it.

I swallowed. "It's fine. But I'm serious. Why waste your time on someone who isn't worth it? Edward's gone, and you'd be better off forgetting he existed rather than giving space in your head to someone who I'm sure isn't thinking of you. Like when you found out I was fired. I'm sure you didn't give me a second thought."

Carson flushed a deep red and chewed his gyoza. "Yeah…well. I am sorry about that. But people can't get away with making me look like a fool. He deliberately sabotaged me." He set down his chopsticks and focused on me with a penetrating stare. "I want loyalty in the people who work for me. Is that too much to ask?"

"Uh, n-no. Of course not. It's just…you have so much to do. I figured it would be better to spend your time concentrating on that, not on some random guy you'll never see again."

Carson took another gyoza without breaking eye contact. "What do you know of my situation? You speak as if you've done some research." Instead of eating, he waited for my answer.

Dammit. I shifted in my seat and toyed with the stem of my glass. "No. Your mother said there were some problems after your father and brother died." The hard line of Carson's mouth drooped, and I immediately tried to backpedal. "Sorry. Forget I mentioned it."

Carson silently finished his food, and when the rolls arrived, he ate without speaking. Feeling awkward as hell, I toyed with my food. Carson pointed a chopstick at my plate.

"Something wrong? I think they're delicious."

"No. They're fine. It's all good."

"So why aren't you eating?"

I picked up a roll and shoved it into my mouth. "Okay?"

"No soy sauce or ginger? Heathen." His cheek creased in a smile, and a dimple winked at me.

Despite my initial reservations, I was enjoying myself. My lips twitched, and I set my chopsticks on my plate. "Look, I don't care what happened. And you don't have to be concerned about loyalty. I work for you now, and however we started off isn't relevant."

"That's very mature," Carson mused.

"You sound surprised." I ate a roll, properly this time, with wasabi, soy sauce, and ginger.

"Well, all I know about you is that you're a whiz with computers, and you shouldn't be allowed to hold more than two plates at once."

"You're never going to let me forget that, are you?"

"I was traumatized. It will take me weeks to recover." There went that charming smile again, and I fought to ignore the flutter in my belly.

"It's going to take me some time to recover from you acting so nice to me." Where the hell I'd gotten the confidence to talk to Carson like this, I had no idea.

"Don't get too used to it. Tomorrow I'll be back to my usual sarcastic, obnoxious self." His smirk grew wider, and he popped another roll into his mouth.

The problem with that was, I enjoyed both Carson Ballards.

Damn. I might be in trouble.

CHAPTER FIVE

Carson

With Davis as my assistant, within a month, the office had turned around completely. I thought Thomas had run everything smoothly, but Davis made him look like an amateur. My appointments were sorted out at the beginning of each week, and there were zero complaints from Davis about typing up notes from my meetings. Thomas had hated having to send me summaries, bitching and moaning while he did them, but with Davis, I didn't even need to ask. After every meeting, they appeared in my inbox.

After work, I joined my mother in her apartment for dinner and sat in her living room, enjoying a cocktail.

"You make a fabulous martini, Mom." I admired the glass. "Cold and dry—just perfect."

"Glad to know if I ever decide to get a job, I have a talent worth selling. Now tell me how Davis is working out." She sipped her drink and set it on the coaster. It might only be the two of us, but she was, as always, beautifully dressed, and

I hoped she'd eventually start dating. My mother was too good a person to live the rest of her life alone, and though my parents had been divorced for years, she hadn't had a steady man that I was aware of. Her social circle was her close women friends and me. "You certainly seem more relaxed than the last time I saw you in the office."

"I didn't think he'd work out, but I can admit when I'm wrong."

"That's a first." She grinned. "I'll mark my calendar."

"Very funny," I groused, but it came with a built-in smile. I could hardly complain when I no longer dreaded waking up in the morning.

"He's working out?"

"Within the first few days, he recovered all the files Edward had attempted to destroy, and since then he's been busy setting up a new filing system. He's got the calendar in order, and he's in the office earlier than I am almost every day. He…is very good. Thank you."

Of course, I didn't mention how much I enjoyed his gorgeous face and the banter we shared. As well as a perfect view of his ass every time he walked out of my office.

Approval shone from her face. "You're very welcome. I had a feeling he'd be an excellent addition. Just what you needed. He's pleasant and very bright. I have no idea why he was working as a waiter when he possesses the skills he does."

Neither did I. And any time I attempted to question him on his past before working at the diner, he deftly changed the subject, or we were interrupted by a phone call.

"I suppose he has his reasons, none of which are my concern. I don't care what he used to do. I only care about now."

"Speaking of now. How are you doing? Aside from the business?"

That answer required more fortification, so I finished

my drink. "I'm fine," was all I could muster.

"Are you? Have you seen any of your college or law-school friends since you came home?"

"Friends is using the term loosely," I responded, unwilling for her to discover how alone I truly was, even if it was by my own design. "Everyone has moved on with their lives. I had as well, until Dad and Dale died."

"True friends stick with you in good times and bad."

"Well, then I guess they weren't really my friends."

I didn't need my mother to point that out to me. The people I believed closest to me proved it with their actions, starting with my former lover, Andrew.

With Dale tormenting me on an almost daily basis, I'd left New York and the firm for the sake of my mental health. I'd easily found a job at the London office of an international firm based in the States. I met Andrew, an investment banker, the first week at an event where people introduced me to him because he came from New York City.

"I guess they think we should know each other." I laughed.

His hot gaze swept over me. "I'd like to," he murmured. "Much better."

We'd talked well into the night, and he came home with me. A month later we were living together. The relationship started out hot and passionate, but as normally happened, the initial lust burned itself out and everyday life took precedence. Andrew, being a bit of a party boy, had chafed at staying home, but I figured he'd settle down.

I'd first suspected Andrew was cheating on me after we'd been together for a year, but I had no proof. I did, however, ignore all the signs—late nights out, secret calls, and marks on his body I knew weren't from me. Was I a fool not to confront him then? Probably, but it had been so damn lonely to be away from everything and everyone that even holding someone I'd thought I loved but proved to be a stranger was preferable to nobody at all.

Eventually Andrew became even more distant, with supposed work pressure claiming his early mornings and late nights. Frustrated by his absence, I went to his office one day, hoping I could get him to talk, but never made it there; from a vantage point across the street, I watched him kiss another man. I hated myself for what I did next, but I went home and searched his jacket pockets, looking for evidence of an affair. Which I found in the form of condoms that weren't the ones we used and a crumpled receipt from a hotel bar.

I confronted him, and that was when he told me he had a new job and was moving home to the States. A week later, he was gone. The saddest thing was that a small part of me missed him, which told me how fucked up I really was.

Months later I received news of the accident and returned home. In a bout of self-pity, I broke down and called Andrew to tell him about the funerals, but he remained silent. I cringed, recalling how needy I'd been to stoop that low in my self-esteem. Andrew was bound to have heard the news, and though we hadn't been together for a while, I'd thought he'd care a little, but those broken dreams had crashed and burned as badly as the car wreck that took my father and brother. I was alone, and I was going to have to get used to it.

"I hate the thought of you having nothing but work in your life. You need to come up for air."

I needed to breathe, which was something I hadn't been able to do since diving into the mess I was taking care of.

"On that note, I should get going. I have an early morning meeting with Lacy Johnson's family, and I need to be on my toes."

"I thought you'd stay for dinner."

Much as I knew my mother wanted my company, my sudden bad mood wouldn't make for a pleasant evening.

"I'd love to, but it's best if I don't. I think I'll go to the office for a little while and prepare for tomorrow. I have to try to convince them that they should ignore what they've read in the press and stay with us."

"You can do it. I have all the faith in you."

Good that someone did, because I didn't believe much in myself these days.

"I appreciate the vote of confidence." I rose to my feet, and my mother joined me and walked me to the door.

"Thank you for coming by. I know you have better things to do than hang around an old lady."

I stooped to kiss her cheek. "If I see someone who fits that description, I'll let you know." She held my arm, and I gazed at her in surprise.

"All I want is for you to be happy."

I left her and walked the ten blocks to the office, passing by loving couples who were out for the evening. Were they happy, or was it all an act, like the rest of us put on for show? When I moved to London, I'd thought I was living my best life, away from the two people who'd tormented me the most, but I discovered you couldn't outrun the pain hurtful words inflict. They lived in your heart and head forever.

In the elevator speeding up to the office, I rested my head on the wall, allowing a brief moment to release all the pent-up tension from carrying the weight of the office on my shoulders. The door opened, revealing a light on inside the office suite. I was certain I'd shut it off before I left. In addition, the printer or copier was humming, as if working.

"Hello?" Puzzled, I called out, "Who's there?"

Davis walked out from behind the receptionist's desk. "What are you doing here?"

I crossed my arms. "I might ask you the same thing. It's almost eight."

"I, uh, I know tomorrow is important, so I figured I'd make sure everything was in order. No chance for glitches. I have duplicate copies of everything for you. They're on your desk."

"You gave up your evening to do this? Why?"

Davis lifted a shoulder. "I had no plans, and I consider it part of my job."

Having no idea how to respond, I walked past him. His computer was on, and an unwrapped sandwich sat on the desk, which reminded me how hungry I was.

I tipped my head. "Where did you get that from? Are they still open?"

He followed my gaze. "What, my sandwich? No, I made it at home." His smile came and went. "Way cheaper." His brows drew together. "You didn't eat yet?"

"No. It's okay. I'll order something." I took off my jacket and rolled up my sleeves, noticing that Davis had not only gone home to make a sandwich, but he'd changed out of his suit into a pair of worn jeans and a plaid shirt. The jeans hugged his strong, muscular thighs, the soft material strained across his broad chest, and with the top buttons undone, I glimpsed a swirl of chest hair.

Greedy hunger rushed through me, and I almost swayed. I'd had neither the time nor desire for sex since I returned home, but my libido roared back to life with Davis in front of me.

"Carson, are you okay?" His worried eyes met mine, and for a brief moment I wondered what he'd do if I kissed him.

Get a grip.

"Yeah. I just need to eat." I rummaged in my desk, but to my dismay, my stash of candy bars was gone. "What the hell happened to them?"

"Are you serious? You've been existing on chocolate and caffeine." Davis laughed. "Today alone you ate three Kit Kats, a Milky Way, and a bag of malted balls. How do you not get sick?"

"They're the dark chocolate ones. And what are you, the candy cops? Sue me, I like chocolate," I grumbled. "But

I'm hungry now. Can you order me a sandwich from the place down the block?"

"They're closed. What about Italian or Chinese?"

"Whatever's fastest." I waved at him and sat heavily in my chair. "I'm starving."

Davis peered at me, shook his head, and left. I heard him rustling around his desk right outside my door but not making a phone call to get my food.

"Hey. I didn't tell you what I want."

I got to my feet and made it to the door, not expecting Davis to be there. We collided, chest to chest.

"Ow. What the hell?" I sprang away and rubbed my shoulder. "What's that?" I asked, pointing to a slightly squashed item in his hand.

Davis blinked. "It's, uh, it's half my sandwich. I figured you need it more than I do. And I was also going to see what you wanted to eat."

"You want to give me your dinner?" Dumbfounded, I stared at him.

"Not all of it." His eyes twinkled. "I already took a bite out of the other half. You wouldn't want it."

Why did the thought of putting my mouth where his had been sound like a good idea?

"I don't want to take your food."

"It's not a big deal. It's just turkey." He offered it. "I want you to have it. Besides, you already squashed it when you ran into me."

"*I* ran into *you*?"

"Glad to see you agree with me. Now, take this and eat while I order you something. What do you want?"

"Damn, you're bossy." But I couldn't resist the sandwich. I was too damn hungry, and when I sank my teeth into the bread, I groaned with satisfaction. "*Mmm*. That's good."

"Yeah, I'm a master sandwich-maker," he joked. "It's a hidden talent. So, food order?"

I chomped another bite before answering. "Egg roll, chicken with mixed vegetables, and brown rice."

"Okay. I'll do that right now." He turned to go.

"And Davis?" He peered over his shoulder at me. "Order for yourself too. And not just a little appetizer. A meal. Use the office account."

"I'm okay. Really."

"I want you to." Sandwich finished, I brushed my hands to get rid of any crumbs. "Didn't anyone ever tell you that you're supposed to agree and just do whatever your boss tells you to do?"

Instead of laughing and coming back at me with a snappy one-liner as he had all week, he paled and gave me a halfhearted smile, then retreated to his desk. I sat and turned on my desktop, waiting for the files to load but not paying attention.

"What was that about?" I muttered to myself. "Everything was fine until I mentioned him doing what I told him to do without questioning me." The files opened, and I had to shelve my curiosity about Davis for another day. The most important thing on my agenda was not to lose this account. If I couldn't persuade the Johnsons that I could undo the damage my father and brother did and win their trust again, it wouldn't take long for the vultures to swoop in and pick at the bones of this firm.

While working on the numbers, I heard the elevator bell ring and the door open. I rubbed my eyes, wondering how long it would be until I needed glasses. At the soft knock, I peered over the computer monitor to see Davis in the doorway, bag in hand.

"Where would you like it?"

I stood and stretched, rolling my shoulders as I pushed in my chair. God, I could use a massage. "Let's eat at the conference table."

He cut a quick glance at me. "It's okay. I-I can eat at my

desk." Looking supremely uncomfortable, he took several steps back.

"That makes no sense. We can work as we eat. I need someone to bounce my plan of action off of."

"Me? I don't understand trust and estates law."

"Maybe you should. If you're going to work here, I think it would be a good idea for you to get a paralegal degree."

"I-I can't afford that."

But I could see his interest. I grinned. "That's not a problem. It's a deduction for the firm. I'll pay for it. Something to think about. Please sit." I walked to the conference table and pulled out a chair. Davis placed the bag on the table and sat but inched away from me. For whatever reason, he now seemed determined to put up a wall between us.

"Here's the issue." I walked as I talked, burning off my nervous energy. "My father and brother were named cotrustees of Ms. Johnson's estate. She left money, stocks, bonds…the usual. But there were other valuable assets—real estate, artwork, and her royalties from the many albums she put out on her own, plus the show tunes."

"Wow. That's got to be—"

"Millions," I interrupted him. "Which proved way too tempting for my father and brother."

Davis's eyes widened. "What did they do?"

I couldn't control the ugly sound that escaped me. "I have no desire to get into it, especially when so much is riding on me being here, ready to prove that the firm is stable and capable of functioning. My father's and brother's failings—as well as my own—are the last thing I want to dwell on."

"Understandable. In any case, what are you going to do?"

What I wanted to do was run as far away as I could and forget the firm and the Ballard name, like Dale and my father had wanted to forget I existed. The first year I lived away from home, I'd reached out on their birthdays with a phone call but was snubbed. When I came home for Christmas, neither acknowledged my presence. I spent the holiday with my mother, who told Dale that if he couldn't be civil to me, not to come. He failed to show up for Christmas dinner, and not wishing to be a burden by making her choose which son to see, I stopped trying after that and stayed in London.

"I plan to transfer the real-estate titles to the trust again and return all the artwork. Whatever money they used will come out of whatever money was in my father's and brother's accounts. I have to make the Johnsons believe I can restore them to whole and try my damnedest to make it happen."

Davis chewed the inside of his cheek. "Sounds like a valid plan of action. Can you?"

I sat and propped my chin in my hand. "I'm hopeful. But I'd better figure it out fast."

CHAPTER SIX

Davis

I awakened at six a.m., showered, shaved, and ate breakfast. Over my second cup of coffee, I slowed down and sipped, replaying the events of the night before. Carson and I had stayed in the office until after ten, and I thought he'd come up with a plan that, on the face of it, should work.

Instead of relaxing in front of the television at home, I took my laptop and researched Lacy Johnson's family, particularly her sister, whom we'd be meeting to discuss Ballard and Melbourne retaining the Johnsons' trust account. I read magazine articles and discovered her favorite foods, drinks, books, and music.

"If you want something badly enough, kill them with kindness." I laughed, thinking how my mother would love knowing I'd used one of her favorite platitudes. With a page full of notes, I made some calls and, after checking off the last item on my list, was satisfied I'd done all I could.

The rest would be up to Carson.

Carson.

Damn, the man confounded me. When I accepted the job, I'd anticipated having to work with a boss I disliked. Instead I was intrigued and excited to come to work. The past month had flown by. I made fun of his dislike of computers and reliance on paper, but it gave me the chance to read and transcribe his notes, and I enjoyed learning about estate and trust planning and forming corporations. Maybe I *should* think about getting a paralegal degree. I did a little research and discovered some excellent nighttime programs where I could continue working full-time while earning my degree. It would help me in my job for sure.

And then there was the other thing I was learning.

Carson Ballard wasn't the rude, obnoxious asshole I'd thought. He could be abrupt and distant, a little pretentious, but he was also generous and unexpectedly funny. I suspected a kind heart beat under those monogrammed shirts.

Did I mention he was gorgeous as well?

Oh, no way. Not again. Don't even think it.

I finished preparing for work.

At seven thirty, I unlocked the office doors and set my bag on my desk. I went to the men's room and stood in front of the mirror, assessing my reflection. When Mrs. Ballard had offered me the job, I'd pulled my old suits out of the closet and brought them to the cleaners. They might not be the expensive designers Carson wore, but I wanted to make sure I fit in, and this navy one was the best of them all. My mother had bought it for me as a Christmas present, and I remembered being so thrilled to have landed a job working for the mayor.

What an idiot I'd been.

Forget that. You've moved on.

I smoothed the tie and tightened the knot to make sure it sat straight, then laughed.

You act as if you're the one meeting with the clients.

I heard a knock at the door and ran. A deliveryman with a load of fresh flowers stood waiting, and I let him in, tipped him, and got to work setting the vases around the office. Soon the perfume of gardenias and jasmine scented the air. The next delivery of the morning arrived, and I entered the conference room to place on the table the platter of scones, crumpets, and croissants, along with fresh strawberries, butter, marmalade, raspberry jam, and clotted cream. Imported English tea awaited, brewing.

Carson walked in as I was removing the clear plastic wrap from the trays of breakfast goodies. His brows knitted together.

"What…are you doing? What is all this? Where did all those flowers in the reception area come from?"

I put up a hand to cut off the rapid-fire questions. "Hear me out. I want to put Ms. Johnson's sister in a good mood when you sit down. Last night I did a little research and discovered she loves fresh flowers, especially gardenias and jasmine, so I ordered some from the florist I saw the firm used. And she loves all things British and breakfast pastries." I crumpled the sticky wrapper into a ball and tossed it into the garbage bin.

Stunned, Carson ran a hand over his face. "You—you did all this? For me?"

"Well, for the firm." I met his mystified eyes with a grin. "My mother always says you never get a second chance to make a first impression. I wanted your client to know that we will do whatever is necessary to regain her trust, and that you plan on paying attention to the smallest detail to make her feel part of a family here." I straightened the fruit platter. "I have no idea if it'll mean anything to her, or if it was the right thing to do, but I figured it couldn't hurt."

"Thank you."

And he turned around and walked out. A little miffed—I'd hoped for a little more appreciation—I was again reminded that I was simply an office assistant. And lemon-drizzled scones and Earl Grey tea, no matter how delicious, weren't enough to seal a multimillion-dollar deal.

Carson's closed door was a signal to keep out, so I kept busy with the never-ending job of sorting through client files—otherwise known as the third pit of organizational hell. I pulled up a case file and winced. No name, only a number, and nothing to indicate who the client was.

"Whoever maintained these files obviously had the intelligence of a flea. Who does something like this? And I thought Brian didn't have a clue. I swear—"

"Who's Brian?"

"What the fuck?" I nearly jumped out of my seat at the sound of Carson's voice at my shoulder and pressed a hand to my pounding chest. I spun in my chair to find Carson laughing at me. "You think it's funny to scare me to death?"

"You were mumbling to yourself about someone named Brian."

I set my jaw. "Yeah. Do you know that there are no names on these files? Who does that? I have to open each file, get the name, and then reenter it in the system. It's a pain in the ass and time-consuming."

"Well, good thing you've got all the time to do it. That is what you're here for."

The snide comment was like a shot to the heart, and all my goodwill toward Carson evaporated. The butterflies I'd felt in my stomach when I thought of Carson's sex appeal morphed into moths.

"I'm perfectly aware of my place." I swiveled to face my computer and picked up where I'd left off, hyperaware that Carson still stood behind me. After a few seconds of typing, I stopped. "Why are you staring at me? What's wrong now?"

"I'm sorry. That was rude of me."

I faced him again. "Yeah, it sure as hell was. I guess I should be used to it by now. So excuse me if I don't need to hear how I'm just the help."

"I didn't mean it. I'm…I'm nervous." He sat on the edge of my desk, and much as I wanted to ignore his words as a play for sympathy, I couldn't. He was telling the truth.

"Understandable. If they leave the firm…"

"We're sunk," he answered bluntly with no attempt to sugarcoat his words. "The negative publicity alone will doom us to bankruptcy."

"Can I ask you something?"

He slid off the desk. "Sure. Fire away."

"What happened to the firm to get to this point? Did they steal money from clients?"

He stopped and balled his hands into fists. "It's much more complicated than that. They sold the real estate to themselves for a minimal amount. They deposited the royalties in the correct bank account but used it as their personal piggy bank. As trustees, they had the power to do what they wanted with the funds within reason and not to the detriment of the trust. It was their fiduciary duty."

"Sounds like they violated those principles."

The harshness of his icy-blue gaze weighed heavily on me. "To the highest degree."

I nodded. "I'm sorry. I didn't mean to pry."

His lips curled. "Yeah, you did. And if we're exchanging cozy secrets, I've got a question for you."

I licked my lips, nervous sweat popping up all over my body. "Sure. Go ahead."

"I already asked you." Still with the ghost of laughter in his voice, he folded his arms. "Who's Brian?"

Shit.

My hesitation proved to be my good fortune, as the elevator dinged. An older woman exited, silver hair in an upsweep and a fine network of lines crisscrossing her face. That would be Lacy's sister, Elise Holloway. A young man I recognized as Amos Johnson, Lacy's son, appeared from behind his aunt. He looked to be around twenty-one, with coal-black hair and eyes, and he seemed to possess a cruel haughtiness ingrained in lips thinned to a slight sneer and a slouch indicating a desire to be anywhere but here.

"Showtime," Carson murmured and placed a smile on his face. "Mrs. Holloway, Mr. Johnson. Welcome. Please come with me and sit. We have a bit of London waiting for you."

"That sounds lovely." Mrs. Holloway beamed and nodded to me as she passed by. "We had a late night with some friends and didn't have time for a cuppa this morning."

I mentally rolled my eyes. Elise and Lacy had grown up in Paterson, New Jersey.

Carson caught my eye, and though I'd only been working for him for a month, I could tell how nervous he was.

"Davis, could you please join us?"

Startled, I jumped to my feet. "Oh, sure. Let me grab my iPad."

Amos Johnson paused by my desk. "Good. I thought I'd have to sit through this boring meeting without anything to do."

I cocked my head. "Pardon?"

"Nothing. Just make sure you sit by me." He bared small white teeth in a grin.

I'd hoped Carson would say something, but he'd already entered the conference room, leaving me to babysit.

"Right this way, Mr. Johnson."

"Call me Amos."

"As you wish, Amos. We have breakfast for you and your aunt."

"Trying to butter us up with pastries?" He flung his long, lean frame into a chair, and though he seemed the type to turn up his nose at everything, he had no issue filling a plate with scones, a croissant, jam, and fruit.

Carson took nothing. I poured myself some tea and kept a careful watch on him.

He cleared his throat. "Thank you for agreeing to meet with me. First, let me assure you that I am now in charge of Ballard and Melbourne, and I'm as appalled as you at the treatment of your trust account. But every penny that was removed from your account has either been returned, with interest, or I'm in the process of fully restoring the account. The trust will not lose a single cent due to the actions of the former partners."

"Your brother and father," Amos said, jumping right into the fray and waving his arm. "Let's cut to the chase. You're afraid we're going to sue your asses. Isn't that what this whole thing is about?" His hand landed on my thigh, and I shifted away, meeting his grin with a stone-cold face.

"Amos, please." Elise Holloway threw Carson an apologetic look. "Please continue, Carson."

Carson's jaw flexed. "Of course I'm hoping it won't come to that. I've been living abroad for many years, so I wasn't part of the firm or aware of what was happening, but I can unequivocally state that if you continue the trust with Ballard and Melbourne under my leadership, our books and records will be open for your inspection whenever you want." Ignoring Amos, he appealed directly to Elise Holloway. "I'm very sorry for this gross abuse and can only hope you'll allow me to handle your family's affairs, knowing that I will always give you an accounting whenever you request it. I will give you two hundred percent." He swallowed. "As a sign of good faith, I'm going to draw up new trust agreements and waive Ballard and Melbourne's fee for the first year."

"Are you dating anyone?" Amos whispered to me.

"Please stop," I murmured, hoping Carson and Mrs. Holloway's conversation would drown out my words.

"Why?" He rolled his chair close enough for me to see the glitter in his eyes and wonder if he was high so early in the morning.

I could've laughed at his crude and childish attempt to seduce me. "I'm here to work."

"*Mmm*. That's boring. Meet me at my place later. 1069 Park Avenue." He leaned in closer. "We can have some fun."

"I can't," I fumbled, hoping to put him off. "I-I have a partner."

"Yeah? Cool. Bring him too."

"No. Please stop, or I'll have to say something."

"Davis? Everything okay?"

Carson's voice broke into my tumbling thoughts. Was Amos implying that if I didn't sleep with him, he'd pull the plug on the firm retaining the trust? Could he do that? From across the table, Carson raised a quizzical brow during a pause in his conversation with Mrs. Holloway, as she selected a pastry. I widened my eyes, hoping he understood the universal signal of distress.

Get me the fuck out of here.

A brief uptick of his lips was the only indication he'd noticed.

Bastard.

"Is there anything else we can do to regain your trust in us and reassure you that your accounts will be completely protected?" Carson asked.

"I'll have Trevor Howard, my personal attorney, look the documents over, so whenever they're ready, you can send them to him," Elise answered.

"Of course. Please give Davis the email address, and he will get them to Mr. Howard as soon as possible."

"I have some questions," Amos piped up, and my heart sank. Brats like him were the worst people to deal with. I gathered myself for him to say something that might sway his aunt's decision.

"Amos, please. You're not twenty-one yet and have no say in the matter," Mrs. Holloway stated decisively.

He pouted and sulked. "That's not fair. I'll be twenty in

two months. Just because I'm not twenty-one doesn't mean my opinions don't count."

I smothered a smile. Nineteen? *Damn.* I knew it was inappropriate, but I couldn't help laughing that someone more than ten years younger was trying to hit on me.

"It does for legal purposes," Mrs. Holloway responded in a brisk, efficient manner, obviously wise to the ways of her bratty nephew. "I'll listen to your ideas, but it doesn't mean I have to follow them."

"I know my mother left me a trust. Is the money still there, or did your family steal that too?"

Carson's face flamed, but he managed to hold it together. "That money is safe. Nothing was touched."

Seemingly satisfied, Amos stuffed a scone into his mouth. "Fine."

Mrs. Holloway touched the diamond necklace at her throat. "Carson, when we heard of the theft and misuse of our property as well as others', my instinctive reaction was to call the police. I hesitated only because I received a letter from you, taking personal responsibility despite the fact that the misappropriation wasn't yours. I respect someone willing to shoulder the burden and right wrongs."

"Thank you, Mrs. Holloway."

Even though the worry wasn't personally mine, my stomach clenched in a painful knot for Carson having to take blow after blow to his pride.

"Since the news broke, I've had very forceful disagreements with my attorney and other family members who don't hold my views, and think I shouldn't continue with your firm. After all, there are hundreds to choose from, all which would be extremely competent and haven't already cheated my family."

Ouch, fuck.

To his credit, Carson remained silent, but I could see the devastation in his blue eyes. A crazy desire to hold him came over me. I wanted to tell him it would be all right. We'd weather this together.

She laced her fingers. "But I'm a great believer in second chances. My sister and I both had pasts we tried to move on from, and without the support from people willing to help us, who recognized we were good, decent people who might've made poor choices, we never would've achieved the success we did."

Elise Holloway had been one of the early magazine cover girls, and while Lacy used her talent onstage, Elise used her perfect bone structure to make a name for herself and married the editor of *House of New York Fashion*, one of the leading couture magazines in the city. They never had children, and Terrance Holloway passed away after twenty-six years of marriage, leaving the bulk of his estate to her.

"If all looks well," Elise continued, "I'm going to stick by you, the way people stuck by us when they were told to walk away. I expect you to use this chance wisely and make sure you don't stray from the right path."

"I appreciate your words more than I can say, Mrs. Holloway." Carson spoke solemnly, and I could only imagine how annoyed he must be. Dammit, I was annoyed for him, knowing again and again he had to sit and take the sins of his father and brother on his chin. Carson, more than anyone, could take care of himself, but this went one step beyond.

Mrs. Holloway gathered her purse and rose to her feet. "Thank you so much for this lovely breakfast. And my compliments to whoever brings in your flowers. The fragrance of gardenias and jasmine always puts me in a good mood."

Carson walked behind her, chatting about the weather and upcoming Broadway shows. Amos and I followed, and he leaned into my shoulder to whisper, "If you change your mind, I'll be waiting."

At this point I could only laugh. "You're a kid."

He pouted and slunk out after her. That behavior might've been cute at four, but at nineteen he was a step away from a sexual harasser. When the elevator door closed, Carson waited a moment and then let out a *whoop*. Before I knew it, he'd grabbed hold of me in a bear hug.

"We did it."

Startled, I clung to him. "Uh…yeah. Congratulations."

His blue eyes warmed, and I froze at the unexpected embrace. A wave of desire swept over me, and I wanted nothing more than to feel his mouth on mine.

A mischievous smile curved his lips, and dimples winked at me.

Does he suspect?

"Tonight we celebrate. Dinner's on me."

Without waiting for my answer, he released me and disappeared into his office, shutting the door behind him.

I collapsed in my chair and waited for my racing heart to settle.

Didn't work. I still wanted to kiss him.

It was easier when I'd thought he was a bastard. This wasn't supposed to happen. I wasn't supposed to like Carson. Or like the feel of his arms around me.

I couldn't let this happen again. I wouldn't fall for my boss.

It might already be too late.

What the hell was I going to do?

CHAPTER SEVEN

Carson

Well.

That was something.

Or something else.

I paced my office, knowing I should call my mother and tell her the good news. With the continuance of the Johnson estate, I knew I'd be able to keep the firm running. Potential and existing clients—the ones who hadn't already jumped ship—would be more likely to stay when a prominent celebrity client showed faith.

And yet…

So much of this win belonged to Davis. I couldn't take all the credit. And he needed to know that, which was why the celebration dinner would also be a thank-you to him for going that extra mile.

But I didn't make a move to look for a special place or call for a reservation. I stopped wearing a path in the carpet and sat behind my desk, head in hands, thinking about Davis.

The scent of his skin.

Soft, silky hair tickling my nose.

His muscles bunching and shifting beneath my grip.

I wanted to hold on tight and never let him go.

What the fuck is that all about?

I ran my hands through my hair and loosened my tie. All that morning it wound around my throat like a snake, pressing against my flesh, cutting off my breath.

Once Elise Holloway stated she wouldn't transfer her account or file charges, the pressure receded, and I could draw in air. Davis's foresight had truly been key in saving the day, and he needed to be rewarded. I picked up the phone.

"Mom?"

"Oh, thank God you finally called." She sounded breathless. "I was sitting here all morning, ready to jump out of my skin."

"It all worked out." I replayed the meeting as well as what Davis had done to help. "Once I send over all the documents and she notifies the court that we're being retained as trustees, this nightmare will be over and I can move on to the next problem child."

"And?" she queried.

"And what?"

"You're not going to play this game with me, Carson Darius Ballard," she responded, her sharp tone and use of my full name an indication of how annoyed she truly was with me. "I'm sure you're going to recompense Davis for his role. Researching the client's likes and dislikes was an extremely intelligent move on his part, and he deserves to be rewarded."

"You think I don't know that? I'm taking him to dinner tonight."

"Good. That's a start."

Now it was my turn to be irritated. "What do you mean, a start? I'm not talking pizza and beer."

"There's nothing wrong with that if it's what he likes. I just hope you're treating him right."

I held my temper in check because she was my mother, and I did love her despite her treating me like a four-year-old sometimes.

"Mother. He's my employee. He's doing a very good job. I tell him that all the time. There's little else I can do. Now I'd better go and tackle the rest of the problem children on my list. Lacy Johnson's trust might've been the biggest one, but it's hardly the only present my father and Dale left me to handle."

"I know, sweetheart, and I'm sorry you have to shoulder the burden. I wish…" She sighed heavily. "I wish you weren't all alone. Isn't there someone you could bring into the firm to help? Another lawyer?"

"Who would want to? Ballard and Melbourne isn't exactly a stellar name to put on your résumé. And why? Don't you think I can do it?" The old insecurities rushed to the surface. Not good enough, not *man enough* to handle it. Those words I'd heard both my father and brother repeat—not only behind my back, but to my face—were the impetus that kept me running to prove them wrong.

Even in death, they taunted me, but if I had to go down, I'd go fighting.

"Of course you can. You're the only one now. I'm just saying that I don't want it to be to the detriment of your personal life. You have to leave the work behind at some point. When was the last time you went out on a date for pure fun?"

If I told my mother the truth, our conversation could go on for hours, with her lecturing me that it was no good to be alone, that I was working too hard. But I knew she didn't want me to become my father—never home, always working, and no lasting relationships. Even though they'd been divorced for longer than they were together, she never confirmed the real reason they split up.

"We grew apart," was always her answer, and I never pressed her on it, although I assumed he'd been unfaithful and mistreated her. He didn't deserve someone as special as my mother.

And now he was dead, and it didn't matter.

But the truth? I missed having a boyfriend. I enjoyed spending weekends together and coming home after work, knowing someone cared enough about me to be there. The fact that Andrew didn't and had cheated on me and abused my heart and trust had only made me harder and more cynical. I'd thought I'd given all of myself. I was loving and faithful. Maybe my first clue should've been that he'd never said *I love you* back.

"I haven't had time for fun, not when there was so much uncertainty. I can breathe a little easier now."

"Now you can take some time for yourself. Maybe tonight, when you and Davis have your dinner date."

"It's not a date." I rolled my eyes. "It's work-related. I'd better go. I've got tons to do. I'll talk to you soon. I just wanted to give you the good news first."

"I appreciate it. Bye, Carson."

I ended the call and chuckled. My mother—she'd never stop. Davis…a date? The man couldn't wait for me to let him go when I held him. I should've apologized for the hug. We'd never had a discussion about sexuality, but I made no secret that I was gay. One thing I'd learned living with a father and brother who couldn't stand the sight of me was that I'd hide from no one.

Tonight I'll tell Davis I'm sorry. In the meantime, we have a lot of work to get through. Apologizing didn't come easy to me but seemed commonplace in my dealings with Davis. My phone buzzed.

"Carson? I have Robert O'Rourke on hold. He wants to talk to you about Britney Valentine's trust."

Britney Valentine was a two-year-old child who was awarded twenty million dollars in damages in a negligence lawsuit against a doctor and hospital. We were trustees for the little girl, and I couldn't have been happier to see that my father and brother hadn't gotten their greedy fingers into it.

"Thanks." I waited a moment. "Mr. O'Rourke? Carson Ballard."

"Mr. Ballard, how are you?"

"Well, thanks. What can I do for you?"

"I'd like to make an appointment to go over the paperwork of the trust and get an accounting."

"Not a problem. I can have that arranged for you by next week."

"Perfect. I know you've been sending the statements on time and everything seems in order, but the family wants to make sure. You understand."

"Of course," I answered smoothly, but the tension swirled in my stomach. Would this ever stop? "I'll put you through to my assistant to set up an appointment."

"Good. I'll see you then."

"Yes. Hold on, please." I buzzed Davis. "Please set up a meeting with Mr. O'Rourke for next week to discuss the Valentine trust account. He's holding on line one."

"Okay, Carson."

I ended the call, thinking not about the meeting earlier nor the Valentine account. Instead, I scrolled through Open Table, searching for a good enough restaurant to take Davis.

* * *

At six thirty, I powered down my computer, shut off the lights, and left my office. Davis sat at his desk, typing away, as he had all afternoon.

"Writing a book?" I whispered by his ear, and he jumped.

"Will you stop sneaking up on me?" He scowled, and I had to stop myself from laughing because he was pretty cute when annoyed.

"Sorry, but it's closing time. And I'm hungry. Are you almost ready?"

His brows drew together. "I—you really don't have to do this. I was just doing my job."

I pointed to the monitor. "Time to shut it off."

"Bossy, aren't you?" he muttered, but I caught the edge of his lips ticking up in a grin that matched my own.

I stuck my hands into the pockets of my slacks and watched him as he saved what he'd been doing and powered down the computer.

"I'm ready, but…" He stood waiting, his face a mixture of confusion and longing.

"Let's get going. I made a reservation. I hope you like steak." He nodded, and we walked to the elevator. "Good. Peter Luger's it is."

Davis's brows rose. "Oh. Wow. I've heard of that place, but I've never been there."

"No?" The car I'd called for sat idling at the curb, and I opened the door. Davis slid inside, and I joined him. The car took off toward downtown.

"No. It's a little more than I can afford. A lot, in fact."

I glanced at his profile in the semidarkness. "You deserve it. Your dedication and research kept the Johnson trust in our hands."

"I don't think so. You worked very hard to keep them with the firm, and I'm sure they would've stayed without the scones and tea I ordered."

"Don't underestimate the power of a good pastry. Those scones were incredible. Even that brat Amos liked them."

Staring straight ahead, Davis didn't take the bait, my attempt at humor falling flat, so I let it go. Traffic was shockingly light, and we were over the Williamsburg Bridge and at the restaurant within thirty minutes. We sat, and I ordered a vodka martini when the waiter asked for our drink order. I turned to him.

"What would you like?"

I could see the struggle behind his eyes—he wanted to enjoy himself but didn't think it was the right thing to do. I decided to take matters into my own hands.

"He'll have a lychee martini. Don't ask."

Davis glared at me while the elderly waiter laughed. "That's a first for me."

The waiter out of earshot, Davis stuck out his jaw. "I don't like people ordering for me."

"Sorry, but you seemed to be having a problem deciding, and I wanted to make it easy for you."

"I knew this was a bad idea," he muttered under his breath.

"Why?" I challenged him. "It's pretty common for people in the office to get together after work." His gaze remained fixed to the table, and I figured now was as good a time as any. "Is it because of what happened earlier?"

A flush crept up his neck and stained his cheeks beneath his evening stubble. "I don't know what you mean," he mumbled.

So I was right. "I'm sorry I made you uncomfortable."

He jerked his head up to meet my eyes. "What're you talking about?"

"You know. After the Johnsons left. When I hugged you." Davis's blush deepened. "I forget that some people aren't comfortable with public displays of affection, especially between two men."

He blinked. "Uh, it's okay."

"Are you sure? I don't hide the fact that I'm gay, and I never will."

"N-no. It's okay. I mean it's okay that you're gay. No— oh God, that sounds so stupid. What I mean is, it's not my place… You don't need my permission…" He gulped his water. "I don't care if you're gay." Red-faced, he buried his face in the menu. "I don't like talking about sex in the office, especially with my boss."

"Understood."

Our drinks came, and the server took out his pad. "What're you having?"

"Can I order for us?" I asked Davis. "It's just that I've been here before, and I know what's good for a first-timer."

Davis met my eyes. "Sure."

"We'll start with iceberg wedge, then do the steak for two, medium rare, creamed spinach, and fries for two. How does that sound?"

"Fine. Good."

The waiter nodded. "All right. Be back soon with your salads."

Davis had returned to avoiding me by scrutinizing the tabletop. I tapped my finger on the breadbasket to get his attention.

"Did you want something else? That's really their classic menu, so it's the perfect thing to start with. You'll have to eat the spinach because even with the pill I took, it's way too heavy for my stomach to handle. The dressing on the salad is bad enough."

"But there was sauteed broccoli on the menu. Why didn't you order that so you could eat it?"

His concern took me aback. "The creamed spinach is what they're famous for. You should have it."

"Not at the expense of you getting sick. That's not right." He frowned. "And…thank you. Again. I still don't understand why you're taking me out to dinner for simply doing my job."

"Because it's the right thing to do. I want you to know I appreciate all your hard work since you started and recognize you've gone the extra mile."

"I know, but really, a simple thank-you is enough."

I sipped my drink, the cold vodka easing the dryness in my throat. "By now you should have realized I don't do simple."

His lips twitched, and the overhead lights picked up the twinkle in his golden-green eyes. "I might've."

"I know we started off on the wrong foot, but from that first day, you saved my ass, beginning with recreating those notes I thought were lost." I set my drink next to my bread plate. "I believe in letting people know when they're doing a good job. I didn't want you to think I'm a total bastard."

"Not a total one for sure." A full-blown smile graced his lips, and I was captured by its warmth. "I'm kidding. I think it's about time to wipe the slate clean and start over."

"Good. Because I really want you to enjoy your meal." In the distance I watched the server approach with our salads.

"I can't imagine I wouldn't." He craned his neck, scanning the bustling restaurant filled with businesspeople and couples on serious dates. I'd seen more anniversary and significant dinners here than anything else. "I've heard about this place, but I never dreamed I'd be eating here one day. Everything looks and smells amazing."

Our salads were placed in front of us.

"Excuse me." Davis got the attention of the waiter. "Could you add a side of broccoli to our main course?"

The waiter shrugged. "Why not?" And walked away.

"You didn't have to do that." I frowned. "It wasn't necessary."

He grinned at me. "I know."

Damn. What the heck was going on? I hadn't enjoyed anyone's company like this in years. Davis was funny, kind, sweet, and smart. Very smart. What the hell had he been doing working at a diner?

I had to ask the question he'd sidestepped earlier. "Who's Brian?"

Davis started coughing and grabbed his water glass.

CHAPTER EIGHT

Davis

Dammit.

I thought he'd forgotten. I guzzled the water as if I'd been stranded in the Sahara for a week and wiped my mouth afterward.

"Brian? He was my old boss." I shrugged. "That's all."

So not true. But I'd be damned if I'd ever let Carson know how stupid I'd been.

"Are you sure?" Carson cut a piece of his wedge and chewed. "If that's true, why do you look like you're ready to puke?"

I wouldn't—couldn't—let Carson know the truth about Brian. It was too humiliating.

"No reason."

A line bisected Carson's forehead. "All right. It was just conversation. Tell me about your old job. You said you worked for the mayor's office in your town? What did you do?"

I shoved some more salad into my mouth, making sure I chewed it to bits before answering. "I guess you could say a little bit of everything? I maintained and updated all the records, managed the calendar for the staff, and was the overall office manager."

Carson continued eating, his thoughtful yet penetrating gaze fixed on my face. Feeling like a bug under a microscope, I let my nerves get to me and drank my martini a bit quicker than usual.

"I'm surprised," he stated, and wiped his lips. His empty salad plate was whisked away.

"At what?" My lips were sticky from the sweet drink, and I licked them, feeling a little light-headed, but whether from nerves or downing my martini, I couldn't be sure.

"You obviously have major computer skills. Even I, with my rudimentary knowledge, can see that."

"Yeah. I'm pretty good."

"Modest as well. But that only confuses me more."

"How so?"

The server stopped by our table. "Another round, gentlemen?"

"Yes, please," Carson answered before I had a chance to say I'd had enough. "What I don't understand is why someone who ran a governmental office, which I know is no small feat, would be working in a diner."

"There's nothing wrong with being a server."

"I never said there was." He came right back at me, as I should've expected. "But with your abilities, you could work at a major tech firm and make big money. Or even a corporation. You mentioned when you first came to work for me that you were struggling to pay rent, so…" He raised a brow and accepted the drink set in front of him. "Thank you."

I gnawed the inside of my cheek, debating how much to reveal. "I-I have my reasons."

"I'm sure you must." A frown settled on his lips, and

his eyes narrowed. "Are you in trouble? Is there anything I can do to help?"

If only. To answer would be to open myself up to the type of scrutiny I wasn't prepared for. I'd broken so many rules—both personal and professional—it was beyond embarrassing. Humiliation and fear were my constant companions. The best thing I could do would be to pretend the affair had never happened and hope Carson would eventually tire from my constant refusals to talk.

"Nah. It was a long time ago, and it no longer matters. I was never interested in working in the high-tech world—sure, the money is better, but I don't like the constant pressure. I'm better off in a smaller environment. Besides, I used to do coding for companies as a side hustle. The pay was great and gave me the extra cash I needed, until the startup market cooled along with the jobs. But I never knew that trusts and estates could be so interesting, and I'm looking forward to learning more."

Did I fool Carson? Not an easy feat—the man could sniff out bullshit pretty easily—but to my surprise, he merely nodded. Those coding jobs were a sweet deal, but their inconsistency made them unreliable, so I couldn't depend on them. The bump up in pay to Carson's assistant should make up for that loss.

"Okay. Ahh. Here comes our food. Good thing, because I'm starving."

Our steak came sizzling hot and beautifully medium rare. The creamed spinach tasted like heaven, the broccoli was deliciously garlicky, and the french fries were perfectly crispy. Hunger won out over pride, and I tucked into that food as if I hadn't eaten for days. When all the plates sat empty, I groaned out a sigh of pure contentment.

"That was…probably the best meal I've ever had." I rubbed my stomach, certain I'd gained five pounds since I walked into the restaurant. "I can't believe how stuffed I am. I ate like a pig."

Carson's eyes gleamed. "I noticed."

I screwed up my face. "Rude. But seriously. Thank you again. I feel like I don't deserve it, but I appreciate your acknowledgment of my work. That's pretty unusual."

"Dessert, gentlemen?" The server appeared before us.

"You're kidding, right?"

Carson snickered. "Don't be a lightweight. We'll do an apple pie and key lime. One black coffee and one cappuccino."

My jaw dropped. "Where do you think I'm going to put all that? And how do you stay in such great shape?"

Carson made a muscle and flashed a cocky grin. "Thanks for noticing. I work out. And I only eat like this on the rare occasion. Most often it's a salad or sushi."

The coffee and cappuccino came, and I sipped slowly, enjoying the cinnamon sprinkled on top. Carson watched me, and feeling self-conscious, I laughed. "What?"

"You mentioned you grew up in Upstate New York?"

"Yeah. It was pretty rural."

"I traveled a lot up there. Went to undergrad at Cornell."

"Really? Bet you couldn't wait to come home to the city. It's fucking cold as hell in the winter."

"You know it." Our pies came, and we split them. Carson cut a hunk of the apple and slid the fork between his lips. "Did you live in Ithaca?" he asked between bites.

"No, Harleyville," I answered without thinking, instantly regretting my slipup. *Shit*. I kept my cool and cursed my stupidity, but I had to stop acting as if I'd committed a crime. I'd had an affair with my boss. Foolish? Yes. But not criminal.

"*Mmm*, isn't the pie good?" He licked his lips, and desire surged through me, which I immediately squashed. No matter how tempting Carson might be, I wouldn't give in. He smiled. "I told you it was worth it."

Beneath my lashes, I studied Carson, wondering what he was up to. In the short time I'd worked for him, I'd learned he wasn't the type to let something go so easily. But he didn't bring it up again, so I ate what I could of the pies and finished my cappuccino.

The *hum* of the busy restaurant rose around us, happy people sitting at the different tables, men and women as well as same-sex couples, enjoying life. I yearned to belong and have what they shared. Unaware of my turmoil, Carson continued to eat his pie, and I followed the movement of his fork to his mouth, losing myself in a sensual daydream, wondering what his kiss would taste like. In the office I couldn't indulge in my fantasy, but at night, when the lights were out, Carson was all I could think of.

I must've made a sound, because his gaze snapped to mine.

"Something wrong?" He searched my face, but I'd grown adept at pretending all was well.

"Not at all." My smile must've satisfied him, and he returned to demolishing the rest of his dessert.

The bill arrived and though I made an attempt to pay something toward the total, as I knew he would, Carson brushed me off and gave over his credit card. He signed the receipt and tucked it away with the credit card.

"Don't worry. It's deductible." He nudged my shoulder and pulled out his phone. "Want to share a car?"

"Uh, sure." I gave him my address on East 115th Street, and he tapped on his screen.

"I'll be getting out first."

"I know. You live on Seventy-ninth."

"Checking up on me?" he murmured in my ear, and a delicious, forbidden thrill ran through me. It had been so long…

"Hardly," I scoffed, gathering my wits and moving a step away. "I saw it in one of the files I recovered. I don't remember which one."

Frowning, he didn't respond except to say, "There's our car."

I waited until we crossed the bridge to the city before speaking. "You know, you've asked me tons of questions about my life, but I haven't heard you talk about yourself."

He lounged against the seat. "Fire away. If you knew anything, you'd realize it's pretty mundane."

"I'm not after gossip," I tried to explain. "But why were you living in London and not working for your family's firm?"

The familiar cocky smile curved his lips. "Would you believe me if I said I had a thing for men with British accents? I do love a bit of the posh."

His British accent failed to hide his pain. "No. I wouldn't."

His face fell, and his jaw worked for a moment. "I'll put it this way. My father and brother couldn't come to terms with the fact that I like men. So much so that dear old Dad pretended I didn't exist, while my brother, who never outgrew the fraternity mindset, threw every woman he knew at me, thinking that by shoving enough breasts in my face, I'd change my mind." His penetrating blue eyes held mine. "But it didn't work. I like what I like."

My breath caught, and a throb hit me low in my belly. "Of course not. You can't change who you are."

"I've known since I was ten. I decided to come out, and I thought I could talk to my brother, but he made fun of me and claimed it was a phase I'd outgrow."

"That can't happen."

"No, it can't," he said. "No matter what."

With every word, I was finding myself drawn further into Carson's suffering. No longer the spoiled, entitled man, his pain was all too real. I'd been lucky enough not to experience it personally, as my parents had accepted me when I came out.

"In the meantime," he continued, "my brother told all his friends, and they made my life miserable all through high school with their teasing until I escaped to college—he stayed in the city. I came home to go to law school and joined the firm, but they never treated me as equal to them when it came to the work. And of course, there were the sly comments about my sexuality."

My heart hurt for Carson. He didn't deserve that. No one did because of who they loved.

Pensive, he went on. "I was always pushed aside and treated like a pariah, a joke. Given the most minor cases. My father couldn't even be in the same room with me, while Dale would constantly tell me what I was missing by not being with a woman. When I told him to stop, he only went harder, telling me that being inside a man's ass couldn't possibly be as good as fucking a woman, describing his dates in detail."

"That's awful. Why couldn't he leave you alone?"

Carson stared into the blackness of the car interior. "He gave me a black eye when I told him he was so obsessed with my sex life, maybe he was into guys as well and just couldn't face it. It all came out then—how embarrassed he and my father were to have me there, and that it would be better if I left home and never came back."

My God. "I'm sorry, Carson. You're close with your mother, though. Didn't she have anything to say about the things your brother said to you?" After meeting Patricia Ballard, I couldn't imagine her standing up for such hatred and bigotry.

"I never told her. I'm not a child who needs to run to his mommy over every little thing."

"This isn't a little thing. It's your life."

"Yeah, well, you know what? I handled it the best way I knew how at the time, which was to remove myself from the situation."

We bounced over the potholes on the FDR, each minute bringing me closer to home and further away from Carson as I sensed his withdrawal.

"So why come back? You didn't owe the firm anything. Why not just let the court seize it and have it go into bankruptcy?"

Carson whipped around. "What I don't owe, is you an explanation for what I did or didn't do."

Anyone else would've said screw you and walked away, but I'd seen enough over the past month to know this Carson—like the jerk in the diner—wasn't the real man. This was the facade he put up to hide the hurt heaped on him by his father and brother and their refusal to accept him. Or love him.

"I never said you did," I responded mildly, hoping he'd settle down. "It was just a question. You don't have to answer it."

We neared the 72nd Street exit ramp, and Carson rubbed his hands on his thighs. "Look. I'm sorry. It's a touchy subject for me."

"And you don't know me, so it's none of my business. I get it."

"Probably not. It's been a great day, and we have tons of work to do tomorrow. Thanks again for the ideas and all the help." A teasing smile lit his eyes. "And sorry about Amos."

"He was a kid trying to play with the grown-ups."

Carson's grin kicked up into high gear. "Can't blame a guy for trying."

Heat rushed over me, and I was never so glad to be in a dark car, as I knew my cheeks were on fire.

"I guess not, but he's barking up the wrong tree with me."

"So you've made it abundantly clear." The car slid to a stop. "Night, Davis. See you tomorrow."

"Good night. And thank you. Again."

I watched through the rear window as he strode into the building, and let the events of the day and evening sink in as we continued uptown to my place. It had definitely been one of the most interesting nights of my life, and I thought I'd managed to put enough into Carson's head to lead him to believe I wasn't into men—and especially not him.

Now I had to make myself believe it as well.

CHAPTER NINE

Carson

News that Lacy Johnson's family was sticking with Ballard and Melbourne spread throughout the legal community fast, and it wasn't long before our fortunes were on the rise. In the month since our meeting, I'd had three new clients set up appointments, and the firm's future looked shaky but promising. Each morning I arrived to Davis sitting at the reception desk, where throughout the day he took phone calls from potential clients, while only a month earlier we'd been losing them every day. The final test would come with the meeting in front of the bar's disciplinary committee, and I could only hope that all the changes and safeguards I put into place would show them I was nothing like my father and brother.

I knew that Davis was working hard to try and help as best he could, but his lack of legal background in general, and education in the estates and trusts field in particular, limited his abilities. I needed a full-fledged paralegal to assist with the day-to-day paperwork. After spending another day drowning in filings, I made a decision, and I hoped Davis would understand and agree it could only benefit us both. I picked up the phone.

"Davis, could you please come in?"

"Sure. Be right there."

He stood at the entrance to my office, waiting for me with a nervous smile. "Is everything all right?"

"Come on in and sit. Don't look so scared. It's nothing bad. You've been working here for a while now, and I wanted to know how you feel about it."

Still uneasy, he parked himself in one of the chairs in front of my desk. "I really like it. I'm learning a lot about estates and trusts law, and it's so interesting to see how the different trusts are structured." He paused, brow furrowed. "I, uh, I know it's been a learning curve for me, and sometimes it takes a little longer than you might like—"

"Which is exactly what I called you in to talk about." I opened the top drawer of my desk and removed several pamphlets. "Your work is exemplary as far as fixing the computer system, answering the phones, and making appointments, but it would be helpful if you had the knowledge and tools to deal with the other aspects as well." I slid the brochures across the desk to him. "So…I'd like you to do a little look-see through these and do your own research and pick a paralegal school."

"Paralegal school? You want me to go back to school?"

I hadn't thought Davis would disagree. "Are you sure you don't want this as a career?" I folded my arms. "You know, I'd say close to fifty percent of the people who go to paralegal school continue on to law school."

His jaw dropped. "Law school? Me?"

"Yes. You." I steepled my fingers under my chin. "You sound surprised. Why not? You're smart, a quick learner, and I can see you're interested in the subject matter. I mentioned it earlier, and you didn't say no."

While I spoke, Davis picked up the brochures and studied them. There was no disguising his doubt, but I also picked up a spark of something else—yearning. He set them on the desk and pushed them toward me, but his gaze lingered on them.

"I-I appreciate the offer, but I can't."

"Because?" I had an inkling, but I wanted to hear it from him.

"Because I can't afford it. I know you said the firm would pay for it, but I don't like being beholden."

"That's foolish and short-sighted—even downright stupid on your part."

"Don't hold back," he mumbled.

"There are other words I could use. I told you already, it's a cost of doing business and the firm can pay."

"I guess I wasn't sure you were telling the truth."

"I don't lie," I snapped. "The only choice you have to make is which program. Apply to a bunch and see where you get in. You can use me as a reference if you want, or a former employer."

Maybe it was the light, but something unpleasant, or maybe fearful, flashed in Davis's eyes. "I think they'll probably prefer a current employer."

And again, as before, I wondered why he kept his past locked so tight. I'd done my own bit of poking around and checked the state court filings to see if he had a record and came up with nothing. Not that I expected to find Davis a hardened criminal, but while my mother blithely and maybe foolishly accepted people by their word, I was a little—okay, *a lot*—more cynical. I trusted no one.

"I'm happy to give you whatever help you need."

He scooped up the pamphlets and rose to his feet, more animated than I'd seen him since he began working for me. "Th-thank you. This is so exciting. I might want to take the classes online so I won't miss work and put you in a bind. Don't worry."

"Considering it's my idea, I'm not. They do have night classes because so many of the students work full-time. I really suggest in-person classes for this."

He hesitated. "I never would've thought…I really appreciate it."

"Not a problem."

Clutching the information, Davis left my office with a smile. A warm feeling filled my chest, knowing I was helping him. It wasn't a savior complex; I knew Davis would excel at any job he held. Well, almost any job. A waiter he was not, for sure.

At lunchtime I walked past his desk and spied him studying the computer screen. He had at least four tabs open with different schools, and he'd set up a chart with the pros and cons of each.

Unnoticed, I leaned in closer. "You're such a computer geek. I should've known you'd do this." Damn, he smelled good. And those green eyes shot through with gold? They glittered like sunlight through stained glass when he became excited. I should excite him more often. I liked it.

Shut up, Carson. Get your mind out of the gutter.

So I said, "If it were me, I'd make columns on a legal pad, but you get all fancy with color coding and shit like that."

He snorted. "Shit like that is what I went to school for and how I'm fixing all your files. I'm three-quarters through them all and creating a new system. I have to say it looks like someone made an attempt to put them in order and then in the middle said 'Fuck it' and gave up. But the good thing is, it shouldn't take me too long. This is nothing compared to what I've done in previous jobs."

"In Harleyville?" I asked casually, hoping he wouldn't shut down as he'd done the previous times. To my surprise, he was actually chatty.

"Yeah. I managed tons of files. It was a mess when I started working there. Worse than you."

I pushed his chair. "Hey. Who're you calling a mess?"

He raised a brow. "I mean…"

"It's not my fault," I protested. "I wasn't even here. I inherited this."

"I'm just kidding. But if you're willing to do this for me, I'm willing to teach you the basics—Excel, Google Docs, saving your files…you really should know how to do the fundamentals."

"I do." I sat my butt on the edge of his desk. "I mean, I'm not a total loser with computers. When I first worked here, the secretaries did everything, and in London I had a fantastic legal secretary. It was easier to let someone else handle it than try and learn it myself. I can use the programs but only to a point. I guess tech is not my strong suit. I can save my docs, but sometimes they disappear and I can't find them, or the computer will crash and I'll lose what I'm working on." I smirked. "Paper never does that. Paper is my friend."

"Until you spill your morning coffee all over it."

I scowled. "That was an accident. I was rushing to answer the phone, and my cup tipped over. The pages dried out. Eventually."

His eyes danced. "Which wouldn't ever happen with a computer file. Case closed."

"Oh, yeah?" I still wasn't convinced. "I seem to recall horror stories of spilling water on keyboards and frying circuit boards or whatever. What about that, huh?"

Who knew computer talk could be so much fun?

"Come here, little grasshopper, and I'll show you something amazing." He waved me over and pointed to his keyboard. "See? I have a shield over it to protect from spills." He arched a brow. "And cookie crumbs."

"Was that a dig?" I made a face. "I'm busy. You know I don't have time most days to go out for lunch. I have to eat at my desk. And I need sugar, otherwise I get weak in the afternoon. Stop picking on me."

"Weak? That's the lamest excuse for being a junk-food addict I've ever heard. Just admit you're a candy fiend. You're anything but weak." Davis fell into his chair, laughing. "And don't pout. I promise I'll teach you how to back everything up."

I'd like to back up…into you.

God, that was awful. I shouldn't be lusting after my assistant. I knew better than to be led around by my dick. It was like bad porn. Davis had been nothing but professional, and I had to stop thinking of him naked and bent over my desk.

"Thanks." I tipped my head to the computer. "So? Did you make any decisions on which program you'd like to attend?"

"So far I think NYU has everything I want, and once I graduate, I can get a specialized certificate in estates and trusts. Plus, it's NYU. Everyone knows the name."

"And they have an excellent law school," I pointed out, "in case you want to take the next step."

"I don't understand." Davis screwed up his face and chewed his lip. "Why're you being so nice to me?"

"Should I not be? Are you trying to tell me something?" I smirked, but apparently Davis didn't find my humor funny. He remained earnest.

"Come on. You're being so helpful, trying to bolster my career. You're nothing like the guy from the diner."

"I'm thinking I ended up doing you a favor." I hopped off his desk. "Now look at you—working in a nice office with a fabulous boss, applying to paralegal school…a whole new future. And you get to wear suits. No more smelling like bacon grease and burnt toast."

The phone rang, but he continued to gaze at me with confusion. "So what you're trying to tell me is that you're really a nice guy."

"I am. A very nice guy." I motioned to the ringing phone. "Now answer that before *I* fire you."

"Don't think I didn't hear the comment about a fabulous boss you sneaked in there." Davis snickered but picked up the phone while I returned to my office. I recalled that one of my father's associates was a dean at NYU, and when I searched online, found him to still be in that position. I hesitated a moment, wondering if my father had ever said anything negative about me to him, but decided I didn't give a damn. Helping Davis was more important than my fragile ego.

"May I speak to Dean Wallace? It's Carson Ballard."

It took less than ten seconds.

"Carson Ballard? You're Lawrence's son, correct?"

"Yes, sir."

"My condolences. I spoke with Patty at the funeral, but I don't believe we had a chance to talk. I had Dale in my Criminal Procedure class. Obviously, my words didn't sink in. For all his likable ways, he was a foolish man."

Patty? I'd never heard anyone call my mother that.

I winced but soldiered on. "Yes, well, I'm here trying to right the wrongs. And because of that, I'm inundated and require the help of a paralegal."

"And you called me about this for what reason?"

I could almost see those bushy gray brows of his raised high.

"A favor. I know you teach classes in the paralegal program, and I was wondering if you could vouch for a student I'm having apply. He works for me now, and he's interested in attending. I know it's a little late in the process, but I was hoping you could get him into the next starting class."

"You never did take my class, did you?"

"No, sir. It was closed when I tried to register for it."

"I guess that's why you never heard my lecture on nepotism and how it hurts the truly qualified."

"I agree." I forged on, "But Davis—my assistant—he *is* truly deserving. He's not some person without a plan. He wants to learn and maybe go on to law school after. I really believe he will be an excellent paralegal."

The silence from Dean Wallace made me uneasy, but I held my tongue and waited for him to respond.

"You're nothing like your brother, are you? I don't ever recall him as the type who'd care much about anyone but himself."

"No," I answered quietly. "I'm nothing like him. Nothing like him at all."

"Give me your assistant's name, and I'll see what I can do."

"Thank you, Dean Wallace. I appreciate it."

"You're a good son, Carson. Many would've walked away from the mess your family left you and not given a damn. I feel terrible for Patty having to face what happened, and I'm glad she has you to help her through this."

"I'm just trying to do what's right. Thank you again, Dean Wallace."

"You're welcome. Good luck."

After the call, I thought about his words. My hard work and determination had nothing to do with being a good son to my father. I was anything but. Aside from not wanting the firm to go under because my mother's grandfather had been a founding partner, it was the fire burning inside me, fed by my father's hatred for who I was, that spurred me on. Wherever he was, he'd know it was his gay son who brought his name back from the ashes.

CHAPTER TEN

Davis

When Carson told me what he'd done, I was more than a little annoyed at his pulling strings for me.

"You didn't think I could get in on my own?" Hurt that he assumed I'd need help, I was ready to quit altogether—paralegal school, the firm…everything.

"Don't be ridiculous," Carson answered mildly, which pissed me off even more.

"Then why did you have to do it?"

"Because," he snapped, clearly irritated with me, "you wanted it, so I tried to help you the only way I knew how. Dean Wallace did nothing but make sure your application was accepted for this term since it was a little late. And I didn't have to do it. I wanted to. You would get in no matter what. I just wanted to make sure it was as soon as possible."

The wind taken out of my sails, and feeling foolish, I hung my head.

"Oh. Well…thank you. I'm sorry for questioning you.

I-I'm just not accustomed to people being that nice and going out on a limb for others when they expect nothing in return."

"But I do expect something." Carson's husky voice sent a tingling thrill through me, and desire pooled low in my belly.

"What?" I hoped he couldn't see how turned-on I'd gotten from those words.

"Hard work and you taking on more responsibility for the paperwork, which will free me up for other things."

Okay. I had my answer. Carson was oblivious to my dirty thoughts and was—as he should be—all about the business. And thank God for that because I was sure he'd be appalled at what I was imagining now. Carson taking me into his office, stripping me naked, and having me get on my knees to suck his cock.

Brian would often call me during the workday for that very reason. We'd find any place we could go to be together—at any time—no matter how inappropriate. And wasn't it more fun and exciting having sex in the office? Being young and dumb, I thought it was daring and an indication of how badly he wanted me. Only now did I see exactly how manipulative he was.

"Other things?" I faced the computer, where I'd opened the *Congratulations and welcome* email from the admissions committee of the paralegal school. "Like what?"

"Like procuring clients so we can make money." He smirked. "Little things like that."

Not little at all. I knew how hard he was working to salvage the clients who hadn't yet cut ties, spending hours on the phone with them. Since I began working, at least a dozen clients had left with veiled threats of lawsuits if their files weren't promptly turned over. Delving into the firm's shoddy recordkeeping before Carson's arrival, I'd determined that those clients' accounts hadn't been touched, but they wanted nothing to do with a firm that had been tainted by fraud and wrongdoing. While I couldn't blame them for wanting to walk away, I knew that each one brought the firm that much closer to collapse.

There was so much riding on Carson's sheer determination and will to right the wrongs of his family, I couldn't begin to imagine the enormity of the weight on his shoulders. The future of the firm rested on the meeting with the disciplinary committee scheduled for later in the month.

"Oh. Well, you don't have anything to worry about when it comes to me. I'm excited to learn more and help you—I mean the firm. I can't tell you how grateful I am for this opportunity, and I want you to know I'm going to do my best."

"I never doubted it for a minute," Carson replied briskly and with none of his former teasing. "Now, how is the Emerson file coming along? I have to provide a full accounting to them by tomorrow."

"I'm almost done. Don't worry. It'll be ready."

A quicksilver smile was directed at me. "I have to worry. From the time I came home to take over the firm, it's the only diet I've existed on. Worry mixed with anger and a touch of fear and shame. When you're ready with those files, bring them to me. And congratulations again."

Maybe that was why he ate half his weight in candy on a daily basis. All that sugar was a good cover-up for the bitterness he wrestled with.

* * *

Two weeks later, excited but nervous as hell, I walked into the lecture hall and took an empty seat. Close to a hundred students fidgeted or sat and scrolled on their phones. I'd put mine away and set it to silent. I wouldn't let anything distract me.

NYU. Who would've believed it? When I told my

parents, they were thrilled, especially when they heard the firm would pay for it. It helped lessen my mother's negativity toward Carson. She refused to believe I bore any responsibility in my own firing.

"It hasn't started yet, has it?" A breathless man, who looked to be in his midthirties, slid into the empty seat next to mine. "I got stuck on the damn A train and almost had a heart attack running here."

"No, it hasn't. You're safe."

"Thanks. I'm Kelly, by the way."

"Davis," I offered with a smile.

"You work for a firm?"

"It's a solo practice, but I know my boss would like to hire more attorneys to help him in the future. How about you?"

"I'm at a three-person practice on Court Street in downtown Brooklyn. Meyers, Cohen, and Stanton. Personal injury, some criminal." Kelly pulled out his laptop and hung his bag over the back of his chair. "I've been there for four years, and I'm hoping after I get my paralegal degree, I can go to law school at night. All the partners in my firm went to Brooklyn Law and say they'll put in a good word for me."

So Carson wasn't making it up. Knowing that made me feel better. "That's great. They must like you."

"I bust my ass for them, but the pay is good, and the promise of a job after graduation is even better. You plan on going to law school?"

It wasn't anything that had ever been on my radar. I'd been happy with my computer programming and spreadsheets. Brian was an attorney, and I'd handled enough subpoenas and filings against the town to know how convoluted the law could be. Plus, I wasn't so sure I could defend someone I personally found repugnant, no matter how much I believed everyone deserved their day in court. But the corporate world and the intricacies of estates and trusts did intrigue me.

"I'm not sure. Right now, I want to learn what I can, and then if I'm good at it, go on to get a specialized certificate."

"What kind?" Kelly asked.

"Estates and trusts."

"That shit can get complicated." Kelly nodded, looking impressed. "Lots of money involved with rich people. Bet you've seen and heard some crazy stuff. I know I have."

"You got that right." I had a feeling Kelly would love me to get into some dirty details, but the first thing I'd learned was discretion. Our clients deserved nothing less. If he expected me to name the firm, he'd be waiting a long time. Nice as Kelly seemed, if he recognized the name, I didn't need to answer a thousand questions on what had happened. My allegiance lay with Carson.

The professor entered and began the introduction to what we could expect from the class.

"You'll learn the mechanics of drafting answers, complaints, and how to prepare interrogatories and research cases to assist the attorneys you work for. Rest assured, you won't always be listening to me drone on and on up here. From time to time, I'll have guest lecturers come to speak in my stead."

Kelly nudged me. "A guy I knew took this course a couple of years ago and said a Court of Appeals judge taught one class, and so did Barry Slotnick."

"Who's that?"

"You're kidding?" I shrugged and shook my head, he continued. "He's old now, but in the '80s he defended all those Mafia bosses and the subway shooter, Bernhard Goetz. Barry Slotnick is a legend in criminal law. You're not from the city?"

"No, upstate. I didn't pay much attention to all the crime here, but I bet he's forgotten more than most people will ever know."

"When it came to defending the Mafia—John Gotti? That's the only way to keep your head. Literally." The man wasn't joking, and I made a face.

"Uh, no thanks. I think I'll stick with estate work. They're dead already—they can't hurt me."

I listened carefully and took notes on my laptop. I'd done some legal work for Brian, but this course was much more intensive and in depth, and I understood why Carson wanted me to take it. By the time it was over, I could see I'd need to improve my writing skills. I'd be learning to draft documents, which would help me not only in the day-to-day at the firm but also if I decided to attend law school. An exciting prospect and one I'd never dreamed of before meeting Carson. I owed him more than I could say.

When the lecture was over, we packed up our laptops, and Kelly took out his phone. "Can I get your number? Maybe we can study together and help each other out."

"Sure." It made sense, and I was glad to have a friend in the class.

He got to his feet. "All righty. I gotta go. It's a long ride to Queens."

My eyes bugged out. "Damn, it sure is. Why're you so far out?"

He slung his laptop case over his shoulder. "My husband's firm is in Jamaica. He's a partner and does criminal work, and most of his clients are from the area, so it makes sense since he's in court two to three times a week. Normally, it's not a big deal, but with this evening class, it's a drag. I won't get home until really late."

"I can imagine. Well, nice to meet you, and see you next week."

"Take care."

It took me less than half an hour to get home, and I lay on the couch, staring at the ceiling. With the paralegal certificate I could make over fifty thousand dollars a year, which still wasn't much in the city, but law school…that could be a game changer. Carson hadn't said if the firm would pick up *that* expense, and without it, I knew I couldn't afford to go unless I got significant aid. But still. *Wow.*

Did I want that? My exposure to lawyers had been minimal: Brian and Carson. As I'd discovered, Brian was a user, and Carson…well, let's say the jury was still out.

But I was definitely interested in finding out what made him tick.

My phone rang.

"Hi, Mom."

"You haven't called this week. Are you all right?"

The overprotectiveness could be a little smothering, which was one of the reasons I hadn't followed them to Florida. Much as I loved them, my parents—well, my mother, actually—could be…overbearing. Weekly phone calls and visits several times a year were plenty for me, although I knew my mother wanted more.

"Yeah, sure. Just busy. You know, new job, and I want to make a good impression. And now I'm taking that paralegal course I told you about. It started tonight."

"I'm sure you're doing wonderfully. You're such a perfectionist. Dad and I are so much happier to see you in a steadier job than waiting tables at the diner. Especially with your degree."

Nothing like a mother to boost your ego. "I hope so. See, Carson's firm is paying for the program, so I have to make sure I do well. I don't want him to think I'm not taking it seriously. He said I should consider law school afterward."

"Law school? I didn't know you were interested in being a lawyer."

"I'm not sure yet, but it's nice to have options. I guess I'll know more after I take this course and see what it's all about. Tonight was only the overview. We haven't gotten into the nitty-gritty of what I'll be learning."

"And Carson is being nice to you?"

Not as nice as I'd have liked, but I didn't plan on revealing my X-rated dreams to anyone. They'd remain my secret fantasy life that I visited every night before I fell asleep. Jerking off to thoughts of Carson was the only way I could relieve the tension of being around someone so fucking sexy all day, but I was determined to be strong and not give in to temptation, considering how badly it had blown up in my face the other time.

"We're not five-year-olds on the playground. Carson doesn't need to be nice to me. The man is my boss, not my best friend, but yes, he's been nothing but professional and helpful."

"Don't get mad. Even though you've been living there almost two years, I still don't like the thought of you on your own in New York City. Every day we read in the papers how dangerous it is. Now you're taking classes at night…I hope you're not riding the subway."

"Mom"—I struggled to hold my temper in check—"I'm fine. I take the train every morning."

"Are you sure you don't want to move down here? The weather is so much nicer, and you could have a pool and play tennis anytime you want. And no snow."

"Just hurricanes, right? Look, we've been over this."

In the background, I heard my father. "Jen, enough already. Leave the poor man alone. Cut the strings."

I grinned to myself. My father, loving as he was, understood. "Listen to Dad. I'm happy, and so are you. Let's leave it at that."

"I guess I'll have to," she answered, but there was no disguising her sigh of regret. "Maybe if you had a boyfriend, someone to spend your time with, I wouldn't have to be so concerned."

"You don't have to be. I'm doing well. Really well. Right now, I'm concentrating on my career. I'm too busy and tired at night when I come home to think about anything else, but I'm enjoying it. The last thing I need or want is for you to worry."

"He's right, Jenny," my father interjected in the background. "Remember what the doctors said. The less stress, the better."

"It's not a crime to be interested in your son," she responded, more sharply than normal. "All I want is for Davis to be happy."

"Which I am." The time had come for the conversation to end. "I'll call you next week and tell you how the class is going. Everything is going to be fine. Bye. Love you."

I ended the call, feeling more guilty than I should. I didn't like arguing, but I also didn't like being treated as though I'd never progressed beyond the fifth grade and playdates. Maybe it was why I'd rebelled, why I had such a screwed-up dating life. My parents only knew about Brian. I hadn't told them about my affair with one of my TAs in college. Or the crush I'd had on my supervisor at my job in the frozen-yogurt store. Yeah, I had a bad habit of falling for the wrong men. Over and over.

Except now. No way was I falling for the boss again.

CHAPTER ELEVEN

Carson

Of everything I'd faced since returning home, the meeting before the disciplinary committee was the sword hanging over my head, and as I proceeded into the conference room, four disapproving faces awaited. I wanted to turn around and run.

Three grueling hours later, I walked out of 61 Broadway, sweaty and drained. I leaned against the concrete building and called the office. Traffic whizzed past me, and though the streets teemed with people, I felt insulated, inside a bubble where no one could touch me.

"Well?" Davis answered on the first ring, breathless and hesitant, and I smiled, imagining him sitting on the edge of his chair, ready to spring, waiting for the phone to ring. "I can't believe they kept you in there so long."

"The only reason they aren't taking action is because with me solely at the helm, they consider Ballard and Melbourne akin to a brand-new firm. With my father and brother no longer part of the management, they're willing to let me continue, but subject to quarterly checks by the court."

The first hour had been me defending myself from the rapid-fire questions posed by the committee. They'd had a difficult time believing I'd had no knowledge of Dale's and my father's activities, and I'd kept my cool, finally convincing them that we'd been estranged to the point of noncommunication. I'd never been happier to be an outcast.

"That's good, right?"

His excitement was contagious. "Yeah. Very good. You've got your job for another day."

"That's ridiculous. I didn't mean that at all and you know it," Davis countered, his voice laced with exasperation.

"Hey," I soothed. "I'm just kidding. I know. I-I appreciate it. Listen, I'm going home first before returning to the office."

"All right. Congratulations, Carson. I'm happy for you."

"See you soon."

Hoping to give my mother the news in person, I stopped by her place but was informed by the concierge that she was out, so I continued on. Once in my apartment, I stripped off my sweaty shirt and underwear and took a shower. Knowing Davis was such a whiz at computers, I wanted no trace on any office computer of what I was about to do, so after dressing in a fresh suit, I opened my laptop and looked up Harleyville, New York.

"Damn, he wasn't kidding. It is small."

Population of less than five thousand—I must've passed more people on Broadway that morning. But that wasn't the information I was after. I clicked around until I came to City Government and found what I was searching for.

Brian Healy. Mayor.

A generically handsome face stared at me from the screen. Blond hair, square, determined jaw, brown eyes. Early forties. I scanned his bio and found nothing out of the ordinary. Married to a pretty brunet, father to a newborn baby girl, and owner of a cute golden retriever and a clapboard house with a picket fence. Typical family.

I scrolled through the organizational charts and found an old one listing Davis as executive assistant to the mayor.

"That explains why you're so good at your job. But why hide it?" I continued my search. "Something isn't adding up."

I scrolled through the township's Facebook page and clicked on their photos, going back to several years earlier.

"Aha." Pictures of a summer picnic popped up, and I enlarged one photo in particular. Brian Healy and a young man who looked like… "Davis. There you are."

He stood by a tree, gazing up at Healy with a serious expression. I clicked on the next picture. People scattered all about the field, children playing soccer, everyone eating barbecue and hanging out. Once again, I zoomed in on the photo and picked out two figures in the background, leaving the picnic and getting into a car. If I squinted, I could make out a blond man with a hand on the dark-haired man's shoulder.

"Now what the hell is that about?" I whispered.

I shut the laptop, finished getting dressed, and left for the office. I had so many questions: Where were the two of them going, and why did Healy have his hand on Davis? Had they been lovers? Could they still be together? My stomach soured at that thought, but I dismissed it outright. Davis had little to no desire to speak about his past. Why did Davis leave and become a waiter? He was qualified to be so much more. And why, if he was gay, did he have such an aversion to me touching him?

The idea of someone deliberately hurting a kind person like Davis made me want to punch a wall. I unclenched my hand from the painful fist I'd made.

Between their body language and the way those two

stared at each other, it was blatantly obvious they'd been sharing a private moment that was inadvertently captured on camera. Not that I had any right to ask him. That didn't stop me from wanting to know more… Hell, I needed to know everything about Davis.

* * *

I pushed through the glass front doors to the office suite and found my mother chatting with Davis. Her face brightened.

"Carson, I heard the wonderful news." She hugged me. "I'm so proud of you. I knew you could do it."

"That makes one of us," I joked but held her tight. "Thanks, Mom," I whispered. It was nice to have someone to lean on and give me support when I'd been fighting alone for so long.

"I called before I came by, and Davis told me you'd be here soon—that you'd gone home first."

I ran a hand through my slightly damp hair. "I was so nervous, I sweated through my shirt. I couldn't stand spending the whole day like that; I took a shower."

"I thought that was a different suit." Davis's gaze swept over me, and I grinned.

"Checking me out?"

Red spots burst over his cheeks. "Don't be ridiculous."

My mother interrupted. "I've ordered lunch for the three of us to celebrate. They should be bringing it any minute."

"Thanks." I sat in one of the swivel chairs and spun around. "They were unpleasant, but I was prepared for that. I'd expected it to be horrible, so the fact that it was only somewhat awful is a win. I think going forward we'll be able to slowly rebuild the practice, and it'll all be okay. Did Davis tell you about the new clients we've slowly been accumulating?"

"No, your mother and I were discussing politics."

"Really?" I decided to push his buttons a little in an effort to get him to spill more information. "I guess you're into that, having worked for the mayor."

"You did?" My mother's brows rose high. "I thought you only worked in the office. I didn't know you worked for the mayor directly, Davis," she said, suitably impressed. "How exciting."

"Not really. Definitely not exciting or all that interesting." His angry eyes focused on me. "I told you that part of my life was over."

"But why? It must've been fast-paced. Especially working as his personal assistant."

Instead of coming back at me with a snippy response, he sagged, and all the energy seemed to drain from him. Refusing to meet my eyes, he shook his head.

"No. It wasn't."

An unfamiliar emotion rolled through me, which I recognized as shame. I might be having fun teasing Davis, but it wasn't a game to him. Not after seeing his response. Something happened to send him running, and it was traumatic enough for him to upend his whole life and hide out here in the city. Because I had no doubts that Davis had a secret. Was he in the closet? Did his family abandon him? My chest tightened, the goodwill from the morning's accomplishment fading.

"Hey, Davis?" He lifted his head, and I didn't like the wariness and pain etched in his face. "I'm sure you had your reasons for leaving, and their loss was my gain. I'm sorry."

The elevator doors opened, and a delivery person with our lunch approached. Davis rose to his feet to handle the food. My mother took my elbow and pulled me aside.

"What's going on?"

"What do you mean? I told you everything that happened

before the committee."

"Don't be ridiculous. I'm talking about between you two."

She always was the most perceptive person in our family.

"Nothing." I shrugged. Over her shoulder, I watched Davis carry the tray of sushi into the conference room.

Lips pursed in annoyance, she gave me the same look as when she'd caught me sneaking home at sixteen at one in the morning smelling like beer and cigarettes. I didn't fool her then, and I wasn't fooling her now. "Davis is a very sweet man, and he's been instrumental in helping you get this office up and running again."

"I agree."

Since he'd started working here, he'd sure as hell gotten me up and running as well. Up first thing in the morning. In the shower. Late at night after staring at that ass all day in those slacks.

Up, up, and away. *Rawr.*

Rein it in. You don't want to get a hard-on in front of your mother.

She eyed me. "You like him."

"Of course I like him. I couldn't work with him if I didn't."

She raised her eyes to the ceiling. "Help me, God," she muttered, then fixed me with that all-knowing stare. "Don't play dumb with me. Your feelings go beyond him being your assistant. Why don't you ask him out?"

Heat suffused me. "I am *not* about to have a conversation about my personal life, at my age, with you. Besides, I'm too busy to date anyone. And that's all I'm going to say."

Arms folded, she refused to let me off the hook and continued on her merry way. "Fine. Don't talk. Just listen. I know Andrew hurt you. I could've told you he wasn't the right man for you."

"You did. Loud and clear." In the time I'd lived abroad,

she'd visited me several times a year, always hoping to meet Andrew. He'd conveniently been busy with work all the times she'd tried to set up dinners, lunches…anything.

"You can't let his cheating ruin your trust in everyone."

"I knew it was a mistake to ever say anything," I grumbled. The one and only time I'd ever discussed my personal life with her had proved my undoing. My mother believed all I needed was a boyfriend and my life would be perfect.

"You didn't have to. I knew." She patted my cheek. "A mother always knows. Have you seen him since you've moved back?"

"No, I haven't." I had no need to tell her I'd tried to contact him. That would lead to a lecture on valuing myself, and I didn't need that. "And by the way, I had a very interesting conversation with Dean Wallace from NYU."

Now it was her turn to turn pink-cheeked. "Charles?"

"Mmhmm." I decided two could play at her game. "He called you Patty. I didn't know you went by that nickname."

"And why would you? I'm your mother." She linked her arm in mine. "Let's go have some sushi."

Neatly sidestepping any further questions, she marched us to the conference room, where Davis had disappeared with our lunch. He'd unpacked the sushi and put it out on the table along with chopsticks, plates, cups, and a pitcher of ice water from the refrigerator.

"Thank you for the lunch, Mrs. Ballard. It's sure better than my peanut butter and jelly sandwich."

"Please call me Patricia. And you deserve it after all the help you've given jumping into the role of office manager on the fly." She selected a roll. "Especially given the way Carson treated you."

"Okay, Mom. We've moved past that. I've apologized numerous times, and Davis has accepted."

Her sunny smile didn't fool me, but she left me alone and

questioned Davis. "Do you have family in the city, Davis? Or are they all still upstate? Do you have any siblings?"

"Might as well give in and answer, Davis." I popped a spicy salmon roll into my mouth. "Resistance is futile."

He finished chewing and drank some water. "No, I'm an only child. My parents retired and moved to Florida. Neither could stand the cold and snow, so now they've traded it for humidity and hurricanes. I can't blame them. It can get wild up there in the winter."

"Is that why you left?" I asked him. "The weather?" Pretending innocence, I played with my chopsticks, waiting for his answer.

"Partly."

Backing off from further interrogation, I changed course and turned to my mother. "Did I tell you Davis is going to paralegal school now?"

"Charles did. He said you spoke very highly of Davis."

"I spoke the truth. He's an incredible asset. My secret weapon."

Davis turned red and choked, coughing up a lung. I sprang into action, slipping one arm around his waist and patting his shoulders with the other. He wheezed, and I murmured, "Take it easy. I've got you."

He coughed, and I held him tighter, hyperaware of his solid, muscular torso pressed to my chest. His silky hair tickled my nose, and I held off rubbing my cheek to his head like a contented cat.

"I'm okay now." He pushed off me, leaving no doubt he wanted me as far away from him as possible.

Ignoring my mother's side-eye and smirk, I continued to ask him questions. "What made you decide to come to the city? It must've been a huge culture shock—from such a small town to being surrounded by so many people."

Eyes on his plate, he lifted a shoulder. "I got used to it."

"That tells me nothing."

That got to him, and he set his chopsticks on the plate and gave me the full force of his stare. "I know. But just because I work for you doesn't mean you get the rights to my life story." He picked up his empty plate and dumped it into the trash, then gave my mother an apologetic smile. "Thank you so much for the delicious lunch, Mrs. Ballard. It was nice to see you again. I'd better get back to my desk. I have some trust agreements to update for you, Carson, and I have to answer the phones."

Without waiting for my answer, he walked out, leaving me even more determined to figure out what the hell had happened between him and the mayor.

"Someone hurt that man very badly," my mother said quietly. "I hope you can help him."

I cleaned up my plate and took hers and dumped the tray in the recycling. "Who says I want to? And even if I did, you saw how he couldn't wait to get away from me." Davis had made his wish for me to stay away painfully clear.

"I say you do." She gathered her purse and kissed me on the cheek. "And perhaps he's running away because he feels too much. He's trying to hide it."

She left me shaking my head, annoyed that she was right. The little I knew about Davis wasn't enough. I wanted more.

CHAPTER TWELVE

Davis

For the first time since I started working at the law firm, I couldn't wait to get home. Carson chipping away at my story set off my desire to flee, leaving me a bundle of nerves on the inside.

I changed and showered, hoping the warm water would soothe me, but all it did was inflame my already heightened emotional state. I finished and dried off, dressed in a T-shirt and boxers, and dug out my phone from my messenger bag to call my friend Tommy.

"Davis? You okay?"

I smiled to myself. Only two years older than me, Tommy and I had grown up next door to each other, and he'd appointed himself as my surrogate big brother. He was the only one I'd confided in when Brian and I started our affair, and he'd begged me to stop and think about the consequences. I'd laughed and told him everything would turn out all right.

I *had* been thinking, just not with the right part of my body.

"Yeah, I'm good. Just haven't talked to you in a while, and I wanted to check in. How're Carrie and the kids?"

Tommy and Carrie met in high school and got married right after graduation. Tommy worked at the auto-parts store in the strip mall next to the TJ Maxx where Carrie was the manager. Carrie was sweet and as fiercely overprotective of me as Tommy. I had to remind her occasionally I was thirty-one, not three like their youngest daughter.

"Great. They're thinking of promoting her to district manager," he said proudly. "And Lizzy just won the county spelling bee."

"She's a smart cookie like her mom."

"So tell me, how's life in the big city? You ready to come home where you belong?"

Of course I'd also told Tommy why I had to leave. He'd tried to talk me out of it, using every argument he could think of—that I should be afraid of muggings and riding the subway, that I couldn't afford it and wasn't mentally prepared to live in a city as big and tough as New York.

"It's been two years, and I'm still making it. Living the life."

He snorted. "Dude, you've got a degree in IT, but you're waiting tables when you could be rolling in the dough."

"You're not living if you're hiding." Carrie's gentle rebuke sent a hot rush of tears to my eyes.

"Wow," I managed to breathe out with a ragged laugh. "Nagging in stereo. Something I don't miss. Love you too, Carrie-Bear."

"Oh, Davis," she sniffled. "I miss you calling me that even if I do hate it."

My smile grew broader as I stretched out on my couch. "I know, but I couldn't resist. And for your information, I'm not waiting tables anymore."

"No?" they chorused. "What happened? Did you get fired? You got another job, or are you coming home? Is that why you called?" Tommy tripped over his words.

"Calm down. It's been over two months. Yes, I got fired, but no, I'm not coming home, because I already have a new job, working in a law firm."

"Lawyers? They're almost as bad as politicians." Distaste dripped from Tommy's words. Over the years, he'd had a few run-ins with law enforcement. Tattoos covered his arms, and his imposing six-foot-six, two-hundred-and-sixty-pound frame made Tommy a target anytime something in town went wrong, even though he was as straight as a ruler and a giant teddy bear of a man with his wife and little girls. They never found anything, but it gave him a permanent mistrust of the legal system.

"What're you doing for them?"

"It's a him."

I explained the situation, leaving out, of course, how attracted I was to Carson. The last thing I needed was a lecture from Tommy and Carrie about playing footsie with my boss again.

"So you're working for the guy who got you fired? Why does that sound weird to me?"

I could picture Tommy scratching his head. "It's unusual, but Carson isn't really a bad guy. He was under tremendous pressure—"

"Listen, Davis. Everyone's got pressure. We get up every day and have to fight for what we need. Some have it much easier than the rest of us, and that makes them feel entitled to take a little walk all over the rest of us. Happens to me every day with the customers."

"Me too," Carrie agreed. "I try and deal with it the best I can, but I have a limit as to how much I can take. I'm not there to be pushed around."

"Carson doesn't push me around. He's a great boss. He

even took me to dinner at one of the best restaurants in the city to show his appreciation for my hard work."

"*Mmmhmm.*"

Hearing the skepticism from Tommy pissed me off. "What?" I snapped.

"Don't get mad. I just want you to be careful. Playing up to you and buying you nice shit was the way it started with Brian."

"I haven't forgotten. I'm not falling for anyone's bullshit again. I was way too trusting and naïve then. I'm not anymore."

"Tommy and me just wanna make sure you're gonna be okay. That's all." Carrie's calm voice settled my annoyance.

"I know. And I appreciate it, but you gotta cut the strings at some point."

"I gotta go help Olivia with her homework," she said, "but please stay in touch, 'kay? Love you."

"Love you too."

Carrie gave me a kiss through the phone, leaving me with Tommy, who loved nothing more than to rant about Brian.

"Meanwhile that bastard is still here, all smug as can be, talking about his wife and baby in the press, as if he wasn't still cornering me in the store, asking if I've been in touch with you or know where you're at."

Dread snaked through me. "He did?"

"Does," Tommy corrected. "This afternoon, in fact. I didn't want to say nothin' in front of Carrie, but yeah."

"What happened?"

I heard Tommy suck his drink through a straw. He never went anywhere without a giant Coke, and despite my nerves, I had to smile. There was comfort in knowing some things never changed.

"You know he loves his BMW. Jerk gets it serviced every three months and washes it at least twice a week. He comes in looking for some fancy-ass, super-expensive tires that need special ordering. I take him to the tire center, and while we're there, he starts chatting me up. How're the kids, how's Carrie doing, blah, blah, blah. I know it's all crap—he don't give a shit about me. I say fine, everything's fine, and walk away. Motherfucker comes running after me, grabs my arm, and gets in my face with a bunch of questions about you."

"What the hell? Are you serious?"

"Uh-huh. 'Where is he? I know you know—you're his best friend. Tell me where he is. I need to see him.' "

Slightly sick, I bit my lip. "What did you say?"

"Don't worry. All I said is you're not in New York no more, that you moved far away but didn't tell nobody. So douchebag has the gall to say, 'You're lying. You know where he is. Next time you speak to him, tell him he needs to come home. He belongs here. With me. He's mine.' "

"Jesus," I breathed. "I can't believe he had the nerve to say that to you."

"I'm telling you, the fucker's obsessed. He's got those wild eyes like in the movies, just when things are about to get hairy."

Normally I'd chalk it up to Tommy being an alarmist, but now I wasn't so sure. Brian had always possessed an ugly jealous streak, and when we were alone, used to lecture me not to be so friendly to the people coming to city hall.

"Now do you understand why I had to get away and disappear?"

"Yeah, but you said he'd forget about you. He hasn't. Dude's got a wife and a baby now, but he still wants you. He's probably fantasizing he can have it all—the family for the cameras, and you for what he really needs but wants to keep on the down-low to preserve his squeaky-clean image."

I clutched the phone in my sweaty hand. "Yeah, well, it's not happening. I've got a good job, and I'm not about to fuck up something special."

If I'd had any qualms that I'd made the right decision, they'd all been put to rest with this conversation. Anonymous in the big city was the best place for me.

"What's so special about it? You're just his assistant, right?"

"Yeah, but he's paying for me to go to paralegal school." I gave Tommy a brief rundown of what had happened to the firm before I stepped in. "He isn't the most computer savvy, and when he came home to take over the firm, it was in crisis. He was losing computer files left and right and was on the brink of collapse because of shit his brother and father did."

"So his mother finds out you're a computer whiz, hires you, and he's okay with that? He one of these prissy boys who does whatever his mommy wants?"

The idea of anyone calling Carson prissy had me laughing out loud. "The furthest thing from it. But they're close. Seems like his father and brother wanted nothing to do with him when he came out. She stood by him when no one else did. She's a very nice lady. And Carson's been working his ass off. I think he feels he has something to prove."

"To who? They're dead."

"Yeah, but sometimes that's not enough. Their negative words live on forever, and you never forget them."

"Well…" I could hear his doubt through the slurp of his soda. "It's cool he's paying for you to get a degree, and that's a great career move, but I hope you know what you're doing. From where I'm sitting, this Carson guy could be no different from Brian, only in a fancier suit. Watch out."

"You don't trust anyone when it comes to me," I brushed him off. "You never have."

"With good reason. You have lousy taste in men. First it was your crush on Ira, the manager at the Froyo place, then that fling with the TA in one of your classes at college—"

"Cooper. But—"

"Yeah, him. And Brian. You got a thing for people you work for. All I'm saying is, be careful."

There was a lot I wanted to say to Tommy, but the front-door buzzer cut me short. "Yeah, sure. Listen, I gotta go. Someone's at the door."

Before he could register a protest, I ended the call. I had no idea who it was and hit the button for the intercom. "Yes? Who is it?"

"Carson."

I stared at the iron box on my wall as if it were on fire. "Carson?"

"Yeah. Remember me? The guy who signs your paycheck? Can I come up?"

"Uh, yeah, sure." I buzzed him in and opened my front door to wait for Carson, who of course couldn't wait for the elevator and took the stairs. A little nonplussed as to why he'd come, I stood at my door, waiting. When he appeared in my view, a grin lit his face.

"Who needs a gym when you can walk up the stairs every day?"

"What're you doing here?" At his approach, I stepped out into the hall.

"Is that a nice way to say hello?" He braced an arm against the wall and searched my face. "I was worried about you."

"About me?" My laughter echoed in the empty hallway. "I'm fine, see?" I moved away from him and spread my arms wide. "Sorry you had to make an unnecessary trip this far uptown."

"I'm not." He glanced over his shoulder as one of my neighbors exited the elevator, giving us a curious look. "Can I come in?"

Much as I wanted to say no, and should, it would be rude to refuse him. Plus, I had little desire to conduct my business in the hall. With a sigh, I opened the door wide.

"Sure."

Two long strides brought him to the center of the living room, while I remained at a safe distance by sitting on the lumpy couch. He took in the entirety of the small studio with his usual penetrating stare.

With my quick escape to the city, I couldn't be choosy as to location—I took the first place I could afford. A studio in an elevator building in Manhattan met my requirements. The sublet was for two years and came fully furnished with the potential to renew. I couldn't have been happier.

"Is this where you've lived since you moved to the city?"

"Yeah. It's a lot different from the Upper East Side."

I could only imagine what Carson—someone who'd grown up on Park Avenue—thought about the dingy paint job and shabby furniture, but he merely nodded, his eyes searching my face.

Nervous, I licked my lips. He'd changed from his corporate attire to jeans, a T-shirt, and a leather jacket, and I couldn't decide which Carson I liked better—the sleek professional or this casual look. Either way he was gorgeous and made my heart race and my thoughts behave in an entirely inappropriate manner. The tension grew between us, expanding and sucking up all the air in the room.

"I feel I upset you this afternoon, and I wanted to apologize, but you left before I had the chance."

"I—you didn't. It's okay. I'm okay." I hoped my immediate, firm response would be enough to satisfy him, but who was I kidding? This was Carson Ballard, who saw everything. The man could spot a fake and a liar a mile away, and I was both.

"Try again." To my surprise, he sat next to me, and my heartbeat kicked up another notch. "You know, if you're in trouble, I can help."

"I'm not."

Grim-faced, he shook his head. "Why don't I believe

you?"

"I don't know, but that's your problem." If I'd only had this kind of courage when I'd been with Brian, things would've been different.

"No, I think it's yours." He shifted closer. "I asked you about Brian, and you said he was your boss, but I think it was something more."

His words hit me like a bucket of ice water dumped over my head. "What the hell are you talking about?"

He shrugged, looking not the least bit embarrassed. "I might've done a little Internet research."

"Since when do you know how to use a computer that well?" I grumbled, and he snickered.

"I might be a fail at keeping a filing system or figuring out how to use an Excel spreadsheet, but I'm a whiz at Google." The laughter faded. "I know something isn't right. I just want to help if I can."

"You can't."

Those blue eyes widened. "You *are* in trouble."

Dammit. I hadn't meant for that to sound the way it did.

"No. Really, I'm not." My lips felt numb as I forced out the words. "It's all good. And I really appreciate you coming all the way up here to check on me, but there's nothing to worry about. I'll be in the office tomorrow, ready to tackle whatever you have for me."

But Carson wasn't stupid, and he checked his watch. "Look at the time. No wonder I'm hungry. How about we order a pizza?"

I rolled my eyes. "Oh, come on. That has to be the fakest segue in the history of the world."

Eyes dancing, he rubbed his stomach. "But I am hungry. All I had today was that sushi."

"And two Kit Kats and a Milky Way. Don't think I don't know about your chocolate addiction."

"Spoilsport," he responded with a sulky pout. I hated

how I noticed his dimples and how full and soft his lips looked. I didn't want to like him. Or want him.

"Did anyone ever tell you how pushy you are?"

With a grin, he took out his phone. "All the time. Pushy, picky, whatever. Just give me pepperoni, and I'm good." He winked. "Mushrooms too?"

"Sure. Knock yourself out. Wait, I thought you were lactose intolerant." I snickered. "Or did I mishear, and you actually said you were intolerable?" I smirked, and his face turned red. "That's more likely to be believed."

"Aren't you the comedian? And sometimes it's worth the stomachache to indulge."

Cackling, he placed the order. Almost immediately after, his phone began buzzing, and he stared at the screen. His jaw hardened and he placed it away from him on the coffee table.

"Bad news? Is everything all right?"

"Yeah, fine. It's nothing."

I narrowed my eyes. Carson's good mood had vanished, and subdued, he stared off into the distance.

"Do you want to go? You seem upset."

"I said I'm fine," he snapped. "Shit. I'm sorry. I didn't mean to tear your head off. Just a text from someone I haven't heard from in forever."

"No need to apologize. Want a beer?"

"Yeah, sure. Gotta have beer with pizza. It's a rule." Unlike during our earlier fun and easy banter, his smile was forced, but I didn't want to press him on it.

"I didn't know that. Guess I'd better write it down." I handed him a cold bottle of Molson.

"Thanks. And yes, you should." Some of his cockiness returned. "I have a few good ones to follow."

I decided two could play his game. "You know…it goes both ways. If something's wrong, I can help."

"What makes you say that?"

"Oh, come on. You got a text, and your whole mood

changed."

"*Pfft.*" He brushed me off and drank his beer. "I told you it was nothing. I'm hungry. That's all."

I believed him like I believed in Santa Claus.

Guess that made two of us with secrets, because his *nothing* looked like a whole lot of something to me.

CHAPTER THIRTEEN

Carson

Dammit.

There I was, enjoying myself with Davis, and this shit had to happen. Why now, after ignoring me for months, did Andrew feel the need to text me?

Hey. Hearing good news about the firm. We should get together and celebrate.

I'd called him at my most vulnerable, and he'd stayed silent as a tomb. Why would he think he could waltz back into my life after disappearing like nothing ever happened?

Because you made it so easy for him all the other times, dumbass.

Determined not to let him spoil my evening, I held up my beer bottle to Davis. "To new beginnings."

His lips twitched. "You know, it's customary to make the toast *before* the first drink."

I smirked. "I'm a rebel."

"Oh brother," Davis groaned. "I think I was better off

when you acted like a jerk in the diner than all corny like this."

The buzzer sounded, and Davis answered it, then stood by the door. I waited for him to return, holding the box in his hands. The apartment was too small to have a real kitchen or a table, so I moved everything over to make room on the coffee table. My stomach growled at the smell of garlic and tomato sauce.

"God, there's nothing better than a greasy slice." Salivating, I flipped open the box and grabbed one.

"Damn, you must be hungry if you're not even waiting for a plate."

"Eh." I waved my hand in the air. "Why stand on formality?" I finished the slice in less than a minute and took another one. Still chewing his first, Davis looked on in amazement.

"Where's the fire?"

"Sorry," I said sheepishly. "I don't do this often, so I forget how good real cheese tastes and I can't control myself."

"It must be hard, having to watch what you eat all the time."

I lifted a shoulder. "Not anymore. When I was young, yeah. It was hard to go to parties and eat the pizza and ice cream, knowing that when I got home, I'd be sick all night."

"Oh, wow, yeah. I'm sorry you had to go through that."

"Worse yet was Dale, who later on attributed my problem to being gay."

Davis's jaw dropped. "What the hell is that supposed to mean?"

I'd never told anyone before, not even my mother, but I found it easy to unburden my secrets to Davis, a virtual stranger, about that kind of hurt. Worse than any physical bruise or hurt to my body was my brother's rejection. It left a scar on my heart that never healed.

"When I came out, my brother said my stomach issues were a sign of weakness, which made sense to him, since I was gay. In fact, he called me a weak link."

The cushion beside me dipped with Davis's weight as he moved closer to me. "Hey. You know that's not true."

Did I?

Playing my emotions close to the vest was how I made it through life, and I willingly kept up the pretense. "Yeah, of course. But it's still hard to fathom my brother having such animosity toward me. Up to and including middle school, we were best friends, but once Dale hit puberty, he became a different person."

"How so?" Davis asked gently.

It shouldn't sit like a lead weight on my chest after all this time. I didn't care. Really. That shooting pain radiating through me must be from the cheese in the pizza.

"You know the type. Trying to be cool. Acting like a jock, playing up to his group of friends."

"By putting you down?"

"Isn't that how bullies operate? Insecure people always push around the people they think are weaker. But the truth is, we're not weak. We don't need to yell the loudest to prove how right we are or that we're smarter. Eventually the truth comes to light. The bullies are defeated."

"Like karma?"

I turned to face him and found my lips dangerously close to his. I froze, and his eyes widened with shock. Lust throbbed low and deep in my belly, and my breath caught. The golden sparks in Davis's kaleidoscope eyes drew me in. Closer and closer. I could almost taste the softness of his mouth, feel the velvet of his tongue sweeping against mine. *Fuck.* I wanted him.

"Davis," I murmured and reached out to tangle my fingers in the hair curling at his nape.

Quicker than a blink, he sprang away from me and

hotfooted it to the tiny kitchen area. Achingly hard, I drew in some air to clear my head of the humiliation of his rejection. When I was able to stand, I wiped my fingers carefully with a napkin.

"Thanks for the dinner, Davis. I'll see you in the office tomorrow."

I shut the front door behind me and took the stairs. My car pulled up within minutes and headed home. In my apartment, I lay on my couch, my stomach cramping not only from the overdose of cheese I'd stuffed in my face, but a deadly combination of reliving my past and screwing up the present.

"God, you're a dope. What the hell made you think Davis wanted to kiss you?" Face hot with humiliation, I buried it in the couch cushions and groaned. "How the hell am I going to explain it to him tomorrow?"

My intercom rang. "Yes?"

"Carson"—the doorman sounded aggravated and concerned—"Mr. Andrew Winthrop is on his way up. I tried to stop him, but he ignored me, and I can't leave the desk."

Of course he was. The evening was already shit. Made perfect sense for it to completely implode on me.

"It's not your fault. He doesn't listen to anyone."

I checked my face in the mirror. A little weary and sleep-deprived, but that was to be expected. My stomach twisted in a knot, but I could breathe through it. I opened the door and watched his confident stride down the hall.

"Carson, baby, you look worn out." He leaned in for a kiss on my lips, but I turned away and he hit my cheek instead. The once-familiar scent of his aftershave tickled my nose as he passed me and entered my apartment.

"What're you doing here?"

"That's not a nice way to greet me after so long." He stuck his hands in his slacks and gave me that charming smile that had fooled so many, myself included, into believing they were important.

Andrew Winthrop, the epitome of preppy good looks with his straight jaw, perfect profile, and precise hairline, hadn't changed since I'd last seen him. There was no shame in him for cheating on me and ignoring my calls. The Andrew Winthrops of the world bore no responsibility for their actions and lived life dancing on a Teflon pan—nothing stuck to them, and any problems slid off their backs, leaving no trace that anything had ever touched them.

"I asked what you're doing here."

He shrugged. "When you didn't answer my text, I decided to come by and see you in person."

"How did you know where I lived?"

A cocky grin curved his lips. "I looked you up, baby."

I made a mental note to get myself unlisted everywhere.

"And what if I had someone here?"

"A date?" His brows drew high. "Do you?" He peered around. "I'm not seeing anyone, unless you have them hidden in the bedroom." A slow smile crept over his face. "I could join you."

Anger and embarrassment heated my face and my words. "Don't be an idiot. No, there's no one here, and you won't be staying."

"Oh, come on, baby, don't be like that." He flopped onto the couch, and I grimaced. I'd forgotten how adept he was at making himself at home, with or without an invitation. "I came to talk. See if we could figure out where we went wrong and patch things up."

"What went *wrong*, as you put it, was your inability to keep your dick in your pants, and your willingness to share it with whomever caught your eye. I'm not interested in a repeat performance."

Unfazed, Andrew yawned. "Yes, well, I've changed. And when I heard how hard you've been working on reviving your family's firm, I figured you must've funneled all that delicious, sexy energy into work." Surprising me, he sprang off the couch and grabbed me by the neck, yanking me against his hard, hot body. "But all work and no play makes Carson a horny boy, I'm betting." He caught my bottom lip between his teeth. "Remember how good it was? How I'd have you screaming for me? We can have that again." He nuzzled my ear, and his fingers inched down toward my zipper.

Alarmed, I knocked away his roaming fingers. "Get your hands off me, or you'll be walking crooked for a month." When he didn't move, I shoved him. "I'm not interested. Leave. And don't come back." To my relief, Andrew didn't pursue things further. The last thing I needed was a physical altercation. I was already on thin ice with the disciplinary board. I kept my temper, walked to the door, and opened it. "Go."

Laughing, Andrew walked past me as if he hadn't a care. "I like a challenge. And I bet you'll dream of me tonight. I'll see you soon, baby." He strode out, leaving me shaken and depressed. I turned the lock and paced my apartment for a while, hoping to burn off the restlessness inside me.

Damn Andrew. I hated that he was right. It had been almost a year since that wild hookup with Sammy in the Med, and I hadn't been with anyone else. Celibacy and job-related stress had left me edgy and horny as hell. I was desperate for someone to hold me, even if it was only for an hour, and I was slightly ashamed that I'd allowed Andrew to get to me. From the first night we'd met, he'd known how.

"I don't need him. I don't need anyone." My stomach cramped, and even though it was after the fact, I took another pill. I lay on my couch, staring into nothingness, when my phone buzzed. *If that's fucking Andrew, I swear I'll get a restraining order.* "Hello?" I growled, wincing at the stabbing pains in my stomach.

"Hi."

It wasn't Andrew.

"Davis?"

"Yeah. I'm sorry. Is this a bad time?"

The twisted knot in my gut loosened, and I managed a grin as I rubbed my aching belly. "Well…I don't know. Why're you calling? Did you miss me?"

"Carson, come on. Stop."

"Stop what? You called me, and I have no idea why."

"I think you do."

A chill shivered through me, and I raised myself to a sitting position. "You mean about that almost kiss?" I frowned. "Is that it?"

"Yeah," he responded softly. "That."

"You're calling me about something that didn't happen. I'm not sure I understand."

"I just…it's not…I'm not sure I should be working for you."

"What the hell are you talking about?"

"I've been thinking—"

"Always dangerous." My attempt at humor fell flat.

"Please, Carson?" Davis seemed genuinely upset, and a second, more intense chill ran through me at his serious tone. "I don't think it's a good thing for me to be your assistant."

"Why? Do you have a problem working for me because I'm gay?"

He sighed. "No, of course not. I'm gay too."

"So what is it? Because I let a moment of weakness take over?" I retorted. Was he willing to give up everything—a job, the paralegal degree—because he didn't want to be near me? "News flash, Davis, you're not the only man in the city. I'll make you a promise to keep my hands off you, if that's what you're concerned about. It was a moment and it passed and won't happen again."

"How can you be sure?"

Dammit, he really wanted to twist the knife so I knew

he wasn't interested. Hurt and humiliation made me angry and cruel, and I behaved like a silly child, striking back. "Because it didn't mean anything. You were there, and I figured, why the hell not? It was a way to pass the time. Now, I hate to cut this fascinating conversation short, but I can't stay on the phone. I'm on my way out. So if you think I'm sitting here, pining away because you didn't want to kiss me, don't worry. I'll get over it. I already have. See you in the morning."

I ended the conversation, and because I needed to prove to myself that someone still wanted me, I placed a call.

"I changed my mind. Want to meet for a drink?"

"When and where?"

"Half an hour. Jacques at the Lowell."

"See you there, baby," Andrew's husky voice filled my ear, but where that used to always put me in the mood, it barely registered.

I tossed the phone aside, ran to the bathroom, and slapped on some cologne. I changed into a suit and tie and called for a car, which was waiting for me outside my building. The drive down Park took relatively no time. I entered the bar, and a hostess greeted me with a smile.

"I'm meeting someone…" I spotted Andrew sitting at a table for two in the corner. "Never mind, I see him."

At my approach, he stood and let out a whistle. "You look good enough to eat, baby." We sat, and he leaned in close, over the fragrant pink rose in a vase set between us. "I'm hoping I get the chance later."

Heat rushed to my face, and I was glad the bar was dimly lit. "I didn't call you to have sex. I said a drink."

He shrugged. "Can't blame a guy for trying."

I ordered a vodka martini, and Andrew ordered a Scotch and soda and a charcuterie board to share. Just what I needed—more cheese. Of course Andrew didn't remember I couldn't have dairy. My needs had never been his priority.

When the drinks came, he raised his glass. "To us."

I met his eyes over the rim of my glass. "Why are you contacting me all of a sudden? I've been home for months. Since the funerals," I added to make a point, which he ignored and sipped his drink.

"I knew you were digging yourself out from under the shit storm your family left. I didn't want to bother you."

The food came, and I nibbled on a cracker.

"All the more reason to want to be with me," I mulled, trying to work through what was formulating in my mind. "A lover or true friend would show their support by being at my side. You couldn't even be bothered to text me after I came home."

Andrew's eyes shifted from my face to the table. "I'm here now. Let's make the best of it. I heard that with the Johnson trust matter settled, you've acquired several new clients. That kind of cash flow should put you in good standing now."

"I'm hopeful." Was I being cautious? Hell, yeah. I knew Andrew, and there was something he wasn't telling me.

He slid his hand over mine. "I am too. Hopeful this could be the start of a new beginning between us."

"I don't trust you. Not after what happened."

"I was wrong. We had a good thing, and I threw it away. I regret it every day." His fingers laced with mine, and he lifted my hand to kiss each knuckle. "I'll do anything to get you back."

I pulled away.

We sat and finished our drinks, and Andrew insisted on paying the bill. We walked outside and he reached for me, but I took a step away.

"Nothing's different because we had a drink."

"Then I guess it's up to me to change your mind." Without warning, he took me by the shoulder and covered my lips with his. I allowed him to hold me for a moment before stepping away.

"Next time, ask."

"Where's the fun in that? You know I love spontaneity." He pulled out his phone. "So? Are you coming home with me?"

I could easily go to his apartment, where I knew he'd do anything and everything to try and please me. The sex between us had always been explosive and hot. The physical part of our relationship had never been the problem.

"No," I responded firmly, and his eyes narrowed. I knew I'd made the right choice. Instead of waiting to call a car, I hopped into a cab discharging passengers at the curb. "Park and Seventy-ninth."

"You got it, buddy."

My phone vibrated. Andrew's text had me rolling my eyes.

I'm not giving up.

I didn't bother to answer. Instead, I texted Davis.

You are coming to work tomorrow, right? You didn't quit?

I could see he read it, but it remained unanswered until I entered the elevator of my building.

I wouldn't just up and leave. I'd make sure you found a replacement.

My lips curved upward. "Not sure that's possible, Davis."

I undressed and got into bed, my thoughts tangled up not with the evening spent with my ex, but in the man with kaleidoscope eyes.

CHAPTER FOURTEEN

Davis

Jesus, I look like shit. Guess that's what a sleepless night will do to you.

I peered into the mirror, wincing at the bags and dark circles under my eyes. I trimmed my scruff, then brushed my teeth and got dressed, all on autopilot. My night hadn't held much in the way of sleep, but holy hell, did I have some amazing fantasies while I'd lain staring at the television.

In one, Carson had followed me after I refused his kiss. He'd crowded me against the refrigerator and taken my mouth, refusing to let me go, and I'd wrapped my arms and legs around him, plunging my tongue past his lips. He'd tasted soft and warm, like the summer sun on your skin.

We'd torn each other's clothes off, and I'd held on to his shoulders as he thrust that big, thick cock inside me. I'd never gone bare, but with Carson I wanted to feel every glorious inch of his hot skin rubbing at my hole. We'd fucked for hours, in every position, and when we were finally sated, he'd cuddled me close and kissed me.

I lost count of how many times I'd jerked off, thinking of Carson fucking me. Kissing me. In the shower, I'd imagined getting on my knees, water streaming over us while I took his beautiful dick to the back of my throat and sucked him until he exploded in my mouth.

I groaned and dropped my head in my hands. "How the hell am I supposed to look him in the eyes today knowing I really didn't mean it, and I do want to kiss him?"

Ignoring the little voice in my head chanting, *Do it, do it*, I rinsed out my cereal bowl and made my peanut butter and jelly sandwich. Carson had turned out not to be who I first believed—cold, obnoxious, arrogant—and the fact that he wasn't made it worse. I could handle a boss I hated. It would make my job unpleasant but still possible.

Working with a boss I wanted to kiss every time I saw him? A way bigger problem. This went beyond Ira, my first crush, or Cooper, the TA I'd looked up to, only to find out he picked one student every semester to sleep with. Brian had pursued me relentlessly, and I'd fallen for him hard. Eventually I'd discovered he was engaged, and he intended to keep me as a sidepiece. Another relationship based on lies.

"I should concentrate on what he said to me. That I was convenient and there. All I'd be for him is a quick, easy fuck. I'm better than that. I can work with him until he finds someone to replace me." A pang hit me at the thought of losing out on the paralegal degree, but it couldn't be helped.

That decision made, but weighing heavily on my shoulders, I left for the office. As usual I was the first one in, and I put my sandwiches away in my desk and made a coffee. At my desk, I reviewed the calendar for the day and saw it was light—Carson had only one meeting scheduled, which meant he'd be underfoot. Vowing to remain resolute, I opened the legal software I'd easily mastered, and began the painstaking search-and-discovery mission into the firm's files.

"Damn, what the hell kind of half-assed filing system did they have here? I should've had this done a month ago," I muttered, then froze at the low, husky chuckle that sent a delicious thrill down my spine. I raised my eyes to meet Carson's amused gaze.

"It's a shit show for sure," he agreed. "But considering the secretary Dale had working here was busier working under his desk than at hers, I'm not surprised."

My cheeks heated. "I-I didn't know that. I thought it was the assistants you hired who quit."

He frowned. "They didn't help the situation, but no, I can't lay the blame completely at their feet. Dale was…shall we say…not the best record keeper? If he even remembered to add his notes to the files, it wasn't contemporaneous, which can be a problem if you have poor recollection." He sighed. "That's what happens when you don't give a damn about anything except the retainer. You forget when you're dealing with wills and trusts that there could be sensitive family issues with long-standing resentments. Similar to the meeting I have scheduled today."

I checked the calendar. "The Zeigler estate? She has a nine o'clock."

"Yeah." He grimaced. "That has the potential to get very ugly."

I'd taken the call from Judy Harris, who hadn't told me anything except she desperately needed an appointment with Carson. I waited for him to elaborate, but when he didn't, I returned to my computer filing. Carson remained standing in front of my desk, and my heart pounded, but I kept silent.

"Davis, about last night—"

"Isn't that the name of a movie?" My joke didn't produce the laughter I'd expected.

"I'll respect your boundaries. Just please don't leave me."

Much as I wanted to reassure him, I had to protect my

heart. I knew how damn easy it would be to fall for a man like Carson, who was the perfect blend of sweet, fun, and snarky, with that sexy brand of confidence all his own. I didn't need to kiss him to know how perfect his lips would feel on mine. But I was a convenience for him. Someone ready, willing, and not only able, but eager to warm his bed. Tommy was right. I had to stop falling for men in a position of authority over me.

"I'll see." It was the best I could give him.

"Okay. I'll be in my office."

I nodded, keeping my eyes on the computer screen, not relaxing until I heard the door shut. "Doesn't he understand I don't want to leave?" I muttered. "But I have to."

The front door opened, and a petite, middle-aged woman entered. Gray threatened to overtake the brown in her hair, which was contained in a simple ponytail, and she wore a plain, white, button-down shirt tucked into a pair of jeans. Her smile was tremulous.

"Hello. I'm here to meet with Carson Ballard? I'm Judy Harris."

Hmm. She didn't look like the greedy, manipulative woman Carson had told me one of the Zeigler daughters had accused her of being.

"Of course." I picked up the phone. "Carson? Ms. Harris is here."

"Send her in, please."

I rose and walked with her to Carson's office and knocked on the door, then opened it.

"Judy," Carson greeted her with affection. "Please come in and sit."

"Can I bring you a drink of water or some coffee, Ms. Harris?"

"No, thank you." Twisting a ring on her finger, she smiled briefly at me.

"Do you want me to stay and take notes?" I addressed

Carson.

Carson barely met my eyes. "No. That won't be necessary. I need you out front."

The cool detachment hurt, but I scolded myself. I couldn't have it both ways—he was adhering to my wishes; it was what I'd asked for. I didn't like it, but as I told Carson, it was for the best. As the Rolling Stones put it, you can't always get what you want. And much as I wanted Carson, I already knew how that story ended. Been there, done that, thank you very much, but no thanks.

"Okay."

I'd just returned to my desk and files, when the front door to the suite opened. A very good-looking man around my age stood before me, his dark, expensively cut hair gleaming in the overhead lights. An arrogant, slight smile tipped up the corner of his generous mouth, immediately putting me on alert.

"Is Carson available?"

"No, I'm sorry, he's in a meeting. Can I take your name and have him call you when he's able?"

The smile broadened. "No. I'll wait. He'll want to see me."

"Did you have an appointment, Mr…" Curious now, I cocked my head, waiting for him to respond.

"I do not." The man took a seat in one of the club chairs and stretched out his long legs.

"His meeting just started. It might take a while."

White teeth flashed at me. "I have time."

With nothing left for me to say, I resumed my work, only to be interrupted by the mystery guest.

"What's your name?"

"Davis."

"Have you been with the firm long?"

My fingers continued to tap the keyboard. "A few months."

"So you don't know Carson that well."

I met his eyes and didn't like the hardness in their brown depths. "Not really."

"He and I go way back. We've known each other a long time. Since London. We're very close."

"That's nice."

So close that Carson hasn't once mentioned you? Liar.

I finished one file, saved it, and moved on to the next. The phone rang.

"Ballard and Melbourne, good morning. How may I help you?"

"Good morning, Davis. It's Patricia. How are you?"

"Very well, thanks. How are you?"

"Fine. I was wondering if I could speak with Carson."

"I'm sorry, he's in a meeting right now, but I'll let him know you called as soon as he's out."

"Thank you so much." Her voice lowered. "It's his birthday on Saturday, and I wanted to take him out to celebrate, but I don't know if he has plans already. Do you see anything on his calendar?"

I scrolled through his business and personal calendars. "Nothing here. I'm sure he'll make time for his mother."

She laughed. "One would hope so. I have to say I'm thrilled you listened to me and took the job. I think it's worked out well, don't you?"

Has it? Debatable, now that I've fallen for my boss. Again. But of course, I couldn't tell Patricia that.

"It's going well, yes."

"Okay, I won't keep you. Have a wonderful day, if I don't speak to you."

"You as well, Patricia. Nice to talk to you."

"Was that Carson's mother?"

The man rose to his feet, crossed the waiting area, and stopped in front of my desk.

"I'm sorry, but I'm not at liberty to discuss Mr. Ballard's

calls."

He leaned forward, sharp eyes boring into mine. "Carson wouldn't mind. Like I've said." He bared his teeth in a grin. "We're very close."

"Then you can ask him yourself when he comes out of his meeting."

Harleyville might be small and no match for New York City, but politics were politics, and I'd learned to hold my ground. The man's eyes narrowed, and he returned to his seat.

Forty more minutes passed.

"Where is the restroom?" he inquired, and I pointed.

"Down the hall, first door on your left."

He disappeared. Carson's door opened, and he walked out with a tearful Judy Harris. "I'll get back to you after I speak with them. I'll do my best, Judy. I know this is what Hal would've wanted."

"I know you will, Carson." She smiled up at him. "He was fond of you and was disappointed when you didn't join the firm."

"He was a good man. I don't like how this turned out, and I know it all happened so suddenly. He never meant for you to get hurt." He turned to me. "Davis, can you get a car for Ms. Harris? Judy, I'll call you as soon as I hear from the family."

When I started working here, Carson had given me access to the firm's car-service account. I tapped in the information. "The car will be downstairs in four minutes, Ms. Harris."

"Thank you."

Carson watched her leave and turned to me. "Any messages?"

"Your mother called."

He rolled his eyes. "Work-related."

My lips twitched. "Be nice. I like Patricia. If it wasn't

for her, I wouldn't have a job."

"I'm well aware. And I am nice. I thought you'd see that by now."

"I do. Look, Carson—"

"Baby, there you are." The man reappeared and headed straight to Carson. I stood and watched as he grabbed him and planted a kiss on his lips. And not a friendly peck either.

Carson pushed him off. "Andrew, what the hell are you doing here?"

Undeterred, Andrew slung an arm around Carson's waist. "Just wanted to see you. Last night wasn't enough."

I blinked and didn't miss Carson's red face.

Last night? What the hell did that mean?

A sick ball twisted in my stomach. Did Carson go to this man because he couldn't get what he wanted from me?

"Please remove your hand."

"He's been waiting an hour," I added.

"Yes, I have. Your sweet assistant wouldn't give me any information. I see you have him well trained to do your bidding."

I grew warm at the insinuation but didn't engage, instead returning to my files while keeping my ears open.

"Don't you have work?" Carson asked, his irritation obvious. "Why are you hanging out in my office? And to that matter, I'm busy."

"I saw. Consoling widows can't be fun for you. Why don't we meet for lunch? Say one o'clock at The Capital Grille? I'll make the reservation."

"No, sorry, I'm too busy. I have a one thirty with a client, right, Davis?"

I met his gaze. "Yes. And the rest of your afternoon is full as well."

Andrew's lips thinned in annoyance. "You're making this very hard, Carson. Come on. Just give me a few minutes? I'm sure you can spare me that."

He checked his watch. "Five is all I can do. Follow me."

With a triumphant smile, Andrew walked with Carson into his office.

Dammit. I wanted to know who this Andrew person was, but without a last name, it was impossible to do anything but wait and see. Whoever he was, he and Carson had been very close.

Lovers.

It shouldn't bother me.

Carson had a life before I knew him, and while he chose not to talk about it, something must've happened between them that caused their relationship—or whatever it was—to end badly. Yet Andrew had shown up this morning, unbothered and talking about the two of them together. And that comment about last night…had they met earlier? Or after Carson tried to kiss me?

That bothered the hell out of me.

And I wanted to know what happened.

# CHAPTER FIFTEEN

Carson

Annoyed as fuck, I shut the door behind Andrew and sat at my desk. "What do you want? And why are you here?"

Andrew sprawled in a chair and grinned. "Cute secretary. Are you fucking him?"

My face grew warm. "Get out."

Of course, he didn't listen. "If you're not, you're a fool. He's hot."

"Answer my questions."

"Oh, stop being such a tight-ass." As if he were a man of leisure, he examined his fingernails. "If you are, I couldn't blame you. And if you're not, maybe I'll take him to lunch. If you say no."

"I said I'm busy. And I told you last night I don't trust you. This…this display"—I waved my hand between us—"is merely proving my point."

Ignoring my words, he posed his own question. "How come he's so friendly with your mother?"

My brow furrowed. "What? How do you know that?"

"I heard the two of them talking, and he called her Patricia. A stranger wouldn't do that."

Fuming over his eavesdropping, I clenched my fists. "Why are you so interested? Why do you care? You never gave a damn about my mother when we were together and she'd come to visit me in London. Almost the whole time we were together, you cheated on me, and now all of a sudden I'm expected to believe you're a changed man? You fooled me before, but now I see it clearly. I won't be fooled again."

An angry flush crept over his face. "People change," he mumbled.

"Maybe so, but not cheaters. And not for me. I don't give second chances when it comes to being unfaithful." I scowled. "And you never answered me. Why are you hanging out here all morning? Don't you have a job?"

He rose to his feet. "Yeah, but I'm on vacation. I'll give you a few days to settle down. I shouldn't have pushed so hard. You need some time to remember how good it was between us."

I skirted a wide circle around him to open the door to my office. When he came close, I stepped out of reach, unwilling to be close enough for him to grab and latch on to me.

Unperturbed, he sauntered out into the reception area and stopped by Davis's desk. "Your boss turned me down for lunch. How about you? Want to join me?"

Stunned by Andrew's fucking audacity, I clenched my hands into fists, waiting for Davis to answer.

"I'm sorry. I can't."

I released a breath of relief.

"Why not? Carson have you on a short leash?"

"Because he's having lunch with me," I heard myself blurt out, and watched Davis's eyes grow wide with surprise.

Andrew's brows shot up high, and his smirk returned. "Of course he is. Have fun, you two." He strolled out of the office, flinging over his shoulder, "I'll talk to you soon, baby."

With Andrew finally gone, I turned toward my office. "I'd better call my mother."

"Who was that?" Davis asked, stopping me in my tracks.

"Andrew? Someone I used to know in London." Once inside my office, I took out my phone. Davis followed me and stood at the door.

"A boyfriend?"

I huffed out a laugh. "I thought so, but considering how much he cheated on me, no."

"I'm sorry. That's rough."

I shrugged. "It was then. It isn't now. Sit, please."

He shook his head. "I have to be able to hear the phone."

I grinned. "I have that same magical invention on my desk that shows all the incoming calls. You can answer from here if need be." At his hesitation, I circled my desk and pointed to one of the two chairs in front of us. "Please, Davis?"

His face full of reluctance, he took one seat and I the other, facing him. Davis perched on the edge, ready to spring up and take flight. "Is there a problem?"

I gazed at him thoughtfully. "Yeah. I think so." I hitched my chair closer. "You think I went to Andrew last night because you turned me away."

"Did you?" Despite his flaming cheeks, he met my gaze without flinching. "And it turns out I was right, considering what you said to me later on the phone."

Now it was my turn to be embarrassed. "Yeah, about that...I'm sorry."

"Yeah? Sorry because you didn't make a better argument? I'm not some easy fuck to play with and walk away. Plus, I take my job seriously. I work hard, and I don't want anyone thinking I'm merely here as your boy toy."

Andrew was wrong about most things, but about Davis

he was spot on. The guy was hot as hell, and never more so than right now when he was annoyed. Those stained-glass eyes glittered, and a flush rested on his high cheekbones.

"If you recall, I didn't hire you."

His jaw hardened. "I know. But I'm here now."

"I'm aware. And just to be perfectly clear, I wasn't even certain you were gay. The attempted kiss was spontaneous. Not planned seduction."

"I didn't think about it one way or the other. But I am gay, and I'm still not going to sleep with you."

"That's fine. I understand that. Have I ever treated you as less than a complete professional?"

"No, but—"

"No buts. You're making assumptions about me. Do I find you attractive? Hell, yes. Did I want to kiss you last night? Also, hell yes. You said no, and I respected that, but then you called me, and I was feeling sorry for myself, so I retaliated by being childish and saying the first thing that came to mind that would hurt you." I looked down, around, and everywhere but at him. "I'm not proud of what I said."

"And?" he asked, his gentle voice running across my skin like a silk feather.

"I really am sorry." I met his eyes. "It was selfish and said in the heat of anger without regard for your feelings and the consequences. Please don't quit." I forced a smile. "Take pity on me. You know I'll be in trouble if you leave."

His lips twitched. "No matter what, you really do need to learn how to use the software. I told you that."

I sensed him weakening and nodded eagerly. "I will. I promise. Will you give up the idea of leaving? Please?" I did my best and batted my lashes.

Davis snorted. "Oh God, you are too pathetic."

My grin grew wider. "Yeah, but is it working?" I could see the war waging behind his eyes, and I made him a promise. "I'll keep my hands off you."

"It's not your hands I'm worried about. No more kissing attempts."

"You drive a hard bargain." But I could see he was serious. And even though I fully intended to find out more about why he was so gun-shy, I agreed. "Okay. No kissing or touching. Can I look at least?"

"Pathetic isn't a pretty look on you, Carson. I'm sure you won't have any trouble finding another man in the city to charm."

"But you do find me charming."

"I didn't say—that's not what I meant. Jesus, you're frustrating." He threw his hands up.

"I've been called worse. Now, and this is work-related, could you stay, please? I'm making a Zoom call, and I need a witness."

"That sounds ominous."

My anger returned from my earlier meeting with Judy Harris. "It could be nasty. Here's what we're dealing with: Hal Zeigler was married and had three children. After twenty years together, his wife, Mary, passed away. Ten years after her death, when he was fifty-five, he met Judy, who was thirty-two. They were together until he died last year. He'd had a stroke, and Judy nursed him throughout the whole ordeal. One morning he had a massive coronary while shaving and died." I winced. "In his file, I discovered a notation my father had made that they were supposed to set up a meeting for him to include Judy in the will."

"They didn't get married?" Davis asked, perching on the edge of my desk.

"There, my friend, is the issue. Hal never married Judy, but he made numerous promises to her that he'd leave her money. Of which he had oodles—more than enough for each of his kids to live a life of slothful luxury. But the greedy little fuckers are now screaming from here to eternity that Judy has no right to the money and it's all theirs."

Davis frowned. "That hardly sounds fair. But isn't it the law that what's in the will is what controls?"

"Very good. I see you've been learning. Yes, the four corners of the document control and oral agreements can't alter it, even if the grantor states they wish it to."

Davis slid off the desk. "So what are you hoping to accomplish by this video call? I don't understand. If you can't change the will, it sucks for her, but it seems pointless."

"I'm going to try and appeal to their better nature. This poor woman wasn't some nobody he had a fling with. They lived together for twenty years. If New York State recognized common-law marriages, we wouldn't be having this conversation, but it doesn't." I checked the time. "Before I make that call, I'd better speak to my mother, so she doesn't decide to pay an in-person visit because she thinks I'm ignoring her."

Davis chuckled. "Let me know when you want me to come in." He walked away.

I called out to him. "So we're good now?"

His voice took on a serious tone. "I hope so."

He walked away, and I picked up the phone.

"Hello, Carson."

"Hi, Mom."

"How are you? Busy, I hope?"

"Yes, we're slowly getting our feet under us."

"Good. I knew you could do it." She turned brisk and efficient. "It's your birthday Saturday, and I want to take you out for dinner to celebrate."

"No, please. It's not necessary." Spending my birthday with my mother—much as I loved her—was somewhat pathetic.

"I know it's not necessary, but I want to."

"Well, I don't." Realizing that came out harsher than intended, I backtracked. "I'm sorry. I didn't mean to sound ungrateful, but I think I'm past the age of celebrations."

"I don't want you to be alone."

The truth hurt, and I couldn't tell her, but I was always alone. From the moment I came out, I'd fought my battles solo. I'd hoped it would be different, that I'd have my brother at my side and my father's acceptance, but once I discovered that would never happen, I'd learned fast that I could only count on myself for my happiness.

Maybe that was the reason I didn't know how to be happy—I didn't really know who I was. And I didn't really like what I saw in the mirror when I took the time to look.

"I'll be fine. I'll have a nice meal, go home, and get a good night's sleep. That'll be the best present."

"Carson, I—"

"Mom," I warned. "Please don't. I'm busy, and I have things to do. I love you for thinking of me, but I have to go. I'll talk to you soon. Love you." Before she could reply, I ended the call. "Davis," I called out. "I'm ready."

A second later he walked in, iPad in hand. "You could've called me on the office phone."

"I know, but I needed to let off some steam. Yelling your name seemed a good way to handle it."

He made a face. "Don't tell me you argued with your mother."

I stared, unseeing, at my desk. "No…not really." To my horror, my throat closed up and I heard my voice wobble. Jesus, I needed to get a grip. After a moment, I explained. "She wanted to take me out to dinner for my birthday, and I declined. Simple as that."

A pucker formed between his brows. "Why did you say no?"

"Why do I have to explain myself?" I groused. "I'm ready to do the phone conference."

I got the three Zeiglers up on the screen and made my argument. "Don't you think it was your father's wish to see Judy taken care of? Judy and your father were married in every sense of the word. She loves you kids. And I know you love her. Don't let money come between you all. She's been part of your family for so long."

Evelyn Hart, Hal's oldest daughter, responded first. "If Daddy had wanted it, he would've changed the will."

"He did want it, Evie," Lillian, the youngest, interjected. "I read the notes. He planned to put her in the will." She sniffed and blinked furiously. "He died before he had the time."

"Lillian's right, Evie," Rob, the middle child and Hal's only son, agreed. "Dad loved Judy. I don't know why you're being such a hard-ass. Judy lived with him, and she was always great to us."

"What Carson said is that Dad wanted to give her a significant amount of money. If Daddy had really loved her, he would've married her."

Wow. I shot a glance at Davis, who sat out of view of the camera. Davis raised his brows and shook his head, making a face of disgust.

I consulted the file in front of me. "You each received twelve million from the estate. How would one or two million less for each of you hurt your bottom line?"

Evelyn gasped. "*Six million dollars?* I was thinking maybe a hundred thousand total."

Thank God I never intended to have children. This avaricious bitch made me weep for humanity.

"It was Judy who took care of your father after his stroke, am I correct?" That necessary tidbit had the desired effect. Evelyn averted her eyes, but I wasn't going to let her get away unscathed. "She was there, night and day with him, feeding him, bathing him. He could've afforded care, but Judy did it all herself because she loved him."

"I couldn't look after him. My children were young and my husband worked late." The excuses from Evelyn Hart came fast and furious.

"Evie, you're being a bitch. We all have more money than we can possibly need." Rob's declaration had me internally cheering him for calling her out. "I'm willing to give her a fair share."

"I am too. Judy came with me to pick out my wedding dress. She's been like a mother to me. I was so young when Mom died." Lillian wiped her eyes.

Sensing weakness, I jumped right in. "I can have the papers drawn up immediately. All we need is everyone's okay."

"Evie, come on," Lillian pleaded. "You know it's the right thing to do. Daddy would've wanted it. He did want it."

Evelyn huffed out a breath. "Fine. Two million dollars. I'll sign whatever you want."

I gave a hand signal to Davis, and he sprang out of his chair and headed to his desk, where I knew he'd prepared the documents.

"Wonderful. My assistant will send the paperwork. Once you sign and notarize it, send it to me, and I'll get the bank transfers processed. You made the right decision. Your father would be very proud of you."

"Thanks, Carson." Rob nodded. "I'm glad you pushed for this. Judy deserves it."

"Okay. I'll talk to you soon. Bye."

They signed off, and I heaved out a sigh of relief. For a moment, I hadn't been sure Evelyn would come around. My computer dinged, and Davis's email with all the forms prepared popped up. Then he walked into my office with a cup of coffee and a Kit Kat bar. King size.

"Here. Job well done." He handed me both. I set the coffee on my desk and opened the candy bar. I snapped off a generous hunk and gave it to him, holding on a little longer than necessary.

"I see you know what I like." I waggled my brows.

"*Carson*," he warned with a groan. "Cut it out."

"What?" Pretending innocence, I raised my brows. "I love Kit Kats. They're my favorite."

"So." He stood before me.

"What?"

"It's your birthday Saturday?"

"Don't." I held up a warning finger. "Don't even think of planning any kind of surprise. I'm serious."

"Not even a cake? Come on. Birthdays are fun."

I snickered. "There's only one kind of cake I'm interested in."

Davis threw up his hands. "You're impossible."

"Birthdays haven't been important to me for years. I prefer to forget I'm getting older."

What was there to celebrate? Another year of one day in, one day out. Over and over.

"No one should be alone on their birthday. It's not right," Davis continued to protest.

"What's not right is this conversation," I grumbled. "Now leave me alone to enjoy my candy." I caught Davis about to open his mouth and put up a hand. "Please, Davis? Let it go."

He shot me a look I recognized as, *You won this battle but not the war*, and left.

I sat chewing my candy. It wouldn't be the first time I'd spent my birthday alone. I'd gotten used to it. I called up 4 Charles Prime Rib and made a reservation.

"Just one, sir?"

"Yes. One."

It sure as hell was the loneliest number.

CHAPTER SIXTEEN

Davis

"Yes, Mom, the new job is going well." I lay on my couch, feet up. Another fascinating Saturday night come and gone for Davis Turner.

"I'm glad you're getting to use your degree, at least. And your boss is nice?"

Nice wasn't exactly the word I'd use for Carson. Frustrating, often annoying, devilishly handsome, and surprisingly observant, I honestly didn't know what to make of him.

"He's fine. I mean, he's my boss, not my friend."

"It's very sad what happened with his father and brother. So sudden and tragic. I'm sure he's still devastated over their loss."

I wasn't. The way Carson had described his relationship with both, they'd been lost to each other years earlier. It couldn't be easy, but aside from that one night, he didn't speak about them.

"I wouldn't know. He keeps things pretty close to the vest. I wouldn't have even known it was his birthday today if his mother hadn't mentioned it."

"So are you doing anything special for him?"

"Mom. He's going to be thirty-five, not five. He specifically said he wanted nothing. Not even a cake."

"I'm sure he didn't mean it." My mother was the queen of birthday parties, and each one had to top the last.

"Oh, I'm pretty sure he did." I chuckled. "He was adamant."

"People say that when they know they're going to be alone and don't want people feeling sorry for them. If you brought him a cake or flowers or something special to the office on Monday, I bet he'd appreciate it."

Maybe she was right. I might not know Carson well, but what I'd discovered in the months working for him was how well he disguised his emotions. And he did have a soft side…

"I'm not sure. His mother would know, but it would be weird for me to ask her, don't you think?"

"No, I don't," my mother stated firmly. "After all, she hired you."

"I'll see. Tell me how you're feeling. That's more important." Her health was always a concern of mine.

"I'm fine. The weather is hot, but you know I love it. I spend my days at the pool or in the clubhouse with my girlfriends, and your father has his cronies. He's there now, playing cards."

"Have you been able to pay off some of the bills? I can send you more, now that I have a better-paying job."

"I don't want you to worry about that." She sighed, and I could almost picture her shaking her head. "We're fine. All I want is to know you're happy and away from that bad situation."

That was what she called my relationship with Brian.

A bad situation. She wasn't wrong.

"I am on both accounts. I'll talk to you next week. Say hi to Dad for me."

"I will. Love you."

"Love you too."

My thoughts returned to my frustrating boss. My mother's suggestion to call Patricia about Carson's birthday was foolish. I shouldn't feel sorry for someone like Carson. He had money, good looks, a fabulous education, and everything he could ever want handed to him.

Except someone to spend his birthday with.

I couldn't help it. Because my parents had always made a big deal over my birthday, the fact that Carson was alone on his didn't sit right with me. No matter what he said, being all alone on your birthday sucked.

To ensure things ran smoothly, I'd set up Carson's calendar to load to mine, so that whenever something was added, I'd get a notification. I'd seen his reservation for dinner when he'd added the time and place on his calendar. How sad was it to spend your birthday eating dinner alone with no one to smile at or share a piece of cake?

Or give a birthday kiss?

"God, I've got it bad… How much of a fool am I going to look?" I muttered to myself, but that didn't stop me from getting dressed and taking the train downtown to the Michelin-starred restaurant where Carson was dining. I'd done it again—fallen hard for my boss—but this time I was lucky. Carson respected my request not to make any more moves.

And now I could suffer in lust alone…

I approached the hostess, hyperaware that my "real silk" tie I'd bought on the corner of 54th and Broadway—three for ten—wasn't going to hold up against the designer labels I spotted.

"Hi. I'm looking for Carson Ballard?"

She nodded. "Yes, this way, sir."

Ignoring my banging heart, I trailed behind her as she led me through the dining room, and I recognized Carson from the set of his broad shoulders and the curl of golden-brown hair at his nape.

"Mr. Ballard, your guest is here." The hostess stood before him while I hung back.

"My guest?" Carson turned around, and when he saw me, his jaw dropped and his eyes narrowed.

"Surprise," I said weakly. "Happy Birthday."

To his credit, he didn't tell me to get the hell out. He maintained his composure and merely pointed with his finger to the chair across from him. A half-empty martini glass sat in front of him.

"Please."

I did as requested and clasped my hands on the tabletop. A busboy appeared immediately and filled my water glass.

"Carson—" I began, but he lifted his hand, and I waited until the busboy left us.

"Let me ask you this," he murmured, his voice steely, despite his unruffled demeanor.

I waited, my heart playing an uneasy rhythm in my chest. This had seemed like a good idea in my apartment, but here, in the wood-paneled dining room, with the tables abuzz with conversation and plates of the most delicious looking and smelling food I'd ever seen? Maybe I'd made a mistake and bitten off more than I could chew. Figuratively and not literally, because damn, I was hungry. All I'd had to eat was some cereal and leftover Chinese takeout from the previous night.

"What part of my telling you I don't celebrate my birthday was in a foreign language? Did you not understand?"

But I refused to retreat. "So why are you here?"

He blinked. "Excuse me?"

I figured if he was going to fire me after this, I might

as well go out swinging. "You made a reservation at an incredible steakhouse—one of the best in the city. On your birthday. To me, it looks like you're celebrating."

He raised a brow. "Maybe I'm hungry and I felt like a steak."

"I don't believe you."

He propped his chin in his hand. "Now I'll ask you the same question you asked me. Why are you here?"

Defiant, I met his blue-eyed gaze. "Because no one should be alone on their birthday. And I know you said you don't like celebrating it, but…dammit, Carson, thinking of you sitting alone makes me sad."

A server appeared at the table. "Can I get your guest a drink?"

Before I could answer, Carson did. "Bring him a lychee martini. And another menu, please. He'll be joining me for dinner."

"Certainly, sir." He vanished, and Carson resumed his study of my face.

"Thank you, but you didn't have to."

"Don't mention it. And it's never fun to drink alone. But how did you know where I was? I didn't tell anyone."

"Your calendar. The miracle of computers strikes again."

"More like a curse," he muttered.

The drink was deposited in front of me and a menu proffered. At the sight of the prices, I almost fell off my chair.

Carson must've suspected what I was thinking, as he chuckled. "I know, but the food is amazing." A wickedly charming smile lit up his face. "Besides, since you're an employee, now I can write the entire meal off as an expense. You did me a favor by showing up."

"So glad I could be of service," I answered him dryly. "But I really would feel guilty ordering steak for a hundred dollars." My eyes popped even wider as I scanned the menu. "And that doesn't even include sides? A meal for two with the drinks could end up costing half my monthly rent."

"But you're here, so now you'll stay. Considering all the trouble you went to, it wouldn't be nice of me to turn you away. And contrary to popular belief, I can be nice."

"Thank you." I sipped my drink. "And I know you can."

That was my problem. He *was* nice. Damned unexpectedly nice. I liked it. I liked him.

"Can I assume your family made a big deal about birthdays when you were a child?"

I couldn't help my lips twitching. "What makes you think they stopped? My mother still calls and sings happy birthday to me, and I get a card and balloons from my parents."

"Really?" The hard lines of his face deepened. "You can't be serious."

Carson's astonishment didn't bother me. "I am. My mother had four miscarriages before I was born. That, coupled with a heart condition and the doctors telling her she shouldn't get pregnant, that it was too dangerous for her…but she didn't listen."

"You were her miracle baby."

"Yeah."

Carson's expression softened. "What's wrong? Is your mother okay now?"

My face had betrayed me. "She takes it easy. I miss them, but it's better for them where they are."

The server reappeared, and at Carson's insistence, I ordered the filet. He ordered the Wagyu beef and several sides for us to share. He also decided we'd split a salad.

"Another martini, sir?"

Carson thought for a moment. "No. Bring a bottle of Roederer. Cristal. Vintage. If I'm going to celebrate, I might as well do it right."

Feeling guilty as hell, I protested one last time. "Carson, I didn't mean to force you."

His smile was enigmatic yet sensual. "Let's get one fact straight. I don't do anything I don't want to. Ever. Understood?" Those blazing blue eyes captured me.

"Understood."

The champagne was popped and poured, and I held up my flute for a toast. "Happy birthday, Carson. I hope your wishes come true."

"We shall see." He clinked his glass to mine, and we sipped.

My experience with champagne was limited to cheap bubbles on New Year's Eve, and at my first sip, I understood why people spent the money on a good bottle. I recklessly drained my glass and met Carson's amused stare. "It sparkles on my tongue. It tastes like a celebration. I've never had anything like it."

"Well, then, be my guest." Carson lifted the bottle and poured me another glass. "Have some more. But take it slow. Champagne can be deceptive. The bubbles go to your head."

I took his advice, savoring this glass. Our salads came, and Carson became more animated, talking about law school and his life in London. Not one mention of his father or brother.

"Can I ask you something?"

Our salad plates were whisked away and replaced by our main courses and sides, which smelled like paradise on a plate. Carson poured me another glass, took some for himself, and ordered a second bottle.

"You can ask me anything. I don't have to answer."

"How did your brother and father die?" The champagne had definitely loosened my tongue and made me brave.

It wasn't my imagination that Carson paled. He resolutely cut into his steak, chewing and swallowing before answering.

"They were on their way to Dale's house in the Hamptons. It was winter, and the weather turned bad. Dale tried to beat the storm by racing his Ferrari down Sunrise

Highway at ninety miles an hour. He lost control around a curve and spun out. The car flipped, and they were crushed when it hit a tree."

My heart did a nose-dive. "That's awful."

"The worst part is that Dale had been drinking. He killed himself and my father because he was drunk. And my father was in the same condition." He stared at the flickering candle between us, and I knew he was miles away, maybe on the windswept stretch of road where his father and brother had lost their lives. "Two fools," he spat out bitterly. "What a goddamn waste."

Then, as if the conversation had never happened, he picked up his fork and knife and began eating.

"I'm sorry," I said quietly after a few heartbeats of time passed without more words between us. "I shouldn't have asked. It's your birthday, and there should be only happy thoughts."

He acknowledged me with barely a glance, but I wasn't offended. In the time I'd been on the job, I'd become accustomed to his mercurial moods, and I knew that in addition to celebration, birthdays could also be a time for introspection. God knew I spent my last one bemoaning my stupidity at wasting too many years over Brian and his lies. An idea came to mind, and after I finished my meal, I excused myself.

When I returned, our plates had been removed and Carson was studying the dessert menu. His serious expression had me second-guessing my decision, but the wheels had been set in motion. Too late to back out now. I was walking on air from a night I knew I'd never forget.

"What looks good?" I asked him as I took my seat.

"They don't have what I like." He set the menu on the table. "I'll just have a coffee."

Dismay filled my chest. "Are you kidding? Everything looks good. I'm sure you want something."

"No. I'm fine."

I gulped. "Well, that might pose a problem."

He raised a brow. "Because?" He folded his arms. "Tell me you didn't do what I think you did."

I allowed a tiny smile. "Maaaaybe?" As the servers approached, I lowered my voice. "Please don't be mad."

Carson blinked when they surrounded the table, one of them holding the biggest piece of chocolate-fudge cake I'd ever seen, complete with lighted sparkler. And I had to admit, Carson was a good sport, thanking them for singing him happy birthday and even ordering some after-dinner port.

We faced each other with that mountain of cake between us. "You did this."

I bit my lip. "Uh, yeah. I thought you needed something birthday-ish."

"And was having four total strangers sing me a cringe-worthy version of that inane song all I could hope for tonight, or is there something else waiting to pop up to surprise me?"

My heart sank. "I'm sorry. I thought it would be nice. It's nondairy, so it should be okay on your stomach."

"Even though I said I didn't like celebrating." He sank his fork into the cake and took a bite. "This is delicious. Taste." He held out his fork.

"I have my own fork, you know."

"Humor me. It's my birthday, after all."

I tasted the piece, and God, it was rich and surprisingly delicious. "*Mmmm*. It's amazing."

"Yes. It is. But you still caused me tremendous embarrassment."

Was he kidding? No smile curved his lips, and he remained stone-faced.

"I said I was sorry."

"Nevertheless, you owe me."

"Owe you?" I sputtered. "What's that supposed to mean?"

"You have to do what I ask. It's my birthday, which means you can't refuse me." A sparkle now lit his eyes, and my heart slammed. "And since you believe I need to celebrate my birthday, we're going dancing."

"Dancing?" I squeaked out. "That's a little extreme, don't you think?"

I loved dancing, but being a little tipsy already, it could get dangerous with a man like Carson. Very dangerous.

"It's my party. The song says I can do what I want." He pointed to the plate. "Let's finish up."

I could be strong. It didn't matter how damned attractive Carson was, or that I was slightly buzzed and horny. I could resist him. Besides, he might find someone at the club he'd rather be with.

Was that his plan? At first I'd thought he wanted to pressure me into being with him. But maybe I had it all wrong. Carson could bring me to the club and hook up with someone in front of me, and there wasn't a damn thing I could do about it.

In either case, I was screwed.

CHAPTER SEVENTEEN

Carson

I should tell him it was all a joke and let the car bring him home. There was nothing I wanted less than to be in a club on a Saturday night. Except if it meant I might get to hold Davis for a moment, and maybe he would kiss me.

I wanted to know. I'd sensed…something brewing between us. Maybe what we needed was a night like this to bring it out in the open.

I couldn't even blame it on the alcohol. I'd wanted Davis for a while now, but he'd made me promise not to push him. And I wouldn't. If anything happened, it had to come from him.

We entered the club and found a table. The server came by.

"How are you tonight, gentlemen, and what can I get you?" There was no getting around bottle service when you sat at a table.

"It's my birthday," I told her. "Bring us some champagne.

But don't go overboard. Keep it at four hundred."

"Happy birthday, and you got it."

"Four hundred dollars for a bottle?" Davis asked, clearly appalled. "That's such a scam. You know it's not going to be worth it."

"It is what it is. Besides, you're the one who loves birthdays."

He muttered something I couldn't hear over the pounding music. Our server returned with the bucket and a bottle, which she opened with a loud *pop*. She poured us each a glass and left.

"To a special night. Thank you." I tipped my glass to Davis.

"It was never my intention to make you spend all this money. I'm sorry."

The man was genuinely upset, and I didn't like that. "Hey. I'm okay with it. Think of it this way—it makes up for all the birthdays I never celebrated before. Now come on. It's bad luck not to drink to a toast."

Davis's smile was wry. "What wise man said that?"

I grinned. "Me. Now bottoms up, and let's dance."

He drank and set the glass on the small, round tabletop. "I don't know if that's such a great idea. I'm a little buzzed."

I rose and took him by the arm. "I'll make sure you don't get into any trouble."

Except with me. I'm already in trouble with how much I want you.

He allowed me to lead him to the crowded floor, where we joined the writhing masses. To my surprise, Davis was a wonderful dancer, and I was captivated by the gyration of his hips and ass. And apparently, I wasn't the only one. Several other men tried to talk to him, spiking my anger. My glares at them didn't work, and after the fourth or fifth man attempted to entice him away, I moved in and rested my hands at his waist.

"This makes more sense, don't you think?"

He gazed into my eyes, and a sweet smile tipped his lips. "Yeah."

I drew him to me, and he raised a questioning brow. I said, "Anything further has to come from you." Still, my promise didn't keep me from grazing his cheek with my nose. A sigh escaped him.

"Why are you doing this?"

"Do you really have to ask? I'll let you go now if you want, but if not, I'm going to take you home with me tonight."

He grasped me by the nape, his gaze locking with mine.

He melted into me, and at the touch of his hot lips, a powerful shock of need stunned me, and I plunged my tongue into his warm mouth. If I was worried he'd push me away, I needn't have been. His hum of pleasure vibrated through me, drowning out the pulse of the music flowing over us. We greedily sucked each other's tongues, and his rock-hard dick rubbed against my thigh.

I might've come into the club sated from a delicious dinner, but now I was starving for Davis. I ground my hips into him, and he responded by wrapping his arms around my shoulders. Our kisses grew frantic. Hungrier with every breath and heartbeat. The pent-up desire I'd squashed roared to the surface. I needed him. I had to have him.

"Carson," he moaned. "How is this happening?"

"You know how," I whispered in his ear. "I want you."

"I want you too, but…"

"But what? That was before." I held his face, drove my tongue deep inside his mouth, and he whimpered even as he licked and sucked it.

"Before what?" he gasped when I let him go.

"Before I touched you. Before you kissed me back. Before I knew how you tasted and felt in my mouth."

I cupped his ass and let him feel my desire. He kissed

me hard, wet and hot, his tongue probing and velvety soft.

"Say no, and I'll let you go and never touch you again."

The music pounded through us as his lust-drunk eyes met mine. He panted, and I waited.

"I can't. I want you more than anyone I've ever wanted."

Triumph surged through me, and I grabbed his hand. "Come." I took out a wad of bills and tossed them onto the table as we passed by. I spied our server and pointed. "Take it in case someone else sees it lying there." We left the club.

A cab sailed by us on the street, its light on, and I hailed it. We tumbled inside, Davis as still as a statue beside me. He remained silent as we entered my apartment, until I shut the door and pushed him up against it.

"Carson," he breathed. "You're my boss."

I nuzzled his jaw and bit his earlobe. "Not like this. Not when we're naked and alone."

He writhed and clutched me tighter. "I'm so fucked."

"Not yet. Give me a chance."

He sighed as I worked at his pants, then opened mine. Our cocks nestled together, only the thin damp fabric of our briefs between us. At his sharp intake of breath, I cupped his face, my lips brushing his.

"If you don't want to go any further, you need to tell me now. Because once I get you naked, I won't be able to stop."

"I shouldn't." The hot press of his mouth to mine silenced my fears. "But I want to. So badly. So no. Don't stop. Don't you dare."

"Follow me." His hand in mine, I led him to my bedroom, and under the shroud of darkness, we stripped off our clothes, my fingers uncharacteristically shaky. Naked, I faced Davis, who stood in front of me, his hard cock rising over his belly.

I kneeled before him, and he shifted, his fingers drifting through my hair. "Carson, you—"

"I'm doing exactly what I've been dying to do since I saw you and that fabulous ass." To prove my point, I reached up and gave him a juicy squeeze, allowing my fingers to trail along his cleft. A violent shudder rolled through him at my touch. "Beautiful." I rested my mouth on his thigh and licked a path up to his bristly groin, loving all the hair. I hated men who shaved themselves. I wanted to feel the scratch and burn against my cheeks.

"I-I don't think I can stand," he said and sat on the bed. "You make me weak."

I licked his balls and moved up his shaft to kiss the sticky, leaking tip. My cock throbbed when I took him to the back of my throat and sucked. Davis's moan of pleasure echoed in the silent room, and I licked his shaft, pressing my tongue along the pulse of the thick vein from root to head.

"*Mmm*," I hummed, swallowing his bittersweet precome. "Better than all the champagne we drank tonight." Davis twisted the comforter into his fists, his hips pumping his dick deeper, and I welcomed it. "Give it to me. You taste so good." I teased the slit and slid over the full length again.

"Oh God, oh God," he cried out, and I swallowed his hot cream, my fingers gripping the taut muscles of his rock-hard thighs.

His chest heaved, and I joined him on the bed, holding him close. Much as I wanted him right at that moment, I knew the longer I waited for my own satisfaction, the better the end would be.

"Carson."

"Mm? What?" I murmured into his hair.

"That was incredible."

I smiled. "I know."

He shook in my arms. "Oh, God. Did I just feed the beast?"

I rolled on top of him, my aching cock trapped between us. "Not yet. I'm just giving you a minute to catch your breath."

He ran his nose down my jaw, and it was my turn to

shiver from his sensual touch. "I'm breathing."

In a flash, I grabbed the condoms and lube from my night table and spread his legs. I slicked my fingers, but first teased the tiny opening with my mouth, loving how he writhed beneath me and tore at the sheets, ripping them off the bed. I never imagined Davis to be wild in bed, but I caught his fever and wanted to see him fly beyond the moon.

"Fuck, Carson. What the hell?"

"Still breathing?" I chuckled, widening his legs and slipping my tongue inside him.

"Nooo." He sighed, and I replaced my tongue with my fingers, loving how tightly he clenched around me. "Please, Carson. Now," Davis begged and flailed, catching my arm and digging his nails into my skin. Pleasure chased the pain, and he didn't need to ask me twice.

I had to take it slow to roll the condom over my aching dick, then teased the head over his hole. Davis slapped the bed twice but urged me on. "Fuck it, Carson. Fuck me. Oh God," he screamed when I thrust deep.

I buried my shaft to the root and rested for a moment, letting him adjust to me, while taking advantage of being inside him. "You're so perfect," I whispered.

"So are you."

I withdrew, returning almost immediately and nudged past his rim, inch by inch. We rocked faster and faster the bedsprings squeaking in protest.

"Harder, dammit. More." He clawed my back, and sweat dripped down my face, falling on his. I licked his cheek. "Again," he rasped, and I licked him a second time. I took his mouth in a claiming, possessive kiss and he met me with unexpected eagerness. I growled as I pummeled harder into his welcoming body. He answered with a rumble of pleasure that blew me up and twisted me into knots I didn't ever want untied.

I exploded, hips jerking endlessly, filling the condom,

and collapsed on top of him. My lips found his cheek and rested there, where I spent several minutes lightly kissing him, until my heart resumed a normal rhythm.

Davis smiled. "Is this real? Am I here with you?"

I ran a hand over his body, playing along the curve of his ass. "In the very delicious, naked flesh." I rolled my shoulders, wincing. "Ouch. You need a manicure." He didn't answer. "What's wrong?" I asked, my lips moving against the scruff of his jaw. "You're too quiet."

"I still don't know how this happened. I don't know if I belong here. If I fit in."

I rolled off him, got rid of the condom, and lay by his side, tangling our legs together. "Why wouldn't you?"

His eyes met mine. "You're kidding. I'm a nobody from Nowheresville upstate. I have nothing to offer you."

How could I tell him that when we made love, he was the one who held the power? When he kissed me, I'd give him anything he wanted. Now that I'd held him, I refused to think of anyone else touching him. A possessiveness I'd never imagined swept over me, and I tightened my arm around him.

"You're somebody to me. You fit perfectly. Right here. Next to me." I kissed his temple, where his sweaty hair lay plastered to his skin. "How about we rest a little, and then we'll take a shower?"

"You want me to stay?"

I hated his uncertainty and threw my leg over his hip. "Yes, I want you to stay."

* * *

I opened my eyes and squinted at the digital clock on the nightstand. Four eighteen a.m. glowed at me. An ugly time to be awake. But now that I was, a shower with Davis sounded like a hell of a reason to get out of bed. I reached for him—and came up empty.

Shit.

Wide awake, I sat up and smacked the bed. *Dammit.* I knew I shouldn't have gone to sleep. Davis had been so wary of the two of us being together, so certain he didn't belong here with me, he must've woken up first and bolted. The sheets were still warm where I ran my hand over them, the pillow indented from his head, and I swung my legs over the side. Maybe I could still catch him downstairs—

The sound of the toilet flushing settled my pounding heart. Laughing at my silliness, I crept to the bathroom and opened the door.

Davis whirled. "Oh, hi. I'm sorry. Did I wake you?"

My attention focused on the clothes folded on the vanity. So I wasn't wrong. "Were you going to at least leave me a note, or did you plan to sneak out without saying anything?"

Cheeks flaming, he hung his head. "I-I didn't know what I was going to do, but I figured I might as well get my stuff together. I put your clothes on the chair in the bedroom."

"That was nice of you." I moved closer. "Do you really want to leave?" I crowded him until our naked bodies pressed together.

"N-no," he choked out when I mouthed the strong cords of his neck. "But I'm not sure what's happening."

Our cocks had thickened and now rubbed, the friction critical to my very existence. Every brain cell I possessed concentrated on keeping Davis right where he was. I wanted him, needed him, and was determined to have him. The need went beyond the purely physical; it lived in my bones and blood.

"I am. I want to make love to you again. And you want me, too. It's as simple as that." My hand guided his to my erection, and he groaned but wrapped his fingers around the stiff length. I did the same to him, and we teased each other faster. He moaned, his cock pulsing out hot come over my stomach. I cried out. "God, Davis." I clung to him and swayed, on the brink of my own explosion, but Davis squeezed me tight at the base, and my climax receded.

"Not yet." He stepped away, leaving me on the edge and frustrated as hell.

"What the fuck," I growled, reaching for him, but he turned on the shower and beckoned me to come under the water with him. My dick ached and it hurt to walk, but I joined him and watched as he dropped to his knees and took my heavy cock between his lips. All was forgiven. It was heaven…paradise…bliss beyond words, seeing my dick slide in and out from those red, wet lips.

His tongue played up and down my shaft, and I no longer felt the water streaming over my head. He sucked and swirled, and I lost it when his teeth scraped the tender, sensitive flesh.

"Davis, fuck, oh fuck." Without warning, my climax crashed over me and I came, seeing stars, the moon, and the whole damn universe. I sank to the cedar bench, and Davis sat next to me. It was the most natural thing in the world to hold him close.

"Incredible. Thank you." I kissed his mouth, tasting myself, and I smiled against his lips. "I hope you're staying now."

"I don't think I could leave."

My heart leaped at his words. "Let's wash off and go back to bed."

We sudsed each other, rinsed, dried off, and made it to bed, yawning. Davis's eyes closed immediately, and he snuggled in with a sigh. I didn't rest until his breathing turned deep and even, and more content than I ever remembered, I shut my eyes.

Davis might not know it yet, but he was here to stay.

CHAPTER EIGHTEEN

Davis

I was sailing on a cloud and feeling so warm. Wonderfully warm and tingly. I moaned and heard a deep chuckle.

"Did you know you smile in your sleep?" Carson asked, and my eyes opened wide.

I was cuddled to his chest, our legs tangled together, and we were stark naked. "I guess last night wasn't a dream?" The pounding beat of his heart rumbled on my lips.

"It was for me."

His tender words rocked me to the core, as did the gentle kiss pressed to my shoulder.

"Me too," I admitted in a whisper. "But what now?" As much as I hated having this conversation, it had to be done. And, as expected, Carson brushed it off.

"Now? I think we get up and dressed and have brunch somewhere. I want waffles."

"I'm serious, Carson." I sat up and brushed the hair out of my eyes. "What happened last night wasn't planned—I just hated the thought of you spending your birthday alone."

"Because your family makes a big deal out of them." Propped up on the headboard, he folded his hands on top of the pillow in his lap. "But you know what? The fact that you chose to do that for me, making sure I wasn't by myself and getting me that cake with the birthday candle, it means you care." His eyes, once icy with disdain, now filled with nothing but warmth. "It was…nice. And I appreciate it. Usually my mother is the only one who remembers."

"And I'm sure she wanted to do something for you," I sympathized. "She's that type of person. She reminds me of my mom." I wondered what my parents would say if they knew I'd become involved with Carson. They already thought Brian had taken advantage of me, but while they weren't totally wrong, I was no innocent.

Carson said, "How about we have some coffee and decide where to eat? It's breakfast time, and I'm starvin' like Marvin."

"So you want to spend the day together? I don't want you to think—*mmph*." My words were lost in Carson's mouth as he covered mine in a lingering kiss. I held on to his shoulders and sighed gustily as he nibbled a hot path down my neck. I cupped his butt and squeezed, feeling his dick lengthen against my thigh.

"I had no intention of letting you go," he rumbled. "And if you keep this up, we may never get out of bed. In fact, DoorDash is looking better and better."

"Worth it." I grinned and ran a finger along the cleft of his ass.

"Bastard," he swore, and kissed me hard.

Eager to feel him inside me again, I responded with fervor. I was his wick and eager to be lit on fire—

A buzzing noise caught my attention, and Carson grunted. "Dammit. What the hell do they want?" His lips and mouth continued to play havoc with mine.

"Ignore it," I panted.

But it continued, and with a growl, he rolled off me and stomped out to the living room to answer it. A moment later he reappeared.

"My mother is on her way up." He opened his dresser drawers and began to pull on clothes. My stomach plummeted to the ground, my blood turned icy cold, and I jumped out of bed so fast, you'd have thought I'd discovered a scorpion in the sheets.

"What? Now? Right now?"

He pulled a T-shirt over his head. "Give or take a minute. Here. We wear the same size." He tossed me a pair of briefs, sweat pants, and a T-shirt. "Get dressed."

"Shit." I scrambled into the clothing and was smoothing my hair down when the doorbell rang.

Looking cool and unruffled, Carson winked at me. "Showtime."

"Not funny. She's gonna know. I mean, I'm here, and it's not even eleven in the morning and—"

Carson swooped in for a quick kiss that settled my racing heart some. "So what? I don't plan on keeping us a secret."

My breath stuttered, and I blinked. For the first time, I was with someone who wasn't afraid to see me in the sunlight after spending the night together.

"Oh...I didn't know..." I shook my head, my insides tumbling with a combination of hope and fear. I'd never had a man say that to me.

The bell rang again, and I hoped I wouldn't get sick.

"That's okay too," Carson said. "We'll just go with our feelings. And I'm feeling pretty damn great." He held out his hand, and I looked at it, then at his eyes, so soft and warm. My bones turned to mush, and I thought I would've done anything he asked. I reached for him, and together we answered the door.

Patricia entered, talking. "Happy birthday, honey. I'm

sorry if I woke you, but I thought—*oh*." She stopped dead, her lips forming a perfect circle. "Oooh," she repeated, drawing out the word with a beaming smile.

"Good morning, Mother," Carson deadpanned, my fingers laced with his in a death grip. "You're forgiven. Next time, please call ahead."

Waves of heat rolled over me, and I knew without needing a mirror that my face was bright red. Carson, of course, was cool as ice, and I wanted to kick him.

She blinked. "So is it even necessary to ask how your birthday was?" Her blue eyes twinkled. "Lovely to see you, Davis."

"Hi," I croaked and cleared my throat. "Good morning."

"It is now. I'd been hoping for this, but I didn't want to push." If possible, her smile grew brighter. "I practiced restraint."

"Is that so?" Carson drawled. "Must've been painful."

"You be quiet." Her glare accomplished nothing, as Carson laughed outright. "I planned to take you out for a birthday brunch, but if you'd rather spend it alone with Davis, I understand."

"No, Patricia. Please. You should be with Carson to celebrate. I can go home and—"

"No," Carson snapped in unison with Patricia's definitive, "Absolutely not. You'll join us. I'd love to get to know you better, now that you and Carson are together."

Together? Were we? He'd said we'd go with our feelings, but I wasn't sure what that meant. For the most part, what I felt was confused.

I waited, unsure if Carson would correct her, but all he did was grin. "I was hoping for waffles."

"Waffles it is. I'll wait for you to get dressed." She perched on the couch, and Carson tipped his head toward the bedroom. Once inside, he shut the door behind him and frowned.

"Why do you look sick?"

"I'm not. This is all just so fast." Which wasn't exactly true. I'd been thinking of Carson for weeks, yet never anticipated acting on my desires. Or Carson acting on his.

"Would you rather I continue to pretend I wasn't interested in you when the exact opposite is true? That's silly and makes no sense. For either of us." Lines deepened his brow. "Or is it something else?"

I blinked. "Like what?"

Carson crossed his arms. "You tell me." With one long stride, he closed the gap between us but didn't touch me. "Are you regretting what happened?" He licked his lips. "Are you sorry you spent the night?"

"No, absolutely not." I ran a hand through my hair. "I-I don't know what I'm feeling. I never expected to be in this position."

Again. And I should tell Carson about Brian, but I don't want to.

If things continued as they were, I'd have to and hope he understood this time was different.

"Because you work for me?" Carson's brows knitted together. "Are you worried things might change?"

"Haven't they already?"

His frown grew. "How so? If you think I'm not going to expect the same hard work I've demanded from the beginning, you're wrong. Many couples work together."

Carson's words came as a relief, but I still had my doubts, thanks to my track record.

"I guess you're right. I'm reading more into things than I need to."

"Just relax and take it as it comes." He winked. "So to speak. Now I'm hungry, and we don't want to keep my mother waiting, because her imagination is bound to run away thinking we're doing all the naughty things in here."

Carson gave me a fresh shirt and a pair of jeans. I slipped

them on and caught him eyeing me.

"What?"

"I like you in my clothes," he said simply, and my heart turned over. Falling for him wasn't supposed to happen, but since when did life follow a lesson plan? I put my arms around his neck and kissed him.

"I like you."

He smiled into my eyes and kissed the tip of my nose. "Let's go get those waffles."

* * *

It took me a few minutes to realize we were on the way to the diner where I'd met Carson and Patricia. The place I was ignominiously fired from. Before entering, I hung back and tugged at his hand.

"I can't go in there," I hissed.

"Why not?"

His lack of insight was astounding. "I can't believe you. It's *embarrassing*."

Carson, the grinning fool, remained supremely unconcerned. "For whom? Look at you now—working in a law-firm office for a fabulous boss who gives you fantastic fringe benefits. The best."

At his wink, I wanted to fall into the nearest manhole.

"Idiot. Don't say that," I shushed him. "Your mother is right here."

"Don't mind me." Patricia gave me a sunny smile. "I think Carson's right. You should walk in with your head held high. You have nothing to be ashamed of."

Knowing I was outnumbered, I decided to suck it up. It had been a few months already. Maybe no one would recognize me. That comforting thought lasted about four seconds. The moment we entered, Peter spotted us, and with a face filled with thunder, came running to the door.

"Davis? Why are you back? I'm sorry, Mr. Ballard, Mrs. Ballard. If he's bothering you—"

"Not at all, Peter," Carson cut him off smoothly. "Davis is with us. Table for three, please."

I gave him my most pleasant face but said nothing. Peter's dark eyes narrowed, but he picked up three menus. "Of course. Follow me."

We settled ourselves in a booth, and a busboy appeared immediately. "Coffee? Regular or decaf?"

"Regular coffee with soy or almond milk," Carson said. "Whatever you've got."

"Regular but milk for me," I answered.

"May I have tea, please?" Patricia asked.

"Right away."

I studied the menu, looking up when Carson dug his elbow into my side. "By the way, that's how you take an order." His smirk threatened to overtake his face.

I rolled my eyes. "Whatever. I never claimed to be a good waiter. This was my third restaurant in two years."

Our coffees, milk, and Patricia's tea were brought. Carson ordered his beloved waffles, I chose banana pancakes, and Patricia chose an egg-white vegetable omelet. She put some of the milk in her tea, sipped, and set it before her.

"Davis, I have to know something. And if it's too personal, please tell me it's none of my business."

Carson snickered. "If he doesn't, I will."

"Don't be rude to your mother." I sipped my coffee. "What would you like to know?"

"Why were you a waiter? From what Carson's told me and I've seen on my own, you're so good at your job at the firm, and it's so obvious your strength isn't waiting tables. Carson told me you have a degree in information technology, and now you're going for your paralegal certificate and maybe law school afterward." Blue eyes as perceptive as

Carson's held mine. "It doesn't make sense."

"Mom, I don't think it's the right time or place for this kind of discussion. Davis's past isn't my concern." His thigh pressed against mine. "I'm all about the present. And beyond."

Did Carson think we had a future? I'd have liked to believe that what was growing between us would make that possible. I knew he'd expect me to tell him about my past, and he was right. Secrets shouldn't exist between friends or lovers, as that was the quickest way to lose both. I wanted… what did I want? I wanted what was growing between Carson and me to be real and not me once again wishing on a star that was nothing more than an illusion, the gleam vanishing before my eyes, leaving no trace it had ever existed.

For now, I settled on alleviating a potential worry. "It's nothing terrible or illegal. I'd never bring shame to the firm."

Carson set his cup down so fast, the hot liquid slopped over the side, but he paid no mind to his wet fingers. "Is that what you believe it's all about? You think that's all that matters?" he growled, fast and furious. "It's got nothing to do with the firm and everything to do with you."

"I—it's silly. But please? Not now? This is supposed to be your birthday breakfast."

"I don't care about that." I'd never seen Carson so grim.

"But I do. And so does your mother." My shaky hands picked up the napkin and wiped my sweaty face. "Here's our food. You've been talking about waffles all morning. Don't let this ruin it. I'm telling you, it's nothing more than me being foolish and naïve."

"I find that hard to believe." Shooting me a dubious look, Carson accepted his plate, and I waited until everyone had their food in front of them before addressing the person I most didn't want to disappoint.

"Patricia, I'm sorry if I spoiled the morning."

"Sweetheart, you did nothing wrong. All I'm hoping

is you're safe."

"I am." My firm reassurance must've satisfied her because she nodded.

"Good. Then let's enjoy our food."

Carson's leg remained by mine, and as he ate, he'd occasionally reach down and squeeze my knee. Having little to no experience with how to act in a normal relationship—if that was what this even was—I tried not to make too much of Carson's thigh pressed to mine and ate my pancakes, thinking only about what Carson might expect from me.

"Well, that was delicious." Carson's plate sat empty. "You're not hungry?" He eyed my half-full plate.

"It's a lot of food." I shrugged. "I guess my eyes were bigger than my stomach."

Patricia wiped her lips. "This was very nice. I'm glad I stopped by. And again, I hope you didn't take offense to my questions."

I reassured her. "Not at all. Trust me, my mother is a master questioner."

Patricia's laugh was merry. "Did she give your dates the third degree?"

A knot formed in my stomach. "Ah, no. I-I didn't date much. It's pretty conservative where I lived. My parents knew, and my best friend, but that's all."

"It's more open in the city," Patricia agreed.

"Somewhat." Carson's cool smile didn't reach his eyes. "But there are still plenty of people who hate people like us and pretend not to. Or…" He jabbed a finger at the table. "They don't even bother to disguise it."

He was talking about his father and his brother. And it hurt me because even after so many years, their rejection still took such a terrible toll on his self-esteem.

"I'll go pay the bill." Patricia picked up the slip of paper the server had dropped off, leaving Carson and me alone.

Carson's troubled eyes met mine. "Maybe one day you'll

feel like you can talk to me."

Unflinching, I challenged him. "Yeah? Well, maybe you'll feel the same."

He blinked. "How about tonight?"

CHAPTER NINETEEN

Carson

Sure, I was a pushy bastard. I didn't need to know about Davis's past to fuck him. I'd been with men whose names I forgot almost as soon as they walked out the door.

But as I'd suspected from the first, Davis was special. Being with him surpassed any of the fantasies I'd fallen asleep to the past two months. Instead of being satisfied after our night together, I wanted him even more.

Seemingly overwhelmed, Davis nevertheless nodded. "Okay. We can talk."

We parted ways with my mother on the sidewalk in front of her apartment. I thought she'd make some excuse to spend time with us and extract more info from Davis, but she surprised me when she stopped.

"I hate to eat and run, but I have plans for dinner tonight and I have a hairdresser appointment." She kissed Davis. "It was a wonderful brunch. I hope we do it again soon."

"Thank you, and me too."

Me, she couldn't foist off so easily. "Dinner? Who with?" I gave her a winning smile. I had a sneaking suspicion and wanted to see if I was proved right. "If you can be nosy, so can I."

She blushed. "Just an old friend."

My grin threatened to split my face in half. "Would his name be Charles?" I kissed her red cheek. "Good for you. I love that you're dating."

Never one to be outdone, she kissed me back and whispered, "I love that you are too. I like Davis. Don't let him get away."

"You want me to handcuff him to my bed? Don't answer that," I swiftly recovered at the dancing light in her eyes. "I'll talk to you later." As she walked inside the building, I called after her, "Be good," then took Davis's hand. "Want to walk a little? It's too beautiful a day to sit inside."

He snickered. "Having waffle regret?" But he laced his fingers with mine, and we strolled up Park Avenue, passing the colorful flowers dotting the median, and turned the corner to Madison. Sweet warmth hit my face, and as we waited on the corner for the light to change, I savored the heat on my skin.

"It's days like this that make me fall in love with the city over and over again. Window-shopping, walking in the park, it's all part of what makes the city magical." I took a step off the curb, but Davis didn't walk with me, forcing me to stop and tug at his hand. "What?"

"I never would've guessed."

"Guessed what?"

He fell into step next to me. "You're a romantic. You managed to hide it so well that morning in the diner when you almost bit my head off."

We stepped onto the sidewalk, and I pulled him close to me. "Now I'd like to bite your tongue. Like this."

He held me and we kissed, slow at first, then deeper and

more passionately, until he panted against my lips. "You need to stop, or else I might do something very bad and very wrong."

"If it feels this good, it has to be right." I wanted to say more, but not here on the street with taxis whizzing by, blaring their horns. "Should we head back?" I asked, my desire to be alone with him intensifying with each passing second.

Davis nodded, and we turned around and crossed the street again, both anxious to be with each other. As we turned the corner to my building, I heard my name.

"Hello, Carson."

Annoyed as hell, I tightened my grip on Davis's hand. "Andrew, what do you want?"

He leaned on a lamppost, a sardonic grin kicking up the corner of his mouth. "I knew it. Can't say I blame you." His predatory gaze swept over Davis. "I wouldn't be able to keep my hands off him either. Maybe we could all get acquainted, hmm? I wouldn't mind sharing."

"I would. Now go away. Leave."

"It's a public sidewalk."

With that truth, I pulled Davis along with me, but Andrew dogged my heels. "Carson, wait."

Only steps from the front entrance of my building, I sighed with exasperation and faced him. "What do you want? I've told you before I'm not interested. We were done when you cheated on me. I'm over it, and over you."

"That's not what I came to talk to you about."

Puzzled, I glanced over at Davis, whose brow was puckered with confusion. "So what do you want?"

For the first time, Andrew's confidence seemed to lag, and he licked his lips. "I, uh, I lost my job. A few months ago."

"Oh. I'm sorry. But what does that have to do with me?" I questioned, perplexed. "I can't hire you, if that's what you're after. You're a banker, not an attorney."

Red crept up Andrew's neck. "Yeah…well…I…I was wondering…I'm short on funds for my bills. I have a few interviews coming up, and hopefully I'll get something, but in the meantime…"

My jaw dropped. "In the meantime you want me to lend you money to tide you over. Is that what this reunion has been all about? You never wanted to be together; you only wanted my money to help you." That was why he'd shown up at my office and called me for drinks. It wasn't me he was after. It was my checkbook.

In a way, I was relieved Andrew had revealed his motivation. Hard facts I could deal with.

"Yeah. It wouldn't be for long."

"But you don't know that," Davis countered, and Andrew, in that pugnacious way he had, thrust out his jaw.

"It's not your concern. This is between myself and Carson."

"Not really. You tried to insinuate yourself into his bed again. You obviously would've slept with him if he'd agreed. Fuck it, you even just insinuated you'd be up for a threesome. So yeah, if it concerns Carson, it concerns me."

Damn. My guy was hot defending me. I liked it. A lot.

"I'm not about to make any decisions, especially ones where large sums of money are involved, standing on the sidewalk. I'm assuming it's a large sum of money and not a thousand dollars?" I raised my brows, and at least Andrew had the decency to flush as he nodded. "Fine. Call me tomorrow, and I'll speak to my financial advisors about setting up a loan."

Andrew paled. "A loan? Baby, we don't need paper between us. You can—"

"Trust you?" I barked out a laugh. "I don't think so. Now we have to get upstairs. If you want the money, you know what to do."

Davis's hand in mine, we left Andrew. Upon entering my apartment, Davis surprised me by leading me into the bedroom and stripping me naked. I tingled with anticipation as he removed his clothes and I saw how excited he was.

"I like it when you're bossy like this," I murmured, running my hands up and down his hot skin, and he held my face between his palms and kissed me hard, plundering my mouth with his tongue. The other times he'd been softer and less aggressive, and while I liked him gentle, I also liked this rough and ready Davis. My cock jumped and throbbed.

"Yeah? Just how in control can I be?" He dipped his fingers into the crease of my ass, sending a full-body shiver through me.

"I told you. Here, when it's you and me, there are no titles between us." I leaned in and kissed him. "Only passion and desire," I whispered. "Whatever you want to take, I'm willing to give."

Light blazed from Davis's eyes, and he backed me up until we hit the bed and rolled onto it together. Underneath him, I wrapped my arms around his neck and pulled him close for a kiss. Our tongues slid and played together, but it was his heavy cock pushing into my belly that had me reeling. I wanted that inside me.

"Fuck me," I breathed into his nape. "Fuck me as hard as you can." At my words, his cock jumped and a trickle of his precum leaked over my stomach. I licked the strong cords of his neck. "You like that?"

Without answering, and with only a wild, almost feral grin on his lips, Davis shoved me into the mattress, pushed my knees to my shoulders, and stuck his tongue in my hole, circling the rim before thrusting in deep. I froze, then moaned at the hungry sounds of him eating me out. My head thrashed on the pillow as he continued to suck me, and I heard myself wailing but didn't care.

He parted my thighs wider, and I grabbed my dick, which

at my first touch exploded in my hand, shooting streams of come across my chest. My toes curled, and I couldn't catch my breath as the most ferocious orgasm I'd ever had split me into pieces.

I barely heard Davis putting on the condom, but he circled my wet and open rim with the sheathed, lubed head for a little while, playing with me. I groaned and he inched inside.

"How is that?"

"*Mmm*, more." I sighed, grabbing for his shoulders. "Give it all to me."

"I will. All of me in all of you."

My eyes flew open as Davis followed my wishes and buried himself completely. "Oh God," I choked out, the burn intense but satisfying. "That's it."

"No, it's not." Davis rolled his hips, moving into me even farther. "I'm just getting started."

He held me down and kissed me everywhere his mouth could reach while he probed my body. His hard shaft pulled out, then hammered in, creating a punishing rhythm. I soared high, Davis the only anchor in the storm battling to break free.

"Davis, fuck, Davis," I cried out, but he was lost above me, his hair in sweaty ringlets eyes alight with golden fire. I fell apart again, he roared and became one with me, his hard, hot cock pulsing and throbbing inside my passage.

"Carson, what the hell," he yelled out, and I held him tight, feeling the scrape of his teeth against my neck. We lay plastered together, sticky with come and sweat, and I never wanted to let him go.

We both came to, and Davis groaned while slowly pulling out of me. I winced, and he must've seen my discomfort because after getting rid of the condom, he sat on the edge of the bed, his anxious eyes searching mine.

"Are you okay? Did I hurt you?"

I trailed my fingers up his arm, tracing the curve of his biceps. "No. It was incredible. It's just been a while for me." I saw a few scratches on his shoulder and grinned. "I hope I didn't damage you too badly."

He leaned in and pressed a soft kiss to my lips. "Worth every drop of blood. Let's take a shower?" He turned, and my eyes widened at the crisscross of red marks over his back. Damn, he made me lose control.

My first attempt at getting out of bed failed. My ass hurt, and my legs were too wobbly. It took two more tries before I could stand and walk. Davis, who'd gone ahead to start the shower, returned to the bedroom and cackled at my wobbly legs.

"You look like you've been ridden rough."

I rolled my eyes. "There's no need to look so pleased with yourself. Come over here and help me."

Still chuckling, he took me by the arm and led me to the shower, where to my surprise, he placed me under the water and washed me with a tenderness I'd never known from any lover. I returned the favor and shampooed and conditioned his hair. When I'd rinsed him clean, I kissed his cheek.

"You were incredible."

"So were you."

We stood under the warm flow of water, holding each other. I didn't want to let go—of him, and this entire day, and this feeling of completeness.

"Stay with me?" I turned off the tap. "Tonight, I mean. We can go into the office together tomorrow."

"I-I don't have clothes or my laptop. I have to go home."

We dried off and dressed in the casual clothes from earlier. Out in the living room, I stretched on the couch, with Davis's head in my lap. I played with the edges of his damp hair. It was all very cozy and comfortable. "You could wear my clothes. You look as good in them as you do out of them."

He shook his head. "I can't keep doing that."

I wanted to snap, "Why not?" But figured that wasn't acting like an adult and refrained.

Davis sat up and faced me. "Are we going to talk about what happened earlier, with Andrew?"

I shrugged. "You saw. It was never about getting back together with me. I knew something was off when he kept popping up after playing the disappearing act." I fingered the fringe of a throw pillow. "Andrew always has a motive behind his actions, and he'll say or do whatever it takes to get what he wants."

"So that thing about a threesome…"

"Oh, I'm sure he meant it. Andrew loves sex." I pushed my toes into Davis's lap. "But that's not going to happen. You're mine. And I don't share."

A tiny smile tipped Davis's lips as he massaged my feet.

My insecurity over his secrecy when it came to past relationships wiggled its way to the surface. "Why? Is that something you're into?"

His brows flew up almost comically. "What? No. If I'm with someone, I don't look at anyone else. Trust me, you're enough of a handful."

His response satisfied me, but only to a point. "At brunch we said we'd talk later about your past relationships. I'm thinking later is now."

A haunted expression darkened Davis's eyes. "Okay." He released my toes and clasped his hands together. "What would you like to know?"

"I'm more interested in why you're acting like there's something to hide. You didn't do anything criminal, right?"

"No, of course not."

"So?" I prodded. "We've all done things that looking back, might've been bad choices we aren't proud of. There's nothing to be ashamed of."

He sighed. "It's—it's not just that. My first job was at a frozen yogurt place, and I developed a massive crush on my supervisor. He never knew it. I think he was straight, anyway. I went away to college, and in one of my computer labs, I had a thing with my TA." His eyes darted to mine. "We had an affair."

"Sex with a teacher is a pretty big no-no," I said mildly. "But more so on his part than yours."

"Cooper was in his midtwenties, and I thought he cared about me. I thought I loved him, but I know now that wasn't the case."

"He was in a power position and abused his authority."

"I didn't see it that way. He made me feel special. Until I discovered that every semester he picked a student and slept with them. Male, female, it didn't matter. I guess he chose whoever was dumb enough to fall for his lines."

"He used you, Davis. I'm sorry you had to go through that. No teacher should ever do that to a student. I gather you didn't report him?"

He shook his head. "No. I knew it was wrong, but…" He shrugged, and I hurt for him. Yeah, he'd been naïve and foolish, but the fact remained that teacher-student affairs were a continuing problem and one, in my opinion, that schools didn't enforce properly or take steps to ensure didn't happen.

"Hey. It was a mistake, but you learned from it."

His sad smile hurt my heart. "I'm not so sure."

"What do you mean?" I remembered and waited. I didn't want to ask him. He had to tell me himself.

"I have to tell you about Brian."

CHAPTER TWENTY

Davis

God, I felt sick, but it was time to tell him everything. I didn't want my mistake to be a wedge between us.

"Brian, the mayor of Harleyville. The man you worked for." Carson waited with expectation.

"Yeah." I chewed on my lip. "He and I…we were lovers. It started about six months after I came to work at city hall. I was hired as their webmaster."

"Pretty prestigious for someone so young."

I lifted a shoulder. "You have no idea how small Harleyville is."

"Go on," he urged.

"After two months, I was asked to join the mayor's office. Naturally, I was impressed and pretty excited. Brian Healy was young and ambitious and had big plans for the town. He wanted to bring business to the area, maybe merge with other smaller villages to increase Harleyville's footprint upstate."

"I understand. It was a résumé builder."

"Brian was interested in learning more about computers. I was happy to show him what I knew. We worked together often." I licked my lips, tearing my gaze away from Carson's to stare at the floor. "It was a Friday, and we'd had big lightning storms. Our systems had gone down, and I was working late. I thought I was alone until Brian came out of his office. He sat next to me and watched as I got us back online. He thanked me and told me he'd take me to dinner as a thank-you. I told him it was part of my job, but he insisted. He told me I'd gone above and beyond what my job required, and he wanted to reward me."

"And that reward went beyond a steak dinner, I'm thinking." Clearly angry, Carson met my eyes. "Is that when it started? Your affair?"

Miserable, I nodded. "Yeah. We went to a nice hotel restaurant about twenty miles out of town. When we finished, the storms started up again. The roads were flooded, and Brian suggested we stay the night. Seemed like other people also had the same idea, because the hotel was full."

"And you were forced to share a room, I'll bet."

"Yes," I whispered. "It—I let it happen. Brian was so kind and gentle. It was so hard being gay in a small town. I'd hear all these homophobic comments, and there was no one I felt safe with, other than my parents and my best friend, Tommy. But he had a family, and I couldn't stand being a third wheel anymore." I blinked. "After that first time, we saw each other almost every night. Brian told me he was in love with me. I'd leave the office first. He gave me a key to his house, and I'd go there and wait for him."

"How long did it last?"

"Over three years."

Carson sighed. "What happened? I'm assuming something went wrong, and that's why you left."

"After three years, Brian said we couldn't see each other

as often. He explained he was up for reelection, and we'd have to be even more discreet, but that once he was reelected, we'd be able to go on as usual. I agreed, but…I saw him at a few functions with a woman. I knew it was silly of me and that I was acting like a teenager, but I'd check his calendar and follow him. And each time he was with her."

"She was his beard," Carson snapped.

"She became his fiancée." My voice caught. "After the election, I saw an announcement in the local paper that they were engaged. A whirlwind romance, he called it." My laugh was bitter. "One January night, there was a blizzard, and my car got stuck in a snowbank, so I started walking home. Brian found me trudging along the side of the road. He had a four-wheel drive and picked me up. I didn't want him to, but the snow was getting worse and the wind made it hard to see."

"You don't need to make excuses to me."

My lip curled. "He took me to his house first, even though I asked him to take me home. Said Kathy, his fiancée, was in Albany for a meeting and was stuck there because of the snow. I told him I wasn't going to sleep with a man who was getting married."

"Of course not."

"He assured me he wouldn't touch me. But it was too dangerous to drive, so we should wait it out at his house. I hated agreeing with him, but he was right. You know how bad it can get up there in the winter. We had sandwiches, and then the power went out. It was freezing, so he made us coffee and said he'd put whiskey in it to keep us warm. He knew I didn't drink that kind of stuff, but it was so damn cold, I needed something."

"Slick motherfucker," Carson muttered.

Feeling miserable, I nodded. "I was weak too. Next thing I knew, he was kissing me. I tried to say no…I thought I did, but I couldn't stop him. I don't know if I was drunk, but it was like I was in slow motion or something. We were lying on the couch, and he took off my clothes…" I shook my head. "I'm not proud of myself. I swear I didn't want to…"

I'd never told anyone the details—not my parents, not even Tommy. I felt so foolish. So violated.

Carson grabbed me tight. "You didn't do anything wrong. He used you. He fed you alcohol—maybe even drugged you. You couldn't give consent."

Cold snaked through me at the words spoken out loud for the first time. "I woke up nauseated, and after I got sick in the bathroom, I put my clothes on and left Brian sleeping. That day I wrote a resignation letter and never returned to the office. Day and night he'd call me. I blocked him, but he knew how to find me anyway. He swore he'd never meant to hurt me. He said he didn't love Kathy, but if he wanted to stay mayor and have a bigger political career, he had to marry her. He couldn't tell anyone he was gay. But he wanted us to be together."

"You deserve more than being someone's down-low, someone to hide." Carson ran his hands over my arms, warming up the parts of me that had been numb from that horrible time.

I'd never felt so safe. So…loved.

"I told him we would never be together again and he had to leave me alone."

"Good for you." Carson kissed my face, my head, and wrapped his arms around me tighter. "You did the right thing."

"He kept insisting he loved me and we'd be together one day. He'd show up at my place, begging to see me. He'd send me emails that he loved me and I'd never be able to get rid of him. That's when I knew I had to leave. I got a new phone number, packed up everything, and came to New York a week later."

"Fucking maniac stalker," Carson growled. "I'll beat

his fucking ass if he ever comes near you."

For the first time since we came back from brunch, I laughed. "You're cute when you're trying to be a tough guy."

"I'm always cute," Carson quipped but became serious. "Let me guess—everything you told me is the reason you chose to disappear here in the concrete jungle. And take those bogus jobs as a waiter."

"Yeeaahhh," I drew out. "I guess that didn't work out too well."

Carson nibbled on my neck. "Debatable. Definitely didn't work out for your customers. But I'm thinking it worked out perfectly for me." He kissed where he'd been nuzzling. "I hate that you went through this. And I knew something was wrong. No one with a degree like yours, who could get a job in any high-tech firm, would struggle like you did."

"There's nothing wrong with being a server. They work long, hard hours and take way too much shit from customers."

"Hey, don't bite my head off. I agree. But you obviously aren't cut out for the service industry." I glared at him but relented at his smirk.

"Okay, yeah. I can admit I was a lousy waiter."

Carson's husky chuckle reverberated through me. "Yes, you were. But like I said, their loss was my gain. In more ways than one."

We locked eyes, and my throat went dry as a scorching wave of heat, then shivering cold rolled over me. I was light-headed, yet grounded enough to press my mouth to Carson's and feel his warm lips soften under mine. I wanted him to take me right there, to grind himself into me until my bones dissolved into his and we became one.

He ran his lips down my cheek, breathing my name like a song. "Davis. Davis."

"What?" I shivered, and he pushed me so I lay beneath

him. His eyes glowed with the brilliance of a cloudless summer sky, and my heart pounded. I was lost in Carson but not looking to be found. My way was his.

I loved him.

"I know it's only been a few months…" Carson cupped my cheek just as my phone buzzed, its ring splitting the silence of the room. It continued to buzz, and Carson pulled himself off me.

"You'd better see who that is."

"Dammit," I growled and pulled it from my pocket to see it was my mother. I took a second to answer it. "Hi, Mom."

"Are you all right?"

"Yeah, why?"

"You didn't call like you usually do on Sunday mornings, and I got worried."

Her anxious voice carried, and Carson's lips twitched. *Sorry*, I mouthed, and he patted my cheek and kissed me before removing himself from the couch. He crossed the room to the kitchen and got two glasses from the cabinet, opened the refrigerator and took out a bottle of wine.

"I figured since we just spoke I could call next week."

"I like our Sunday calls. I hope I didn't interrupt you."

Only from realizing I'm in love with my boss.

A few minutes later and we would not have been having this conversation, as I would've been naked and under Carson. I closed my eyes briefly at my fantasy.

"No, it's all good. Nothing that I can't get back to."

Carson winked, poured two glasses, and brought them over, handing one to me.

"I was thinking about what you said about your boss."

"I told you, it's good. Everything is going well."

Carson's grin spread across his face, and he took off his shirt. My face grew hot as my mother didn't exactly have the quietest of voices.

"Well…I want to make sure he doesn't take advantage

of you. He needs to know you're important and a valuable asset."

Listening to my mother speak and knowing Carson was able to hear every word she said was particularly mortifying.

"Mom, he does. It's all good."

"Except for the distance. We're still not used to being so far away."

Guilt rushed through me, as I didn't miss her well-intentioned yet slightly overbearing presence in my life. "I know, but things are going well for me here."

In the background I heard my father grumbling, "Let the boy live his life. You don't want to be one of *those* mothers." I pressed my lips together to keep from laughing.

"Tell Dad hi and I love him. I'll try to call during the week. I'd better get going, though. I have to prepare for my course and finish up something I started."

Carson drank his wine and took off his pants. He walked away, wearing only his black briefs. Was there anything sexier? Not in my world. God, he had a gorgeous ass, and I wanted to pounce on him. He must've sensed my eyes on him, as he turned around and gave me a beaming smile before disappearing into the bedroom.

"Okay, don't forget."

"I won't," I promised. "Bye, love you."

"Love you too."

I tossed the phone and practically ran into the bedroom to find Carson naked on the bed. I pulled off my clothes and joined him. He held me to him, and I cuddled close.

"Thank you for sharing your story with me." His lips brushed my hair.

I squeezed my eyes shut, knowing what I had to say wouldn't go over well. "It's not everything."

"Oh?" he questioned, his voice taut. "What, then?"

"My best friend Tommy, who still lives up there, said Brian still asks about me. Tommy, of course, blows him off every time."

"Okay, so what's the problem?"

I sat up. "The last time, a few weeks ago, Brian confronted Tommy where he works—it's an auto-body place, and Brian brings his car there to be serviced. He said that Tommy should tell me that no matter what, I couldn't run away. That I was his and he was going to have me." An involuntary shudder ran through me, and Carson's wary eyes sparked with anger.

"The fucking hell he is. That's bullshit. The man is threatening you. You need an order of protection from that bastard."

"No." I shook my head. "I can't. Brian doesn't know where I am. If I get a protective order or file anything against him, he'll discover I'm in the city, only a train or car ride away, and come after me."

Carson took me by the shoulders. "Do you think I'd let him come near you or hurt you?"

"I'm not a child who needs protection. I can handle my own shit." Irritated, I scowled.

"I never said you were, and I know you can. I'm not here to fight your battles for you. But if you let me, I'll be by your side to help you."

"Why?" I had to know if his feelings ran as deeply as mine.

Carson tangled his fingers in the hair curling at my nape and brought our lips together. "Because." He touched his mouth to mine, and I felt his heart in the press of his lips and his soul in the brush of his fingers to my heated skin. I fell into his touch as if this was the beginning of forever.

"*Hmm*," I debated with a pretend frown. "That's not an argument that would win you your case in court, Counselor."

"But will it win your heart?" He kissed me again, and I clung to him. "I'm thinking that's the only thing that matters."

"You already have it. A unanimous verdict." I kissed him over and over. "I wasn't planning on falling for you, but maybe some things are inevitable."

CHAPTER TWENTY-ONE

Carson

Monday mornings were never my favorite, but I entered the office with a spring in my step and a smile. Fact was, for the past month since Davis and I started seeing each other, I'd been viewing the world differently.

Work had ceased to be the driving force in my life, as it had been upon my return home. My focus had shifted to living my life instead of going through the motions. I looked forward to the office because it was time with Davis. Our days were spent working hard—Davis had finally gotten the files under control and was creating databases for them. He insisted I learn record-keeping, and though it was tough to wrap my head around it, his patience made it possible. All that while staying on top of his paralegal studies, which, as I'd predicted, were proving to be an invaluable asset to the firm.

And my nights? My nights were filled with passion rather than resentment of what tomorrow might bring.

When Davis and I left the office, we'd go out to dinner or, more often than not, order dinner in and spend the night learning each other's likes and dislikes, emotionally as well as physically.

Davis loved his parents but was happy they'd moved—as much as he loved his mother, she could be smothering. I was slowly letting go of the hostility toward my father and brother. As Davis had said at the Japanese restaurant that first week, what purpose would it serve to hold on to anger?

Did I mention Davis was also stubborn as hell? He refused to allow me to pay for everything, even though I could easily afford it. Every night I'd ask him to stay with me, and every night he'd refuse and drag himself out of my bed and back to his crappy little studio, leaving us both alone and lonely in our respective apartments.

The night before, we'd ordered in sushi, and Davis had stayed till nearly two a.m.—we'd shared the sushi in bed, and then I made love to him, teasing my tongue over his gorgeous body until I was afraid the neighbors would call the police from his screams.

"Please stay. You know you want to." I watched him roll out of the bed and head for the shower.

"I can't."

"You mean you won't." And I knew why. Brian had made him leery of believing he deserved a normal, healthy relationship. It would take lots of time and loving reassurance that I was there for the long haul. I had plenty of both.

This morning I was surprised to see his chair empty, as he was almost always at work earlier than me. The elevator dinged and he trudged out, yawning, with bags under his eyes.

"Late night?" I inquired with a cackle, and he glared.

"If you think you're cute, you're not. I don't do well on less than six hours of sleep."

"That's why you should've stayed."

He covered up another yawn and sat in his chair. "No. Next time I'll have to leave earlier."

I bent to whisper in his ear. "We'll see about that."

He swiveled to face me with a serious expression. "You know how I feel about this. I don't want flirting between us in the office. The last thing I need is for people to think we're a couple—"

"Even though we are?" I responded with a raised brow.

"I've been through this enough. I don't want my personal life bleeding over to the professional. No hand-holding or kissing." A stern frown was directed at me.

"Agreed. We're here to work. That'll only make our downtime so much more pleasurable." I understood his position.

The elevator door opened, and a woman entered the office. Uncertain brown eyes met mine, and she tucked a strand of blond hair behind her ear.

"May I help you?"

Her smile was shy. She was very beautiful and very young—early twenties, I'd guess—and dressed simply in dark jeans, a white linen shirt, and with a heavy gold rope chain around her neck. A large diamond ring glittered on her finger, and she clutched the handles of a designer tote bag hanging on her shoulder.

"Are you Carson?"

I raised my brows, glancing at Davis for a split second before answering. He shook his head, indicating he had no clue to her identity.

"Yes. Carson Ballard. May I help you with something, Ms.…?"

"Fontaine. Lia Fontaine." She blinked, her large eyes framed by ridiculously long lashes, and played with the edges of her hair. "Can we talk in private?"

I blinked, my senses on high alert. "Can you tell me what this is in reference to?"

"I'd rather wait until we sit down."

"Very well. Follow me. Davis, hold my calls, please."

He nodded, and Lia Fontaine passed by me. I waited by the door for her to take a seat in one of the chairs in front of my desk.

"Okay. Now, how can I help? Do you have an estate question or a trust issue?" My smile was pleasant, but my nerves were dancing on edge. The casual way she'd said my name had set off my internal antennae.

"No. I wanted to talk about Dale."

"Dale?" I blinked. "What about him?"

"He and I…we were together."

I couldn't say I was shocked. Dale loved beautiful women, and Lia Fontaine was gorgeous.

"I see. And you're here to tell me this, why?"

"Because of this." She reached into her bag and pulled out her phone. After tapping the screen, she handed it to me, and my stomach did a deep dive to my knees. A baby lay sleeping in a crib. I swiped to see pictures of Lia holding the child—a girl—and wheeling her in a carriage.

"You're saying the baby is Dale's."

"I'm not saying. She is."

"How long were you with my brother? How did you meet him?"

She lifted her chin. "I'm a dancer at a club on the West Side. Not one of those with signs above the taxicabs. Luxe is a very private, very expensive, members-only club. Dale used to come in like, twice a week, minimum. We met two years ago, and he'd always ask for me. Soon he and I were meeting outside of the club. He paid for the rent on my apartment. We were in love."

Anything was possible when it came to my brother. Except that. Dale being faithful to a woman—any woman— was about as plausible as me getting pregnant.

"And he was the only man you were with during that

time?"

Her face turned bright red. "It's not easy for a single woman to make it alone. I'm not ashamed if men like to give me gifts."

"You didn't answer my question, Ms. Fontaine."

She flung her head back. "Sure I gave them lap dances and let them touch me. That's the only way I could make big tips. But I never had sex with any other man. That's how I know it's Dale's baby. And I need help because I have to pay someone to watch her when I go to work. With the baby now, there's all these expenses. I can't afford my rent and a sitter and her formula…" Her voice trailed off, and she twisted her diamond ring around and around. "Dale said he would help me."

I took notes as she spoke. "So, if I understand correctly, you claim you only had unprotected sex with my brother."

Her face flushed. "I know what you're thinking, but it wasn't like that. I stopped all the extra other stuff when I fell in love with Dale. He said he wanted to marry me. He wanted a baby. I loved him." She sniffled. "We were going to be a family."

From what I knew of my brother, he'd say anything to get a woman into his bed, but telling a stripper he'd marry her seemed a little far-fetched. And as far as him wanting a child? I didn't see it either, but what did I know?

"Why don't you sell the diamond ring you're wearing? That would bring in enough money for you to live on for a while."

A tear rolled down her cheek. "Dale gave it to me. I can't." She met my eyes with fierceness and crossed her arms. "I just want what's right for my baby."

"And what is it you think will make it right?"

"A million dollars." Defiance brewed in her brown eyes. "I know he had the money."

I had to hand it to her. She had balls. "Cash, check, or

money order?" I joked, unable to help myself. "Did you really think you'd just be able to walk in here, make a demand like that, and expect me to simply nod my head and hand you the money?"

I pretended nonchalance, but dammit. Could this be true? Was that baby Dale's? My niece? God, what a mess. And if it was true, how ironic to have me, the gay brother he hated, left to take care of his child.

She shrugged. "That's not my problem."

"*Au contraire*, my lovely Lia. It most certainly is," I drawled. "Why should I believe you?" I had little doubt my brother had slept with Lia Fontaine, along with half the strippers in Manhattan. Did I believe he was stupid enough to not have used protection? Yes, especially if he was drinking. That still didn't mean the baby was his or her story was true. I refused to be swayed by her pretty pleading. "I have no proof that the two of you were ever together."

With her long red nails, she swiped at her phone screen. After a second, she handed it to me. "Here, see? There's a picture of us together."

I took it from her, and sure enough, it was her in a skimpy outfit, cuddled on my brother's lap. One of his hands cupped her mostly exposed ass, and their cheeks were pressed together as they smiled for the camera. In the background I saw a dancer on a pole. I studied the photo. No matter that Dale and I were estranged for years before his death, seeing my brother laughing and alive hurt my heart.

"Where was this taken? It looks like a strip club." I handed the phone to her. "I'm sorry, but this proves nothing—only that Dale was at the club you worked for."

She shoved the phone in my face. A little baby in a pink outfit gazed up at me. "She's his. Look at her—she has Dale's face. That's your niece. She needs her family."

As babies went, she was adorable. "Maybe so, but I'll need a DNA test to prove it."

For the first time since walking into my office, her confidence faltered. "Uh, okay. But Dale is dead."

"Not to worry. My DNA will suffice as a match." This touchy subject matter would often arise while drawing up wills and trusts for clients. Unknown family members had a habit of popping up out of the woodwork where large sums of money were to be had. I'd discovered that the firm had a testing company, and I pulled their name from the database Davis had set up. "I can give you the name and address of the center, and they'll do a test. It's painless." I scribbled out the information and handed it to her, then rose from my seat, hoping she'd get the hint that the conversation was over. "Until then, I'm afraid there's nothing I can do for you, Ms. Fontaine."

She remained in the chair, so I walked over and opened the door. She blinked, grabbed her bag, and stalked past me. As she reached Davis's desk, she stopped and whirled around. The elevator dinged, and my stomach went into freefall when my mother walked out and entered the office.

Shit.

"Brooke is Dale's baby," Lia cried out. Davis's shocked expression didn't concern me as much as my mother's reaction, and I rushed to her side.

"Carson, what's going on?"

Lia's eyes opened wide, her gaze traveled between my mother and me, and she burst into tears. "I have Dale's baby, and he won't help me. You're her grandmother, aren't you? I saw pictures of you and Dale together. You have to do something for us."

My mother clutched my arm. "Carson, is this true?"

Calm but grim, I shrugged. "We'll have to see. She came here demanding money, but I'm not giving her anything before the DNA test."

The tears continued to flow down Lia's face. "That could take weeks, and my baby needs help now." She put the phone up to my mother's face. "That's your granddaughter. You need to take care of her. I'm behind on my rent, and they can evict us. We have nowhere to go."

This was turning into a living soap opera.

To her credit, my mother kept her composure. "She's a beautiful girl. But Carson's right. Without proof, there's nothing I can do. Where is your baby now?"

Lia sniffled. "With my neighbor."

"Why don't I send you home in a car, and you make the appointment for the DNA test, like Carson said." My mother continued to dart glances at the phone, and anxiety swirled in my stomach.

"I'll call the service," Davis offered, then spoke quietly into the phone. "They'll be waiting outside in two minutes."

Without another word, Lia turned and walked away. After she disappeared into the elevator, I heaved a great sigh of relief. Davis helped my mother into a chair and brought her a cup of cold water.

"Tell me what happened, please," she demanded, and after I repeated the entirety of my conversation with Lia, my mother shook her head. "Your brother...I just don't know what to think. Do you believe her?"

"The million-dollar question. Literally. On the one hand, do I believe Dale slept with her? Yes. Dale, from what I heard, liked surrounding himself with beautiful women. Was he that incredibly foolish to not protect himself?" I shrugged. "I have no idea. She said they were in love. I have my doubts about that." Mostly because Dale only loved himself.

"Why?" Davis asked.

"She hardly looked like someone who'd just lost their lover. I saw a single tear, but that was it. She wanted a million dollars."

"Oh."

With my mother wavering on her immediate support of Lia, I pressed on. "Yeah, oh. It was all about the money for the baby. Now, I understand she's worried about how to take care of her, but I have to assume Dale knew she was pregnant—it's awfully hard to hide something like that. She said he paid for her apartment. I can check the books. I wouldn't be surprised if he had the firm pay for it. He never mentioned anything to you?"

"Not a word. And he didn't seem concerned or worried about anything in the last few months."

"I guess we'll have to wait and see if she goes through with the test. If she doesn't, we'll have our answer." But I could see the uneasiness in her eyes.

"I hope the baby will be okay. Do you think she has enough to eat? Do you know where the woman lives? Is it safe? What if they do evict her?"

My mother, always the softest heart in the world, was now concerned about a baby that may not be any relation to her.

"I'm assuming she does. I have no idea where she lives, but we can find out the address from the car service."

"What if it's true, Carson?" Her fingers tightened around the handle of her purse. "What if that is Dale's child and I'm her grandmother?"

"Mom," I warned, but I could see it was too late.

"If I let any time pass where she might need food or medical attention…we have so much, what would it hurt to help her?"

"But you heard what I said. She was with other men besides Dale. Why would you take the word of a stranger?"

"What does it matter, if she proves to be his daughter? That little girl could be all I have left of Dale." I recognized that steely determination in her eyes. "And even if it turns out she isn't ours, I couldn't bear to think of an innocent child suffering because of money. Money that we can well afford to give." She handed me the cup and rose to her feet. "I need to see what's truly going on there. Davis"—she turned to him—"please find out the address from the car company."

I could see it was a waste of time to argue with her, so when Davis looked to me for confirmation, I nodded. "You heard her. Go ahead. Since when does anyone listen to me?"

My mother put a hand on my arm. "I'm only doing what I feel in my heart is right."

I bent to kiss her cheek. "I know, Mom. Call me later to tell me what happened."

With a quick nod and a wave good-bye, she was gone. I settled myself on Davis's desk. "Well. That's a Monday morning I didn't expect."

"Here's my question for you. Do you think she's telling the truth?"

I drummed my fingers on my thigh. "Who's to say? I automatically think she's lying, but I know nothing about my brother. He was a stranger to me alive, and nothing's changed with his death. It's entirely possible Lia was his secret girlfriend and he knew all about the baby and kept it from my mother."

The phone rang, and I slid off the desk. "But I have a business to run. So let's get to that, and if she consents to the DNA test, we'll have the answer."

Davis picked up the phone. "Ballard and Melbourne. May I help you?" On my way to my office I heard him schedule an appointment with a new client. The morning bombshell couldn't distract me. We were getting back on track, and that was what mattered.

Once behind my desk, I turned on my computer, and while waiting for it to boot up, I opened the bottom drawer of my desk. A picture stared up at me. My father and brother, side by side, arms over each other's shoulders, so close that not a ray of sunlight could slip between them. No room for anyone else in their lives.

Another fine mess you've gotten me into.

Davis buzzed me, and I shut the drawer.

CHAPTER TWENTY-TWO

Davis

I spotted Kelly in our usual seats in the classroom and waved from the doorway. He removed his backpack from the chair so I could sit.

"Hey, Kelly. You're here early. I'm almost always here first." I set my laptop on the desk and opened it to connect to the Wi-Fi.

"Yeah. I got lucky with the trains. There's a first time for everything."

I pulled out the two bottles of water I'd picked up for us, and Kelly handed me a protein bar. We'd become good friends since that first day. We shared drinks and snacks for the lectures and had a weekly study session to go over the lessons and prep each other for tests. Over FaceTime, Carson and I chatted with his husband, Mark, and we'd all agreed to go out once Mark's trial ended.

"How's your week been?" Kelly checked his phone before shutting it off and putting it away. The professor was late, so we had time to catch up. "Any interesting clients?"

Since Mark handled family-law cases, I'd asked Carson ahead of time if it would be okay for me to mention his meeting with Lia. Knowing how private he was, I had no intention of revealing anything without permission, but he was more than willing to hear Mark's opinion.

"Not sure about clients, but we had a bombshell on Monday, and Carson's been trying to figure out how to deal with it."

I relayed the information of Carson's meeting with Lia, and Kelly whistled.

"Damn. Well, I'm not surprised Carson's skeptical. All of a sudden, *boom*. This woman pops up with a baby and demands a million dollars? Shit, I wouldn't pay her either."

I chewed a fingernail. "And then we have Patricia, Carson's mom, who has decided to be a grandmother to the baby without a definitive test result."

"She wants something to hold on to from her son. I get it. Mark's seen this in a lot of cases where the man passes away before paternity can be decided. Is she gonna take the test?"

That had been the main focus of the week. Carson had been distracted and not the best company, which heightened my overall uncertainty about our still-new relationship. I figured if he wanted to talk, he'd come to me, but he didn't. Instead he withdrew and stayed in his office or went home. Alone. Not being one to push, I let him be, but now it was Thursday and after a month of spending every evening together, I missed him.

"I don't really know. Carson hasn't said."

"Well, it's the only way he's going to get any resolution. How're things going with you two otherwise?"

It was nice to have a friend to talk to. Tommy was my best friend, but he was still unhappy with me living in the city, and I hadn't told him about my involvement with

Carson, since I already knew he'd be against it. With my track record, I couldn't blame him, but it was good to have someone who was positive about my relationship.

"Great before all this happened. Now he's preoccupied with the situation, which I get, but instead of talking to me, he's shut me out."

The professor walked in, and the classroom quieted, but Kelly leaned in closer. "So make sure you open that door and let yourself in."

* * *

I took Kelly's words to heart, and after class, decided to stop by my place first, pick up a few things, then go to Carson and confront him. This was different from my previous relationships, which made me determined to fight for what we were building. I'd just stepped out of the shower when my buzzer sounded.

"Who is it?"

"Me. Can I come up?"

Hearing Carson's voice through the intercom, I almost dropped my towel, but I gathered my wits, tucked it in tighter around my waist, and hit the button. A minute or so later, he rang the bell, and I peeped through the spyhole to see him standing there, head down, hands shoved into his pockets. I opened the door.

"Come on in."

A slight smile ticked up his lips. "Do you answer the door for everyone in a towel?"

"Only the special ones."

We stood in the small space, facing each other. I could see the dark circles under his eyes and the deepening lines in his face. I couldn't stand our awkward silence.

"I've missed you this week."

Carson's eyes flashed to mine. "I've been at the office."
I shook my head. "Not really. In body only."
"This body missed you."
Using sex as a way to escape wasn't how I planned to deal with Carson's emotions. "Nice try, but it ain't gonna happen unless we talk."
Carson slipped his fingers into the knot of the towel at my waist and pulled me close. "Then put some clothes on because seeing you half-naked after being without you all week is too dangerous."
With his hands on my bare skin, brushing the trail of hair leading to my rapidly stiffening dick, I almost gave in to the savage desire scorching through me. I pulled away before he could see the full-body goose bumps that had risen over me, and left him to get dressed. When I returned, half a room away couldn't hide the yearning in his eyes. I wanted him so badly it hurt, but I was proud of myself for staying strong. I joined him on the couch.
He grinned. "I liked you better in the towel. Or nothing."
"Don't," I said simply. "You're using sex and humor to hide, and that's never good."
The humor faded from his lips. "I'm sorry."
"For?" I waited.
"For this whole week. I know I've been a shit to deal with."
"Yeah, you have." His apology loosened the knot of anxiety in my stomach. "Why are you shutting me out?"
His hands twisted in his lap. "I-I don't know. I guess it's because I don't know any other way. I'm not used to having someone to lean on or talk to. Except for my mother, I've always had to do everything on my own."
"What if you don't have to anymore?" The risk was mine, but I'd rather take a chance with my heart than never know love at all.
"What do you mean?"

"I want you to share everything with me. The good and the bad. The ugly as well as the beautiful. Life can be hard." I scooted over to take his hand and lace our fingers together. "But love can give us strength."

"Is that what we're talking about here? Because if love means needing you with me all the time, wanting you so bad I can't think straight, and wishing I never have to let you go, then…I love you. So damn much."

My heart might've stopped because the next thing I knew, I was kissing him. "I love you too, Carson. Love is also hard—if it were easy, it wouldn't be so special when you find the right one."

He tightened his grip on me. "I didn't like being without you."

"You weren't. I was right there, the whole time, thinking of you and wishing you would talk to me, but you made it impossible. Tonight I decided to hell with you shutting me out. I was planning on coming over and not leaving without you speaking to me."

He hung his head. "I don't want you leaving at all. Having you with me helps me deal with all the chaos."

I knew this had to do with the baby. "So lean on me."

"I'd rather hold you."

He slid his arm around me, and I settled into the familiar place I loved best—cheek to his chest so I could listen to the comforting sound of his heart.

"Better?" I asked.

"The best." His lips touched my hair. "Lia had the baby tested. We'll know soon if she's telling the truth. My biggest fear right now is my mother. She's been at Lia's every day since she came into the office. I think she's convinced herself the baby is Dale's. And if she's disappointed, I'm worried it will hit her almost as hard as Dale's death."

"You've spoken about it with her?"

He shrugged, and from the hitch in his breath, I gathered

the conversation hadn't gone too well.

"What? Tell me."

Tension grew as the time he remained silent ticked on. "She won't talk to me."

"What happened?"

"I told her she was only hurting herself by getting so close with the baby, and that she should stay away until we get the test results. That Lia was playing on her sympathy by allowing her to think the baby was Dale's without any proof."

"That's nothing different from what you said on Monday. Something else must've happened."

His face flushed red. "I-I said some…things."

"Things?" I sat up and faced eyes filled with shame and regret. "What things?" I frowned. Patricia was a wonderful person who didn't deserve to be attacked for wanting a grandchild, whether it was a fool's paradise or not.

Carson's sigh filled the air. "I called her ridiculous and foolish. Naïve and desperate. I told her she was acting like one of those people you see on television who get scammed." He peeked at me from beneath his lashes. "I said her nickname should be Patsy, not Patty."

I winced and glared at him. "I can't believe you said those things to her."

"She told me I'm so blinded by my anger toward Dale that I can't see past it. And until I understand and work it out, I shouldn't call her." He took me by the shoulders. "But I'm not. Really."

"No? Are you sure?" I wouldn't let him get away with talking to his mother like that. "Because you don't know yet. And what business of yours is it if your mother wants to get close to the baby? Are you worried about your inheritance? Is it all about the money?"

He made a face. "No. I have my own money from a trust. I don't care about that, although I'm not saying I want my mother to give this person all her money. Obviously, if I saw something shady happening, I'd step in."

"What is it? Talk to me."

He looked right, then left before hanging his head. "My mother's all I have left. She's the only person who's always been by my side, one hundred percent, loving me unconditionally. I don't want to see her get her hopes up, only to be hurt. I know she's always wanted grandchildren, and I guess with me being gay and not interested in having kids and Dale gone, this child represents her last chance at being a grandmother. And if the baby's not Dale's, she'll be devastated."

I touched his cheek. "I know it's hard for you to sit by and say nothing, but you have to stay out of it." He opened his mouth, but I put my fingers over his lips. "Carson. This isn't your battle to fight."

"I know, I know. I hate this. I've never had this kind of argument with her. Little disagreements, sure, but she's never refused to speak to me." He pressed his cheek to mine. "Can you call her? Try and get her to see my point?"

"Nope."

"But—"

"But nothing." I scowled. "First of all, I think you're wrong. And second, you're not going to use me as a go-between. You need to tell her everything yourself. Not only about the baby, but about how Dale spoke to you and how your father shut you out."

"You're supposed to be on my side."

"There is no side. I care about both of you." I took his face between my hands and kissed him. "Call her and apologize. Or better yet, go over and do it in person. Talk to her."

"Will you come with me?" he appealed. "I don't know if I can face her alone, and I don't want to screw this up. You're the one who knows the right thing to say. I know you said you're not taking sides, but…I need you with me. At my side."

Who wouldn't fall in love with someone who said that?

"If you need me, I'll be there for you."

His smile was tentative at best, and I hated knowing he and Patricia were on the outs.

"Let's go now." He jumped to his feet, anxious to leave, but I remained uncertain.

"Don't you think you should call her first and let her know we're coming?"

"No. She'll tell me not to. If I show up, especially with you, she won't turn me away. At least, I don't think so."

"I'll do whatever you want if it helps."

More serious than I'd ever seen him, Carson took my hand in his. "You being with me is all I want."

I laced my fingers with his, and we left. The car he'd ordered sat waiting at the curb, and all through the drive downtown, Carson didn't speak but held on to my hand.

"Hey," I said as the car pulled in front of his mother's apartment. "It'll be all right. Families go through things all the time, and you and your mother love each other. It'll work out."

He grimaced. I wasn't sure he believed me.

The doorman didn't announce us, and Carson's Adam's apple bobbed as he stood before the apartment door and swallowed hard. He rang the bell twice and clung to me as if I was the only thing keeping him from falling.

The door opened. "Carson?" Patricia's troubled gaze met mine and softened imperceptibly. "Davis. Please come in."

"Thank you, Mom." Head bowed, Carson passed by her without stopping, but I held her gaze.

"How are you, Patricia?"

"I've been better."

It was my first time at Patricia's home, and it was as elegant as she was. The pale walls were offset by dark wooden floors and simple furniture with clean lines. Fine artwork hung on the walls, and when I glanced into the dining room, I spied heavy silver pieces I knew without a doubt were sterling. Carson made light of the extreme wealth he came from, and it hadn't made a difference, but now, confronted with all the signs, I suddenly had the urge to run home and change into something more appropriate than my faded jeans and T-shirt.

My steps slowed, and perhaps Carson was attuned to my feelings, because he took my hand and whispered, "Don't." Curiously, that single word settled my nerves.

Upon entering the spacious living room, Carson stopped short. "Dean Wallace?"

"Hello, Carson. Nice to see you again."

"It's good to see you too. This is my partner, Davis Turner."

"Good to meet you. I hear you're in paralegal training."

"Yes, sir. I'm enjoying the class very much and learning a tremendous amount."

"Excellent. It's a good stepping stone for law school."

"And that will be one step at a time," I said with a smile, which he returned.

"Understood."

"Charles and I were about to have an after-dinner drink. Will you join us?"

"I can make my own." Carson crossed the room to the bar, and I watched him make himself a martini. "Davis, what would you like?"

"Just club soda for me, thanks."

"Coming right up."

We took our seats across from Patricia and Dean Wallace. I waited for Carson to take a sip of his drink, hoping he would make the overture to his mother and not wait for her to speak.

"Mom, I'm sorry. I had no right to talk to you like that.

I was only thinking of myself and not how you were feeling about the baby. I apologize." In a sure sign of nerves, he clasped and unclasped his hands. Carson could face down the disciplinary committee like a lion, but when it came to his mother, he was a pussycat. "You have the right to deal with the situation any way you want. I was only trying to prevent you from getting hurt."

Her lips trembled. "Thank you. I understand how you feel because it's your brother involved, but I truly believe Brooke is Dale's baby. She looks exactly like he did as a baby. But even if the tests prove she isn't, I want to help her. No young mother should have to accept gifts from men to make ends meet. She shouldn't have to choose between formula or rent."

Carson looked to me, and I nodded at him while squeezing his hand for reassurance. "I'm not sure you understand how I feel."

"About the baby?"

He waved his hand. "No, no. About everything…Dale and Dad."

Her face paled under her makeup, but she held his gaze. "What do you mean?"

"The divide between us was deeper and wider than I led you to believe. Dale often said…hurtful things. Called me less than a man, a weak link. Dad told me many times he didn't believe I was man enough to run the firm with them."

Tears fell down her cheeks. "I'm so sorry, Carson. I never knew."

"I didn't want you to. But it's why I'm trying so damn hard to bring the firm back from the ashes. Because this gay man, the weak link, is going to be the one to do it. It's not your fault, Mom. I love you, and I always felt your love in return. You were the only one I've been able to count on to be by my side."

"Until now?" She wiped her cheeks, then smiled at

Carson and me.

Carson tightened his grip on my fingers. "Yes. Now I have two people in my corner."

"I imagine Lia must feel a similar loneliness, having the world she planned end before it began."

"I agree with you, but Lia isn't the only woman in that position, Mom."

She met his gaze steadily. "I am aware. Which is why I'm going to start a foundation to help single mothers. It pains me to think of so many women in that position. Charles will assist me with the legalities."

Charles favored her with a look anyone could see went beyond simple friendship.

And because it was Carson, he couldn't help himself. "Is that all he's helping you with?" he asked with a cheeky grin that brought a pretty blush to Patricia's face.

"Don't you tease me like that."

"I'm happy you've found someone."

Charles smiled. "I'm happy to help Patty with whatever she wishes. I've been an admirer of hers for years. As you know, she's a wonderful woman."

"Oh, stop." Blushing at Charles's words, she eyed me. "Thank you. And I can say the same for you, Carson. Don't think I didn't notice how you introduced Davis. I'm glad you finally opened your eyes to see what was in front of you all along."

I jumped in to defend Carson. "It wasn't all his fault, Patricia. I've had a habit of making bad choices and falling for the wrong person."

"He wasn't the only one." Carson took my hand. "But this time, we both finally got it right."

CHAPTER TWENTY-THREE

Carson

"Stay with me tonight," I whispered in Davis's ear as I kissed him. "I don't want you to leave."

We'd left my mother and Charles, and while I still had reservations about the baby and Lia and their place in my mother's world, I wisely kept them to myself and gave her the support she needed. Whether the baby was Dale's or not, my mother was determined to make her part of the family, and if that was what she needed so she could come to terms with Dale's death, then I'd stand by her.

Right now, I was more interested in the man in front of me. Davis's glittering eyes held nothing but desire, and his lips softened under mine.

"I-I don't have clothes for tomorrow."

"Good. I like you better naked anyway."

"Idiot," he joked but wound his arms around my neck. The push of his hard cock sent a blaze of hunger through me, and I yanked at the tab of his jeans and zipper.

"Call me anything you want, just don't go home. Not after tonight and what we said."

His smile gleamed in the dim light of the living room. "I couldn't."

I kissed him again, our tongues meeting and touching playfully. "I want you. I love you. I've never said it, but I like saying it. To you."

"And I like hearing it from you," Davis murmured. "And I've never said it to the right person."

I pulled him across the apartment to the bedroom, where we tore off our clothes and got on the bed. Naked, hot skin met naked, hot skin. Davis's rigid length rested against my belly, and his balls lay soft on my thigh. I cupped his ass.

"Yes." He sighed, and I played with him until he buried his lips in my neck, breathing hot and heavy. "Now."

"Not yet." I teased his rim, circling the quivering edges. Davis's hips rolled, his cock spurting a sticky, hot release that seemed to go on forever. "That's it, that's it," I urged. "I love watching you come."

"Inside me," he managed to choke out as he shook in my arms.

"Never say I don't listen to you." I reached for the lube and condoms. Davis lay curled in my arms, watching me. He plucked them out of my grasp.

"Let me," he whispered and took the condom, but before he opened it, he licked around the crown of my dick and sucked me. I moaned, struggling not to burst apart. Davis's hot, wet mouth was a place of pleasure I willingly lost myself in.

"God, you're killing me."

With one last swirl of his tongue, Davis released me. "But what a way to go." He opened the condom and rolled it down my aching cock, slowly dragging his teasing fingers along the length of my shaft. "Now I'm ready."

I coated my fingers with lube, then pushed them deep

within him. He yelped in surprise, but I soon had him purring when I replaced my fingers with my cock, sliding in to the root. "You got me."

"Give me more," he demanded and flung his legs over my hips. "Harder."

"I like it when you're bossy." Passion like I'd never known tore through me, and I pinned him to the mattress as I plundered his mouth with my tongue and his body with my cock. I thrust into him over and over, his cries mixing with mine as the bed slammed against the wall. "You're mine. Don't leave me."

"I won't," he gasped. "I can't."

My climax ripped me to shreds, and I pumped inside him several more times before I collapsed on top of him. My spent cock twitched, and I held Davis closer, our sweat-slick bodies melding together. Davis's thundering heart beat the same rhythm as mine, and I pressed my lips to the fluttering vein at his neck. "I don't think I can move."

"Who says you have to?" Davis nuzzled me, and I slid an arm around him, finally content.

* * *

The next day, the first of the quarterly audits required by the disciplinary committee was due, and despite having Davis next to me all night, I was on edge. I woke up at five, my mind racing.

"Too nervous to sleep?" Davis crawled on top of me. "Let me calm you." He took me in his mouth, his lips working their magic. I was buffeted from all sides—his hot, wet mouth on me and his firm, knowing hands on my body. I splintered apart and erupted. He swallowed me fully, licking me clean.

I pulled him close. "You really are the perfect man."

I kissed him, my tongue rubbing his as I gripped his erect cock and began a firm up-and-down stroke while kissing his lips, his jaw, and the shell of his ear.

"Carson, oh God," he moaned, and came hard and heavy between us.

"Like I said," I whispered against his lips. "Perfect."

As Davis hadn't brought any clothes, I gave him one of my suits, a shirt and tie, and caught him preening in front of the mirror.

"I've never worn anything so nice."

"It looks better on you. Keep it."

His jaw dropped. "What?"

"It's not a big deal. I've told you I like seeing you in my clothes."

His gaze lingered in the mirror. "I shouldn't. I know this designer is very expensive."

"You'll make me happy by accepting it."

Davis tweaked the tie. "Ready to go?"

"Yep. They'll be at the office by ten."

"You'll do fine, Carson. Everything is in order, and I have printouts of all the documents they requested in the conference room."

I hugged him and gave him a kiss that left us both gasping for breath. "If I haven't told you thank you already, consider yourself thanked."

* * *

At ten on the dot they showed up—an older, gray-haired woman with a pleasant smile, and a dour-faced, skinny man in a black suit who looked as if he were attending a funeral.

"Mr. Ballard? I'm Janet Reed, and this is Morris Cicero. We're here from the First District."

"Of course. Come right into the conference room and

have a seat. Would you like coffee, tea, or water?"

"Not for me," Morris said with a pinched expression, as if it hurt to move his lips.

"I'd love a hot tea if it wouldn't be too much trouble," Janet asked.

"I'll bring it right in for you," Davis offered, and I met his eyes. His reassuring face settled my banging heart. It would be all right. It had to be. Everything I'd done since coming home and taking over the firm had been by the book.

Davis brought the steaming cup and placed it before Janet. Morris pursed his thin lips.

"We have what we need, so if you'll excuse us?" Janet's smile was apologetic, as if she were used to his rudeness. "We'll need time to go through all the paperwork, and if we have any questions, we'll be sure to let you know."

I forced myself to be pleasant. "Of course."

I withdrew and returned to my office, although I'd be damned if I got any work done. Instead, I paced. The day had begun on a high of positivity, but after an hour and a half had passed, my confidence began to wane, and all sorts of terrible things passed through my mind—they would find accounting errors, clients had secretly complained to them about how I was handling their accounts and they'd decided I was as guilty as my brother and father and they'd institute disbarment proceedings against me. Worst of all, Davis would decide he'd had enough and quit, not only the firm but me as well.

My cell rang, and I grabbed it. "Hello?"

"Carson? She's ours. The baby is Dale's." My mother hadn't sounded so joyful since I'd announced I was coming home.

"The DNA test is back already?"

"Yes. Lia called and forwarded me the email. I'll send it to you. It's a ninety-nine point eight percent match. She's Dale's daughter."

Hearing her sniffles, I could let go of the last bit of resentment toward my brother. He'd given my mother a grandchild to lavish her love and attention on.

"I'm happy, Mom."

"You don't sound it."

My grip on the phone tightened. "Right now, two members of the disciplinary committee are sitting in the conference room for the quarterly audit, so you'll have to forgive me if I'm not more enthusiastic."

"Oh, I'm so sorry. With all the upheaval over the baby, it slipped my mind. I'm sure everything will be fine. You and Davis worked miracles getting the firm sorted and in working order again."

My mother had always looked at the world with glass-half-full optimism, but I was too nervous. All I saw was spilled water.

"I wish it were that simple. They've been in there a long time."

On cue, Davis buzzed me. "Carson, they're ready to speak with you."

My stomach clenched. "Mom, I have to go."

I ended the call, sprang to my feet, and rushed out of the office so as not to keep them waiting. Janet and Morris stood in the reception area. Her smile was comforting but meant nothing to me. I needed to hear what they had to say.

"We're all finished, Carson, and everything looks in order. Your record-keeping is meticulous, a far cry from what we were presented with prior to you taking over."

"All thanks to Davis, my assistant. He saved us from complete disaster with his computer-skills wizardry. I couldn't do this without him."

To my surprise, Morris agreed. "A good paralegal is worth their weight in gold. I know I couldn't function without mine." He eyed Davis, who sat straight in his chair, hands clasped. "Make sure you pay him well, or he might go elsewhere."

"I have no intention of letting him go. Davis knows how much I value him."

He nodded. "We'll be on our way, and I will be recommending to the committee that the firm is operating as per the agreement."

Janet nodded to me. "Have a lovely day."

I waited for the elevator doors to close before releasing a huge sigh. "Thank God." Relief like I'd never known flooded through me. "I thought I was going to puke when you called me. I was on the phone with my mother and hung up on her. I should call her." I scrubbed my face with my hands. "The DNA test came back. The baby is Dale's. No doubt."

"Oh, wow. I don't know why, but I wasn't expecting that." Davis pulled over a chair so I could sit by his side.

"Me either." So many thoughts whirled in my head, I felt dizzy. "I was all set to wash my hands of Lia as an opportunist, and now I have to eat my words."

"How does that make you feel? You have a niece."

I rubbed my chin. "Is it strange that I don't really have any feelings about it one way or the other? Does that make me a terrible person for being ambivalent about a baby?"

A chuckle escaped Davis. "Of course not. You're being honest."

"My mother, as expected, is over the moon. And I get it. But I don't want her thinking I'm going to be all goo-goo gaga over her. She'll be taken care of, and I'm sure Lia will be at all the family functions. I'll be polite, but that'll be the extent of it."

"Carson. No one is expecting you to take the child on trips to Disney World. I mean, we went when I was young, and yeah, it was fun, but if you're not into it, you're not into it."

"Oh, God." The mere thought of the crowds, lines, and hordes of screaming children was enough to make me shudder. "Yeah, that's not happening."

The phone rang. "Ballard and Melbourne," Davis answered. "How may I help you?… Hi, Patricia… Yes. It all turned out well… I know, but it's hard to say how they'll feel on any given day, even if Carson did have everything ready for them and on point." He threw back his head and laughed. "Okay, *I* had everything ready."

I made a face, and he stuck out his tongue at me. Damn, he was cute.

"Yes, he told me. I can't imagine how thrilled you are. A little girl to spoil after having two boys." He paused, and his gaze slid to mine. "Tonight?"

It was to be expected, and I shrugged and nodded at Davis, who gave me a big thumbs-up.

"Yes, of course we'll come by and meet her. It's all so exciting… See you at seven. Bye."

I rolled my eyes. "So exciting."

"Don't be an ass. Think of it this way. You never made peace with your brother. Maybe this little girl is the universe's way of giving you a second chance. She's an innocent, Carson. And I know if I had the opportunity to have an uncle like you, I'd want that." He put his arms around me, and I held him close.

"Maybe you're right. You are pretty smart."

"I know. I got you to fall for me, didn't I?"

I rubbed my cheek to his. "Here I thought I was lucky to get you to look past everything and fall for me."

Davis kissed me and rested his lips against mine. "Guess we're both lucky."

* * *

At 7:15 that night, I rang the bell to my mother's apartment. Davis held the shopping bag filled with gifts he'd left early to buy. Good thing his best friend had little girls, as I hadn't a clue what to get her. Or a boy, for that matter. My experience with babies was running away as fast as I could the minute one started squawking.

The door opened to my mother's beaming face. "Come in. We've been waiting."

Davis held my hand, and we walked into the living room. It looked like a toy store had exploded in there. Davis handed over the shopping bag. "Here. We brought some gifts, although I'm thinking she might already have everything she needs."

I scanned the room. "Good thing you know how to show restraint, Mom," I joked, and she swatted me.

"Don't be a brat. Come meet your niece." She tugged on my free hand.

The three of us approached the playpen set in the middle of the room. Lia sat on the floor next to it. Mistrustful eyes met mine, but I couldn't blame her. The last time we spoke I'd basically called her a gold digger and a liar.

"Hi, Lia. Welcome to the family."

Her brows shot up high, and she gracefully rose to her feet. "Thanks. I'm glad we got this all settled." She held out her hand. "I know I came at you the wrong way and made it all about the money. I was scared to meet you, and I didn't know what to say. But Dale was excited to be a father. I'm just sad Brooke will never know him." She brushed at her eyes.

"I am as well. And she'll have us to help her." And I meant it. I had no animus toward Lia. She'd done what she had to in order to protect her child. "This is my partner, Davis."

"Hi, Lia. Nice to meet you. Brooke's such a cutie." With his natural warmth, Davis waved at her, then leaned over the playpen and wiggled his fingers. "Hi, sweetie. Aren't you pretty? My best friend has three little girls," he explained.

"I don't think I'd know what to do with a little boy."

A tiny human in green-and-white footie pajamas lay on her back, kicking her feet in the air. A pink headband with a giant bow held the wispy blond curls off her face.

"This is Brooke." My mother lifted the baby and kissed her cheek. "Here's your uncle Carson, sweetheart."

Big blue eyes met mine, and a gummy smile split her chubby cheeks. "Ba ba," she sang.

"She's adorable," Davis cooed. "Look at those eyes. Big and blue like yours, Carson."

Without any warning, my mother plopped her in my arms. Instinctively, I held her close, and she settled against me with a sigh. A light sweet scent tickled my nose.

"What if I drop her? Or she starts crying?" Panicked, I sought help, my gaze darting between my mother and Lia, both of whom gave me indulgent looks. Davis, traitor that he was, was too busy laughing at me.

"Don't worry, Carson," Lia said. "She's a very happy baby. She rarely cries. And from how you're holding her, I doubt she's going anywhere. She just had her bottle, so you might want to get a burp cloth."

"What's that?" It sounded ominous and icky.

"Babies tend to spit up after they eat," Davis explained and draped a towel over my shoulder.

"Spit up?"

As if to prove the point, Brooke's little body grew rigid, a horrible noise came from both her top and bottom, and warm wetness spread dangerously close to my neck.

"Uh…help? Someone, please."

"Just a second." Davis cackled, and I caught him taking a video.

"Are you kidding me?" I fumed, then almost gagged. "What is that smell?"

"Come here, honey. Don't mind your uncle." My mother lifted Brooke off me and wiped her face. "Someone needs a diaper change," she sang and carried her off.

"You'll get used to it." Davis gleefully informed me. "I was a master diaper changer by the time Tommy and Carrie's third daughter was born."

"Good. That'll be your job."

Several minutes later, my mother returned with the baby in a clean outfit, but when she brought her to Lia, Brooke squirmed and cried.

"What's the matter?"

"Nuuh," she squealed, and I winced as Lia walked over to me. Brooke waved her little arms, and Lia grinned at me.

"I think she wants you to hold her again, Carson. Here."

"Uh…well, okay." I had no choice but to take the baby, and sure enough, the moment she came into my arms, she quieted down. Within a minute, she was asleep.

"I love it," Davis said and gave her a gentle kiss. "She feels safe with you. Babies know who's going to protect them."

"I never pictured myself holding a baby, never mind being an uncle, so I guess stranger things could happen." I smirked. "Look at us. Who would've thought after you dumped a load of dishes on my head, we'd end up together?"

"And if you're lucky, I might let you hold me too."

"Oh, trust me, I know I'm the lucky one." Davis put his arm around me and I kissed his cheek. "And I'm not about to let you go."

CHAPTER TWENTY-FOUR

Carson

For the past few days, Davis had seemed a little off, but no matter how many times I asked if something was bothering him, he denied it. He'd agreed to move into my apartment, but even that didn't help settle my anxious thoughts. All sorts of scenarios ran through my mind, the main one being that he'd only agreed to move in to humor me, but he really wanted to move on. I'd been down that road before and knew the signs.

When I caught him checking flights, I knew I had to confront him. At lunchtime, I heard him talking on the phone and crept up behind him to listen.

"Yeah, I'm really looking forward to seeing you too. Of course I miss you. I know it's been a long time. Okay, bye. I love you too."

My stomach soured, and I waited to speak until he set his phone on the desk.

"Who're you missing?"

He swiveled around in his chair and glared at me. "Were you listening in on my conversation?"

I shoved my hands into my pants pockets. "Yeah. So, who do you love and miss so much?"

Davis's lips tipped up, and his eyes crinkled shut. "Are you…jealous?"

"No…yes…should I be?"

We'd kept our promise to refrain from public displays of affection in the office. It surprised me, then, when Davis rose to is feet and nudged my cheek with his nose.

"Not at all. *At all,*" he emphasized. "I was talking to my mom. She and my father booked flights to come to the city. It's been a while since we've had a visit, and my mother is a little…no, that's a lie. She's a lot anxious to see me. And meet you—she wasn't waiting any longer, now that she knows we're living together."

"Oh." *Damn.* Not what I'd expected. "I've never met anyone's parents. What if she doesn't like me? I didn't know you told them you moved in."

"Aw, look at you. So cute when you're all nervous." Davis was having way too much fun at my expense.

"I'm always cute."

"And modest too. My parents will love you. My father wasn't surprised I moved in with you. My mother…don't worry. It'll be fine." He grinned and I gulped.

"Don't worry? When are they going to be here?"

"Uh…"

"Davis." I glared at him. "When?"

"Next Friday night."

"You're kidding, right? I only have a week to prepare to meet your parents? And where will they stay?"

"Plenty of time," he said brightly. "It'll be fine. We'll figure it out. Don't worry."

"You owe me," I pointed at him. "Big-time."

"Can't wait to pay up."

* * *

Of course the flight was delayed, resulting in us waiting an hour and a half before the plane touched down at LaGuardia. I knew Davis was excited to see his parents, but I was nervous as hell. I didn't know what to expect, especially from his mother, who was extremely overprotective. I'd heard snatches of conversations where she'd question if he was getting enough rest and eating properly. And of course, how quickly he'd moved in with me.

Obviously, I kept my wise-ass comments to myself because I wanted to say that I was to blame for her darling Davis losing hours of precious sleep, but it was so, so worth it.

"There they are." Davis sped away from me to greet them as they came through baggage claim, wheeling their suitcases behind them. I hadn't told anyone—not even Davis—but I planned to treat them to a suite at The St. Regis. I thought that was a nice way to show them I was happy to meet them and yet have them at arm's distance from Davis and me and our nighttime fun and games.

I was no fool.

Smiling from ear to ear and pulling his mother's bag behind him, Davis brought them over to me.

"Mom, Dad, this is Carson."

"Glad to finally meet you, Carson. I'm Greg."

"Same here, Greg. I hope the flight wasn't too bad. There are always delays these days." I shook his father's hand and liked his kind eyes and firm grip.

"That's the truth. We're really looking forward to being here, that's for sure. I haven't been to the city in over twenty years."

"I can say that it has most definitely changed since your last visit."

"Mom, meet Carson."

Davis brought his mother over, and I stooped to kiss her cheek. "So nice to meet you. How are you feeling?"

Pretty hazel eyes like Davis's met mine. "I'm fine, thank you. Nice to meet you too. We're looking forward to getting to know you better."

Maybe it took her some time to warm up to people. I'd called for a limo and had received the notification that it was waiting in the pickup area. Once the luggage was loaded and we were on our way, I decided it was a good time to reveal the first part of my surprise.

"Jenny and Greg, I wanted to do something special for your visit, so instead of staying with us in the apartment, I booked you a suite at The St. Regis."

"Wow, Carson, that's incredibly generous of you." Greg's effusive enthusiasm puffed me up. "The St. Regis. That's a special place. Isn't that wonderful, Jen? It's a luxury hotel on Fifth Avenue. The best of the best."

Jenny, unfortunately, wasn't so enthusiastic. "Oh. I was hoping we'd be staying with you. I'm sure The St. Regis is very nice, but I haven't seen Davis in so long. I want to spend as much time together as possible, and if we're staying so far away, that can't happen."

I wanted to tell her The St. Regis was less than a mile away from my place, but I had a feeling that was a mile too far for Jenny.

In profile, Davis's jaw flexed. "Mom. The St. Regis is one of the nicest hotels in the city, and I'm sure the suite is gorgeous. And you're still going to come over to the apartment and spend as much time as you want."

"But it's not the same as being with you."

She sounded miffed, and as I didn't want to be the cause of any conflict, I said, a little more heartily than I felt, "Not to worry. I can cancel it. You'll come home with us. I have a second bedroom."

"Carson…" Davis put a hand on my arm, while Greg's

mouth pulled down in a frown.

"Jenny, come on. Carson went to all that trouble to do something nice for us. We should just stay there."

But Jenny was stubborn, and I could see from whom Davis had inherited that trait. "Thank you, Carson. I'm sure you think I'm a silly woman, but I've missed my son." Ignoring me, she beamed at Davis. "I'm sure you can understand."

Not really, but I wasn't about to get in between Jenny and Davis. It would be like taking a cub away from a lioness.

I informed the limo driver of the change in plans, and when we arrived, Davis took his mother's suitcase, while I handled Greg's. Inside the apartment, Jenny walked around and nodded with approval.

"This is very nice. Do you own or rent, Carson?"

Out of the corner of my eye, I watched Davis cringe at her probing questions, but I took it in stride. "I own it, Jenny."

"Smart to get a two-bedroom. Room for children."

I saw Greg roll his eyes and shake his head, but I decided to be honest. "I'm not sure about that."

"What?" Her brow furrowed. "You don't want a family?"

"Mom," Davis warned, but I held up a hand.

"It's fine. Davis and I haven't discussed that. We haven't been living together long, so I think one step at a time is working out best for us."

"I agree," Greg said, and I could've cheered. "Let the kids live their life, Jenny. Carson seems like a man who has his head on straight and isn't into playing games like the other one."

"You mean Brian?" I offered.

"Oh?" Jenny sounded surprised. "Davis told you about him?"

"We have no secrets. Davis knows about my past, and I know about his."

"Have you had many serious relationships?" She frowned, radiating disapproval.

"Jenny, enough," Greg rebuked her. "Carson doesn't have to answer to you." He took her hand. "I think we should go into the bedroom so you can rest. It was a longer trip than we thought, and you haven't been traveling much lately."

"I didn't think it was such a bad question," I heard her say to Greg as they left the room.

Groaning, Davis fell onto the sofa and put his head in his hands. "God, she's worse than I remembered. I'm sorry."

Chuckling, I sat next to him and slid an arm around his shoulders. "It's okay. All I could think of is that the disciplinary committee has nothing on your mother."

"She's relentless," he muttered. "I can't believe how nosy she was, with all the questions about children and your apartment and your past."

I trailed my fingers along his jawline. "But you know what? It's something we've never discussed. What do you want? Are you looking to get married? Do you want kids?"

"I love being with you, and right now I have everything I want. Eventually, that might change into wanting something more official and permanent." He met my eyes with pure honesty, which was what I loved about him. "You're not into that, though, are you?"

No matter how much I cared for him, I wasn't about to lie to make him feel better. "I don't know. It's still pretty new between us, and marriage and kids aren't the number-one things on my mind." I grinned. "My main concern is always getting you naked and under me as quickly as possible."

Eyes wide, Davis glanced toward the second bedroom. "Shh. Don't say that. I don't want my parents hearing that."

"What? That we have sex? News flash, Davis"—I smirked—"I think they know."

Red-faced, Davis raised his eyes to the ceiling, muttering to himself, "God help me. But I don't have to shove it in their faces, do I? I can't think about having sex with you when my parents are in the next room."

Well, damn. This was going to be a long two days.

Now it was my turn to be honest. "Tell me how to behave. You know I've never met the parents or done this kind of stuff before."

"You've been the perfect boyfriend so far."

I chuckled. "A whole two hours."

Davis kissed my cheek. "It was very sweet of you to arrange that suite for my parents. I'm sorry my mother didn't want it and you have to cancel it."

A sudden thought hit me. "*Hmm*. Maybe not. Maybe… we could use it. You know…once they go to bed, we can sneak out and have it all to ourselves."

His eyes sparkled. "Who said you weren't brilliant? I love it. They're bound to go to sleep early tonight."

"I hope so. And wait a minute." I frowned. "Someone said I wasn't brilliant?"

Laughter bubbled out from him. "I'm just kidding. I love you, Carson. I know this isn't how you planned to spend the weekend. Thanks for being a good sport."

I ran my nose down his cheek. "I love you too. And I do want you to understand that just because I don't have an answer about marriage and family right now, doesn't mean I'm going anywhere. You know that, don't you?"

He nodded and shrugged. "But it isn't something you're interested in."

"Thinking about my father and how poorly he'd treated my mother, it's not exactly an institution I have much faith in."

"My parents have been married for over forty years, and they still love each other like crazy. When my mother was sick, my father never left her bedside at the hospital. He still brings her flowers every weekend and makes a big deal over Valentine's Day."

"And those things matter to you?" All that was a foreign concept to me.

Sad eyes met mine. "I think it's nice."

And I thought it was silly, but what did I know? After all, there was a whole industry built on this stuff. Maybe Davis was right and I should try to be more romantic.

He pressed on as if he'd read my mind. "*But* I never want to force you into something you're not comfortable with. I'm not planning on leaving even if you never want to get married."

"How about we take things one step at a time? I'm committed to you and you to me. That's huge in my book. A first for me. Someone I can trust implicitly."

"I agree. And you're the first healthy relationship I've ever had. I know my parents are thrilled about that."

"I have to admit, your mother scares the hell out of me."

His eyes twinkled. "Just be yourself, and she'll love you as much as I do."

I reached for him. "How about a little loving right now?" Those sweet lips near mine were so kissable, I couldn't help it. I settled my mouth over his, welcoming the hot push of his silky tongue. Sighing with pleasure, he wound his arms around my neck, and I readied myself for a little hot and heavy make-out session.

"Excuse me."

We sprang apart at the sound of Jenny's stilted voice.

"Sorry," I mumbled, my face hot as the sun.

"I just wanted a glass of water."

"Of course." I jumped up from the couch.

Yep. It was going to be a looong two days.

* * *

That evening, my mother had us at her apartment for

dinner. She was excited to meet Davis's parents and brushed aside my warning about Jenny's forthright behavior.

"I appreciate a person who speaks her mind. I'm sure we'll get along."

Now, watching everyone interact, I was still on edge. I had no idea why, as my mother was the consummate hostess, and the dinner she'd catered should be perfect, according to Davis, with some of his parents' favorite dishes.

We were in the living room for drinks. Because of her weakened heart, Jenny drank only club soda. Greg had a beer, and I fixed my mother and myself vodka martinis and Davis his favorite, a lychee martini.

"Here, Mom. I think I got it the way you like it."

She tasted it. "Delicious as always." She held up her glass. "To a special night filled with new friends and family."

"Do you drink very often, Davis?" Jenny asked. "I don't remember you enjoying alcohol that much." She sipped her club soda. "Maybe that's the influence of living in the city. At home, we'd only have liquor on special occasions or on holidays."

Davis's jaw tightened, and a flush rose to his cheeks.

My mother, sensing the tension, fixed Jenny with a bright smile. "I consider meeting you and Greg a very special occasion."

Greg said, "I agree, Patricia. Thank you for having us to your beautiful home." Greg's appreciative gaze swept over the space. "I imagine you must do a lot of entertaining."

"Not that much lately. Since Dale and my ex-husband passed, I haven't gone out much."

"Our deepest sympathies on your loss. Davis told us about the terrible tragedy." Jenny set her glass on the table.

"Thank you. I'm slowly learning to deal with it."

Jenny shook her head. "I don't think I'd ever be able to deal with losing my husband or child. I can't imagine how you managed."

"*Ex*-husband." I jumped in to defend my mother. "And everyone handles grief in their own way. I don't think we can know how we'd respond until it happens to us. And I hope you never have to experience it."

"I agree, Carson." Greg shot Jenny a troubled look. "Patricia deserves our care and concern."

"Really, Mom. That was a little harsh."

Gracious as ever, my mother sought to soothe hurt feelings. "It's okay, Davis. I understand what your mother means, and I agree. I don't think we can ever get over losing a child. But the alternative would be to give up on my own life. And I have Carson, who's been the most wonderful son, leaving a thriving career in London to come home and take over the family firm. In the interim, we've grown closer than ever. I feel as if I have a lot to live for, even though I've lost so much."

My throat closed up. "I did what anyone would. You needed me, and I was there. Like you were always there for me."

I felt the weight of Jenny's stare on me, and I met her eyes. "Jenny, I feel that you don't like me all that much."

"Carson," my mother gasped, and Davis, sitting next to me, hissed, "What the heck are you doing?"

Jenny set her glass on the coaster and tipped up her chin. "I don't dislike you. But I have a hard time with the fact that you got Davis fired from his job. That doesn't sit right with me."

"Mom," Davis agonized. "It ended up being the best thing that ever happened."

"But what kind of man does that? It wasn't nice. Maybe one day he'll turn on you again for making a mistake and fire you."

"I deserved it, Mom. You didn't really know the whole story. I was a lousy waiter—Carson wasn't wrong to be angry with me. Plus, he never asked Peter to fire me, just never serve him. We might've started off on the wrong foot, but we're way past that, and it's time for you to stop thinking about it as well."

"Don't be upset with your mother," I soothed Davis, and didn't miss how Jenny watched me touching him. "She's right. It wasn't nice of me to behave as I did. I acted like a spoiled, selfish child that morning. And the fact that you ended up working for me and we're together doesn't negate my bad behavior. Even the stress I was under wasn't an excuse. But here's the thing. I'm no longer that arrogant person walking around with a chip on my shoulder. There is zero connection between the man who threw a tantrum because someone dumped dirty plates on him and the man I am now. I've been humbled in many different ways since then and learned something from every mistake I've made. But the common denominator in all this is Davis. He's the wind lifting my sails."

If I thought my explanation would satisfy Jenny, I was wrong. "He's been hurt before, you know. I don't want him hurt again."

"Mom," Davis snapped. "Stop. It's time you let go." He gentled his tone but remained firm. "I'm an adult. I make my own choices and decisions. Have I made mistakes? Definitely. But I own up to them. They're mine and part of what makes me who I am today. Much as you love me, you can't cover me in Bubble Wrap and protect me from life." He took my hand. "I'm staying in New York City. With Carson. My life is here now. And whatever the future holds for us, whether it's marriage and a family or not, that's for us to decide. Not you or Dad or Patricia or anyone else except Carson and myself."

"He's right, Jenny," Greg stated with a firm nod. "We raise our children the best we can, and give them the values we think, or hope, they should have, but in the end, they make their own choices. Sometimes they're good, and other times they're not. But from where I'm sitting, Carson cares for Davis, and that's all we can hope for. Let them live their lives. Their way."

The housekeeper walked in. "Dinner is ready, Miss Patricia."

"Saved by the prime rib," I joked. "Jenny? Will you walk in with me to dinner?"

She slipped her arm through mine, and once in the dining room, I sat her next to my mother and took my place next to Davis. He leaned in close to whisper, "Can I tell you how happy I am to have that suite later tonight?"

"Talk is cheap. You're going to have to show me."

His lips tugged up in a wicked smile. "Challenge accepted."

CHAPTER TWENTY-FIVE

Davis

Carson was right about one thing. It was going to be a very long two days. I'd never had to run all around the city, showing all the sights. And because I wasn't a native, born and bred, I needed Carson's help, which entailed him waking up on Saturday and Sunday much earlier than usual, as my parents didn't want to miss a thing.

"It's barely eight a.m." He stuffed his head under the pillow.

We'd returned home late from the suite, and my body still hummed from his hands and mouth. There wasn't a patch of skin Carson hadn't touched with his lips and tongue. I reveled in my soreness and loved the ache of pleasure left in its wake.

"Come on. If we get them up and out now, they'll go to sleep by ten."

Blue eyes peeked out at me from under the pillow. "And?"

"You're so predictable. And yes, then we'll go to the suite and have fun."

Carson wagged a finger. "Fun? *Hmm.* Not so sure what I have planned for you will be fun." He reached out and dragged me close so our mouths touched. "You must pay the price for denying me my sleep."

My eyes slid shut in anticipation of a kiss and maybe a quickie. "*Mmm.* Give me a taste of what I have to look forward to."

Carson's grin was deliciously wicked, and I nestled my hips to line up with his.

"Davis? Are you awake? Dad and I want to get an early start."

Nothing like your mother's voice to deflate a raging hard-on.

I flopped onto the bed and stared at the ceiling, taking deep breaths. "Be there in a few, Mom."

Carson groaned and palmed his erection. "You are in such trouble…"

I kissed him. "Promises, promises."

The day proved more fun than I'd anticipated. We went boating in Central Park and walked through the zoo. Ignoring my mother's warnings, my father insisted on a dirty-water dog from one of the vendors, and Carson was happy to join him. I loved seeing them bond, and my heart beat warm and happy, knowing how badly Carson wanted a father in his life.

We took them to the Empire State Building, Rockefeller Center, St. Patrick's Cathedral, and Macy's. For dinner they wanted pizza, so we took them to Patsy's, where Carson suffered through a personal no-cheese pizza. I knew he wanted the real thing, but I hated seeing him in pain.

"You're too good to me," he murmured, playing with the ends of my hair. "I could take a pill. It's no big deal."

"They don't always work, and I know you feel weird after taking them. I don't need you feeling uncomfortable just to fit in."

His smile was wry. "Old habits are hard to break."

I squeezed his hand. "Time to make new ones. Together."

"I think we're off to a good start." Carson raised his glass. "To a memorable day."

"To family," Dad toasted.

After dinner, we dropped my exhausted parents off at the apartment.

"See you later," I called out through the window. "Carson and I are going to catch a late movie."

"We'll definitely be asleep by the time you get home. I'm zonked," my dad said.

The car drove on, and we grinned to each other. It pulled up in front of The St. Regis, where once we closed the door and locked it, we played a game of naked catch me if you can in the hotel suite.

He caught me. Twice.

Sunday morning was brunch from Barney Greengrass, and by Sunday night, we'd hit Ellis Island, the 9/11 Memorial, walked over the Brooklyn Bridge, and gone to the Met and the Guggenheim. We all agreed we were too tired to sit in a restaurant, so we ordered Chinese food from Mr. Chow to be delivered.

"Thank you so much for an amazing weekend. And thank you too, Carson, for being the best tour guide." My mother took another scallion pancake. "I'll never forget it."

Chopsticks in hand, Carson picked out a lobster shumai and popped it into his mouth. "My pleasure. To be honest, it's been years since I've been to half the places we took you to, so it was fun for me as well."

My father wiggled his toes. "Good God, my feet hurt. I don't want to sound ungrateful, but I'll be glad to do nothing next week except sit and play cards."

"Greg, that sounds damn good to me. I wish I could join you," Carson joked.

"Anytime, Carson. You and Davis have an open invite. Davis doesn't play golf, but you and I can play eighteen holes. They have a nice little course by us."

"We might take you up on that." The speed with which Carson accepted the invitation made my heart ache with equal parts joy and sadness. If my dad could fill the void within him, I was thrilled, but I wished his own father could've provided the love he so desperately sought.

Monday morning we accompanied them to LaGuardia for their flight home. I hugged my father, and when he and Carson said their good-byes, discussing their golf games, I took my mother aside.

"I hope you're feeling better about Carson and me now. You do like him, right?"

Both my hands in hers, she squeezed them. "Yes, I do. I was wrong. I can see how much he cares for you, and he treats you like an equal."

"He does. And we're happy."

Carson approached us, blue eyes wary. "Jenny, it was great having you. I hope you had a good time."

I watched as she held out her arms. "The best. Can I have a hug?"

Carson brightened. "You sure can. Make sure you let us know when you arrive home."

Her eyes twinkled. "As an overprotective mama bear, isn't that supposed to be my line?"

We walked them over to the desk and made sure they checked in. At the security gate, we gave my father one last hug. My mother gave us a good-bye kiss and held each of our hands in hers.

"I'm glad you didn't let the suite go to waste and you got to use it for yourselves."

My jaw dropped, and I darted a glance at Carson, whose eyes danced.

"How did you know?"

Her smile was smug as she showed the TSA agent her ticket. "A mother always knows. And never gives away her secrets." With a laugh and a wave of her hand, she and my father entered the line, and Carson stood at my side until they passed through security and disappeared.

"Well," I said. "That's that."

Carson draped his arm over my shoulders as we walked out of the terminal. "I'm exhausted, but we'd better get into the office. I have a meeting with the Fontanas."

I thought for a moment. "Oh, that's an interesting case. The grandmother was a Holocaust survivor, and the family became wealthy from the diamond business. She set up trusts for all the grandchildren."

"Yes." Carson's mouth twisted in a grimace. "Which my illustrious father and brother used for themselves. They took some of the assets—artwork and jewelry—for their personal use."

"So what're you going to tell them?"

His mouth twisted in a grimace. "I got lucky. While scrolling through Dale's social media, I saw pictures of the missing items. I located and retrieved them all, and I plan to let the family know the trusts are now one hundred percent properly funded."

"That should satisfy them." My overconfidence didn't relieve Carson's tense face.

"Yeah? I'm glad you think so. Let's hope they feel the same."

Back at the office, Carson's clients came a bit early, and he disappeared into his office with them, but not before giving my shoulder a squeeze.

"Thank you for preparing everything ahead of time. I'd be lost without you."

Snickering, I winked. "I know. But I'll always know where to find you. You're stuck with me."

"Lucky for me, stuck with you is my favorite place to

be."

Could it get any better than this? After a somewhat rocky start, my mother and Carson got along, and my dad was helping Carson deal with the pain he'd carried for years for not having a loving and supportive father. I'd finally found someone who wanted me as more than a shadow lover, someone who was proud to walk with me in the sunlight.

An hour later, Carson escorted the Fontanas out of his office, and I could see the relief in his eyes.

"Thank you so much for allowing us to regain your trust. I promise you'll never have to worry about your assets with Ballard and Melbourne. I'll have my assistant send you all the paperwork, and we can consider this a new beginning."

Lucy Fontana, the oldest grandchild, put out her hand. "My grandmother was a great believer in redemption and new beginnings. Even though she witnessed the worst of humanity, she was always willing to see the best in people. We're satisfied that with you running the firm, everything will be handled properly this time."

They left, and Carson rolled his shoulders. "Thank God those people are the forgiving type. I'm not sure I could be so nice."

"I am. You're very nice. Like last night? You were amazingly, incredibly nice."

Red-faced, he brushed his fingers against my cheek. "You make it very hard for me to keep to the no-funny-business-in-the-office rule."

I tangled my fingers with his and held them to my lips. "There's nothing funny about how I feel with you."

He traced my lips for a brief moment, then let go. "I have a phone call with a client in five minutes. I'll see you later." One last lingering look, and he left me.

With Brian, he'd often call me into his office and we'd have quick, hot sex—his excuse was an inability to keep his hands off me, and I'd been flattered and eager to please him and had gone along with it. I'd thought it was exciting and sexy. We never got caught, but once I'd let it slip to Tommy, and he'd become enraged.

"That bastard is using you. No way should you be having sex in the office. The next time tell him no. I can't believe you're doing this with him while you're working."

The following day, when the inevitable call to come to Brian's office occurred, I'd tried to say no, but Brian had held me close and told me that he loved me so much, he couldn't help himself. He said I didn't understand the pressure he was under, and having me there for him during the day was the only way he could function. Didn't I love him? In between his kisses, I reassured him I did, and he'd locked the door and unzipped his pants.

Now, I cringed at my naïveté. I'd been too anxious for Brian's love to ever think of saying no. In direct contrast, during work hours, Carson had never asked for sex. He'd rarely been physical at all—a slight brush of his fingers or a hand to my shoulder was the limit. Those touches meant more to me than anything. They were a signal that he was thinking of me but respected who I was.

I'd just finished reorganizing the files and was now setting up a website for the firm, something it lacked and sorely needed. Carson had given me *carte blanche*, and I was settling into it with a coffee. The elevator opened and my best friend, Tommy, walked out, a Big Gulp in one hand.

"What the fuck…Tommy?" I jumped up from behind my desk to meet him at the door. "What the hell are you doing here?"

"Dude, you're so corporate. Fancy suit."

It was a little disconcerting seeing Tommy in my workspace. I was used to him at home, working in the auto-parts store or in his house with the kids and Carrie.

"I can't believe you're here. You swore you'd never step foot in the city. What's wrong?" I immediately jumped to the worst possible conclusions. "Is it Carrie or one of the girls? Are they all right?" Medical care was the only reason I could think of for Tommy to be persuaded to come to New York City, a place he'd always looked down on as dirty, overcrowded, and overpriced.

"Everyone's fine. And sometimes you gotta do shit you hate to keep someone from making another dumbass mistake."

My fears now alleviated, I could breathe. And get annoyed. I crossed my arms and leaned against my desk. "And that someone making a dumbass mistake would be me, I gather?"

His lip curled. "I don't see no one else falling for their boss. *Again.*"

My phone rang. "Hold on, I have to answer that." I picked up the receiver. "Ballard and Melbourne. How may I help you?"

"This is Judy Harris. I was in a month or so ago. Is this Davis?"

"Yes, it is. How are you, Ms. Harris?" I was shocked she'd remembered my name.

"I'm well, and I hope you are too. Is Carson available?"

"I'm sorry, but he's in the middle of something right now. Can I have him call you back?"

"No. I just wanted to let him know that the money came through and everything worked out well with the children. Please thank him for everything for me."

"I will. I'm glad to hear that."

"Thank you, Davis. Have a lovely day."

"You as well."

Tommy had wandered around the reception area during my conversation, and now took a seat. "Dude, you're pretty official-sounding."

"It's my job. I'm Carson's personal assistant and the receptionist for the law firm."

"Yeah?" He quirked a brow. "Lemme ask you. How personal do you two get?"

My face burned. "It's not what you think."

Tommy scowled. "You're bullshitting me. I know what I know. Every guy you've worked for, you've had a thing with. You even had the hots for the straight Froyo guy. I don't want the same shit happening again. You're in love with him, ain'tcha?"

"Yes, but—"

"No buts. This ain't gonna happen again." His big hand curled into a fist by his side. "I'll be goddamned if I'm gonna stand by and watch you get screwed over again, this time by some rich asshole."

"Usually people meet me before calling me an asshole."

I peered behind me to see Carson standing in the doorway of his office. A smile tugged at his lips.

"Carson, I-I'm sorry. This is Tommy. He's come from Harleyville to the city for the first time."

Carson turned to Tommy. "Because you were so, so worried about Davis?"

Tommy rose to his feet and eyed him. "Yeah."

"And because you think I'm a rich asshole who's taking advantage of him?"

I pressed my lips together. From his appearance alone, Tommy could be intimidating, but Carson seemed amused more than anything. And knowing how sharp his tongue was, I waited to see what would happen between them.

"Well…yeah." Tommy's gaze cut to me, but I refused to help him out. It wasn't often I saw Tommy taken down a notch, and usually I'd be a hundred percent behind my best friend, but not this time.

Carson strolled over and stood behind me, several feet away from Tommy. "I mean, you're right. I am rich. And there have been occasions when I've been an asshole."

My lips twitched, but I kept silent. I did enjoy me some

snarky Carson.

Tommy, however, didn't know Carson or his sense of humor and narrowed his eyes, certain he was being made fun of but unable to figure out exactly how.

Carson wasn't done. "So you came allllll the way to the big, bad city to warn Davis because you're afraid I'm going to hurt him. And you know what I say to that? Fuck you." The snarky smile faded, replaced by fire and flash. Angry Carson had rarely shown his face since that first day in the diner, and I wasn't prepared.

"Whoa, wait a second," I tried to intervene, but he brushed me aside.

"No. Who the hell is this guy to come here with a preconceived idea of who I am based on the number of zeros in my bank account, and accuse me of being the same person as that cheating, lying son of a bitch who used you?"

Shaking and flushed with anger, Carson got up in Tommy's face.

"Listen, Grizzly Adams or whoever you are. Davis is a man. A grown man. And he doesn't need you to tell him who he should love. Did he make mistakes in the past? Yes. Am I the same as those other people? No. But you won't even give it a chance. You want to hate me because that's easier than getting to know me."

"I don't hate you."

"No? You said I was a rich asshole who would screw him over. That doesn't sound very kind and caring to me. You're a big shot because you're the lucky one who fell in love with your childhood sweetheart and have the life you wanted. Well, not everyone gets it right the first time. Some of us get screwed along the way or we get our heart broken."

"Davis is my best friend. I don't want to see him waste his time on someone who only wants one thing. You have no idea what kind of a person Davis is." Tommy's ferocious glare would normally make anyone quake in their shoes, but

Carson wasn't just anyone and stood toe to toe with him, an equally merciless expression on his face.

"The hell I don't. I know how he gives himself a thousand percent in everything he does. I know he's kind and considerate and the sweetest fucking guy on the planet, and I am so damn lucky he even looks at me." The smile he sent my way was filled with so much tenderness, it took my breath away.

A bit disconcerted, Tommy blinked and mumbled, "I just want him to be with someone who cares about him and treats him right."

"I fucking care. I care more than I'm going to share with you, because it's none of your damn business. It's about Davis and me and how we are together. Not me proving myself to you."

I sat quiet and watched them face off. Tommy looked as though he wanted to take Carson's head off and eat it for breakfast, when a funny thing happened. Tommy grinned.

"Well, okay. I'm thinking you're the real deal." He held out a hand. "Looks like Davis finally got himself a man with some balls."

"Last time I checked, yeah." Carson smirked, and they shook, and then Carson put his arm around me. I didn't mind him showing affection in the office this time.

"Well, I gotta get back on the road home. Got my car in some garage, and parking in this fucking city is ridiculous. Davis, I'll call you."

Once he left, Carson said, "First the parents, now the best friend. Anyone else you've got ready to pop out of the woodwork?"

"Nope. I think you're safe."

Brian was upstate and had no idea where I was, and I had every intention of keeping it that way.

CHAPTER TWENTY-SIX

Davis

"We're having a guest speaker tonight. Any idea who it is?" I asked Kelly, who'd gotten to class before me. Patricia had stopped by the office with Brooke on their way home from the park, and I'd lost track of the time playing with her.

"Nah. Probably some judge or lawyer again. How's things? It was nice finally getting the guys together. Mark really liked Carson."

"Same here. Carson said we should do it again soon. Mark's a cool guy."

The four of us had managed to coordinate our schedules and meet for dinner over the past weekend—Carson had wanted to thank Mark for expediting the change of Brooke's birth certificate, which would allow her to take Dale's last name, and he was still working on whether she was entitled to Dale's death benefits. Patricia had moved Lia and the baby in with her—Lia was finishing up her GED and working at Saks Fifth Avenue, leaving a more than happy and willing

Patricia to take care of Brooke during the day.

Kelly winked. "I only hang out with the best."

The door to the lecture hall opened, and our professor walked in with a man two steps behind him. My stomach bottomed out.

Fuck, no. It can't be.

I ducked my head behind my laptop as our professor made the introductions.

"Ladies and gentlemen, tonight's guest speaker is Mayor Brian Healy, who is also the president of the upstate bar association, which encompasses over ten counties and includes the capital city of Albany. At the age of thirty, he was elected mayor of Harleyville, New York, and has since been reelected three times. He's in town for a conference and has graciously agreed to come here tonight to teach you about governmental filings and the importance of business record-keeping."

Oh God, I'm going to be sick.

My head spun, and Kelly leaned in close. "Are you okay? You look like you're about to throw up."

I wanted to get up and run, but if I did that, I'd only draw more attention to myself.

"I'm fine."

Brian hadn't lost any of his charm, and for thirty minutes kept the class enthralled, weaving stories of actual case law with examples of the correct way to handle confidential government files. He easily fielded questions from the audience, and with the time inching closer to the end of class, I was able to breathe a little easier, but wouldn't feel safe until I was up and gone.

Of course, Kelly had to ask a question.

"Mayor Healy, how do you verify chain of custody?"

All I could do was keep my face buried behind my laptop screen, my head down, and pray Brian answered the question quickly.

I should've known better.

"That's a great question, and I have a story." He launched into a retelling of a case that occurred while I was working for him. I'd discovered a major fault in how our sheriff's office had handled the collection of evidence. It ended up a big scandal with the sheriff resigning and Brian looking like a hero for catching a corrupt public official. In actuality, I was the one who'd caught the lying bastard.

"I'm afraid our time is up," our professor stated. "Join me in thanking Mayor Healy for his excellent lecture."

Everyone applauded and Brian waited for the adoration to die down before speaking. "Thank you for allowing me to come tonight and speak with you. If you have any questions, I'll put my email up on the board. Feel free to contact me anytime."

I waited for a large group to surround Brian before shoving my laptop into my bag. "I gotta go," I mumbled to Kelly.

"Yeah, take it easy tonight. Hope you feel better."

I threw him a quick smile and hurried out of the lecture hall. Anxiety nipping at my heels, I waited for the elevator to come, but when it finally opened, too many pushed their way in ahead of me, and I was stuck waiting.

I was being foolish. Brian was busy with the people bombarding him with questions, and there were also close to a hundred students in the class. Most likely, he hadn't even seen me.

"Davis. It is you."

A heavy hand fell on my shoulder and held me firmly in its grasp. Panic erupted inside me at his touch, and I twisted out from his grip.

"I'm sorry, but I have to leave." The elevator came, and I rushed inside, only to have Brian slip in behind me.

"I recognized you the moment I walked in. I sensed you there, and when I looked up, you were right in front of me."

I said nothing and stared straight ahead.

"You look wonderful."

I blinked and cursed the fact that the class was on the sixth floor.

"I missed you," he whispered and reached for me.

"Don't touch me," I spat out, batting away his hand. "Leave me alone."

The elevator doors opened and I dashed out, pushing past the lingering students in the hallway. Out on the sidewalk, I didn't want to take the chance of waiting for a car, so I headed for the subway two blocks away. Across the street from the school, Brian caught up to me.

"Please talk to me." He took my arm, and before I could break free, kissed me full on the mouth. Stunned, I hesitated a moment, which he took advantage of by pushing his tongue past my lips. I shoved him off me.

"Don't you ever fucking touch me again, or I'll bite it off next time you try and stick it in my mouth," I snarled and strode off, but my threats didn't deter him and he kept pace.

"Why won't you talk to me?"

Sick to my stomach from the feel of his tongue in my mouth, I rounded on him. "You're married. Leave me alone. I'm with someone else now."

"I don't love her," he whined, his mouth drooping with petulance. How weak and pathetic he was, and I wondered what I ever saw in him. "I love you."

"No, you don't. You love yourself. The only thing you care about is having everything you want and to hell with the rest of us."

"That's not true. Come back home with me. Don't you remember how good it was between us?" He followed me down the street.

"What I remember is that you're married, and I don't sleep with married men. What don't you understand about that?"

"I'll get you a job in Albany and an apartment. I'm there twice a month. We can be together."

"You're out of your mind. You think I'm going to settle for being some back-door boyfriend?" I shook my head. "And didn't you hear what I said? I have a partner now, and we love each other. Please. Just leave me alone and go home."

"I'll leave her."

"What?" Despite myself, I stopped midstride.

"I'll divorce her, and we can be together."

"You'll divorce her," I repeated. "The mother of your child. You're going to walk away from your wife and baby even though I've told you I don't want you."

"Yes, you do. You told me you loved me."

"What I'm telling you *for the last time* is to leave me alone. If you don't, I'll get a restraining order against you. I don't want you. I don't love you. Is it worth losing your career, wife, and child for someone who doesn't give a damn?"

"You loved me once."

"No." I made sure to meet him face on. "That wasn't love. Go home, Brian. Forget about me, the way I forgot about you."

"Davis? Is everything okay?"

Kelly stood a few steps away, his brows pulled together. Relief such as I've never known filled my chest.

"Kelly, sorry, I forgot about our coffee study session. It's not too late, right?"

"No, I'm ready if you are. Thanks for the lecture again, Mayor Healy."

God bless him for picking up on my hidden signals.

Brian grunted and stomped away. I scrubbed my face with my hands and heaved out a sigh. "I have never been so glad to see you. That was hairy."

"What the hell was that all about? Do you *know* him?"

I spotted a Starbucks half a block away. "Do you have time to sit for a few?"

"Yeah, sure, lemme just text Mark and let him know I'm gonna be late."

We got to the coffee shop where Kelly found us seats, and I waited in line to order, then texted Carson.

Be home soon.

Why so late?

I debated telling him but didn't want it to be over text because I knew he'd call me immediately and demand the entire story. As much as I loved Carson, I needed a few minutes to decompress.

Something happened in class. Nothing's wrong, and it's all fine now. I'll be home in less than an hour.

Okay, but we'll talk then.

Yes, sir.

I added a winky-face, and he responded with a frown.

I picked up our coffees, joined Kelly, and gave him an abbreviated version of my relationship with Brian. As I spoke, his eyes grew wider and wider, and he kept muttering, "I don't fucking believe it," over and over. I finished and gulped my now-cold coffee, while he rubbed his chin, studying me.

"What?" I asked him.

"Does Carson know?"

"About Brian? Yeah. I've told him."

Kelly chewed his lip. "Wow, I'm like…still fucking floored. He seemed so cool and nice. I would've thought he'd be a dream to work for."

"He was," I said grimly. "Until he became a nightmare I almost couldn't escape."

"Hopefully, he'll leave you alone now. You told him no and that you're with someone. That should be enough."

But I wasn't so sure. Brian didn't give up easily. And after what he'd told Tommy that time? That I belonged with him? An involuntary shiver prickled through me.

"It has to be. I'd better go. I sent Carson a cryptic message, and knowing him, he's already pacing the floor, waiting for me to get home so we can talk."

"I'm glad to hear you're going to tell him you saw Brian tonight. Secrets between partners are never good."

Something in Kelly's tone made me guess he was speaking from experience.

"You and Mark had a problem?"

Darkness clouded Kelly's eyes. "Yeah. A few months into our relationship, Mark cheated. He got drunk at an office holiday party, and someone in his office blew him in the bathroom."

"Jesus, Kel. I'm sorry." That admission rocked me to the core.

"It hurt like fucking hell, but I was glad he came and told me, instead of trying to hide it."

"I guess…"

The pain on Kelly's face was evident. "He apologized and cried, but I almost broke it off. Mark swore it was the one and only time, but it made me doubt myself. Like, why would that happen? Wasn't I enough for him?"

I didn't like seeing my friend hurting, and I put my hand over his. "Sure you are. And drunk is never an excuse. How has it been since? Do you trust him now?"

"Yes. I do." His smile was genuine. "It took a while, but we're celebrating our five-year wedding anniversary this year. We've been together nine years, so the incident—as I like to call it—is almost a faded memory. Maybe before that happened, he was a bit of a flirt, but he's settled down. Mark's loving and devoted and is always coming home with flowers or little gifts to surprise me. I know he does it as a gesture to show how much he loves me, but I don't need that. All I want is the man I love, at my side and in my bed."

"I understand. And I'm so glad you two worked it out,

because I can tell you really do love each other."

"So do you and Carson. When we had dinner, I could see he's totally into you and your needs. Make sure when you go home tonight, you tell him everything."

"Everything?" My brow puckered. "What're you talking about?"

"I saw Brian kiss you."

My jaw dropped. "I didn't want that. He forced himself on me."

"I know, but if I saw it, someone else might have too. And Brian might run into Carson one day and try and twist it around. Get in front of it now and tell Carson exactly what happened."

"I plan to. I'd better get home. Knowing Carson, he might send out a search party." I called for a car.

"Yeah. Me too. Text me tomorrow and let me know how it went."

"I will," I promised, and we said good-bye, separating in front of the coffee shop. Kelly walked to the train station, and I got into my car.

I opened the door to the apartment, and Carson was waiting for me. He pounced on me and held me at arm's length, his gaze locked on mine. "You look okay. So what happened?"

"Can I come inside, at least?" I laughed. "And I am okay." I set my laptop bag on the table, and with Carson at my heels, sat on the couch in the living room. I clasped my hands. "Tonight's guest lecture in class was given by Brian."

"Brian?" he repeated, his brow furrowed, and then recognition hit him and his brows flew up. "Brian. Fuck."

"That was my initial response too. And I thought I did a good job of hiding behind my laptop, but it wasn't good enough. He followed me out of the classroom, into the elevator, and out to the street."

To his credit, Carson held his temper until I told him

about the kiss. As expected, that was when he lost it.

"The fucking hell he touched you," he raged. "That's assault. He needs to be arrested."

"No, please, Carson. It's done, and all I want is to forget it."

"But he thinks—"

"I don't care what he thinks. You know why? Because we love each other, which means he can't hurt us. I told him if he didn't stay away, I would get a restraining order."

"And I'd go right over to the precinct with you. He had no right to accost you like that. I'm telling you, the man is dangerous."

"He's pathetic," I insisted. "Imagine living a lie your whole life and being too scared to be yourself, simply for a career. Nothing is worth that, no amount of money or title. I hated being Brian's secret. It made me feel dirty. Like a second-class citizen."

"You deserve everything. The best."

"I've got that. I have you."

"That calls for a hug." Carson pulled me in close, and I settled against him with a sigh. "You're never second with me. First in my thoughts and always first in my heart. By the way, I spoke to your parents today—they called when you were in class." Carson's lips tickled my jaw.

"Yeah? What's going on? I know my mother's checkup last week went well."

"Why didn't you tell me about their medical bills?"

I stiffened. "What're you talking about?"

Solemn eyes met mine. "Your father let it slip that the preferred medicine for your mother's condition was too expensive because of the debt they're already dealing with."

"I've helped where I can, but I can't pay it all off for them. With interest, it's ballooned to over fifty thousand dollars."

He touched my lips with a gentle kiss. "Not anymore."

Stunned, I pushed him away. "What do you mean?"

"I'm paying it off for them. Greg was reluctant to accept right away, but I told him that's what family does for each other—help when you have the means necessary. You know I have assets from my great-grandmother's trust, more than I can use in a lifetime."

Still unable to wrap my head around that, I rubbed my face. "But…you paid their debt? Carson, that's the most incredibly generous, selfless thing anyone's ever done for us."

His cheeks flushed bright red. "I just wanted to make you happy. And them. It can't be good for your parents to have that kind of stress hanging over their heads. And no one should have to sacrifice proper medical care because of money." His lips kicked up in a devilish grin. "And I'm not completely selfless. I know you're usually tired after class, but I figured maybe I'll get lucky tonight." He winked at me, and I fell against him, whooping with laughter.

"You're such a sap." I rubbed my cheek to his chest, thinking how incredibly lucky we were to have each other.

Bright eyes twinkling, Carson kissed the tip of my nose. "I prefer to think of myself as romantic."

"You are. And not because of what you've done tonight, but because of all the little things you do that make me fall for you, every day, over and over again."

"I only want the best for you. And that's me." That teasing grin grew wide and wicked, and my heart hurt from all the happiness it held inside.

"Oh, brother." I snorted. "Quit while you're ahead, lover boy. Now let's go to bed so I can thank you properly."

He pulled me to standing. "I thought you'd never ask."

EPILOGUE

Carson

"Shh, shh." I put my fingers to my lips. "He'll be here in five minutes."

Everyone quieted down, and Jenny asked, "Do you really think he's going to be surprised?"

"He has no clue. He knows I'm not into parties, and we went out to dinner on the night of his actual graduation. This morning I played to perfection the part of having the world's worst stomach virus. He couldn't wait to get out of the apartment."

Eyes dancing, she shook her finger at me. "You are terrible. But brilliant."

"Why, thank you. I'll take that as a compliment."

"You already know I think you're wonderful. And not simply for paying off our medical bills, which still makes me tear up." She squeezed my arm. "I've never seen Davis so happy. He told me you weren't into parties, and for you to throw him this party and include us…it means everything to me."

I knew she'd be delirious if I told her what else I had planned, but she and everyone else would have to be satisfied with a hearsay rendition. That moment would be for Davis and me alone.

"I'm happy you're happy."

Davis had graduated with his paralegal certificate two days earlier, and I'd been planning his graduation party for three months. I knew he was stressing about the results of the LSAT he took, which were due any day now, so I figured having everyone he loved around to celebrate his accomplishment would make him feel better and take his mind off waiting for the email from the Law School Admissions Council.

Jenny and Greg had flown in the day before, and this time were happy to stay in the suite I'd booked for them. Giving credit where it was due, my mother had offered her apartment as a venue and helped with the menu and flowers, and she and Charles, now her steady companion, were busy chatting with Davis's parents. Tommy and his wife, Carrie, along with their girls, had made the trip into the city, and Lia had introduced Brooke to them. All four little girls were having a great time in the play area my mother had set aside for them, along with her housekeeper to watch over them.

Patrick the doorman sent me the prearranged signal that Davis was on his way up.

"He's here," I announced and shushed everyone.

They ran to the dining room, where my mother had an incredible buffet set up. I waited by the door, and when the bell rang, I opened it to his tired, smiling face.

"Hi."

"Hi, yourself." I leaned in for a kiss, but he took a step away. "How's your stomach?"

"Fine. I guess I should come clean and admit that in the middle of the night, I had an ice-cream craving. I might've demolished your pint of coffee chip."

His eyes grew wide. "You did not. I was saving it for tonight."

I took advantage of those full, pouting lips to snag a kiss. "Oh, don't whine. I'm sure my mother will have a little something special in her refrigerator. She always keeps treats for Brooke."

"Not coffee chip ice cream," he complained.

"Aw, poor baby. Come on. Let's go to the kitchen and see. If you want, we can order some later when we get home."

Hand in hand, we walked into the dim apartment, and as we turned the corner, Davis had only enough time to ask, "Where's Pa—" before everyone jumped out of the dining room to yell, "Surprise!"

He dropped my hand. "What? What's going on? Wait… what's happening?"

Jenny rushed up to get the first hug. "Carson planned this surprise graduation party for you, and we're all here. Isn't that amazing?"

"He is amazing." Eyes shiny with tears, Davis mouthed, *Thank you*, over Jenny's head. I hung back, watching him accept everyone's congratulations. Tommy and Carrie approached, Tommy giving him a shoulder slap I'd wager set Davis's ears ringing.

"Dude, you did it. Way to go."

"Ouch. Thanks." Davis rubbed his shoulder. "Keep those moose hands to yourself."

"We're so proud of you," Carrie gushed and hugged him tight. "And the girls love Carson's little niece."

Brooke was certainly her father's daughter, possessing a charming smile when things went her way, but if you told her no, look out. I'd swear my eardrums were permanently scarred. To her credit, Lia was doing her best not to spoil her, despite my mother's way-too-frequent trips to the toy store.

"I still can't believe you're all here. Mom, Dad, I want you to meet everyone. Kelly and Mark—Kelly graduated with me." A glass of champagne was shoved in his hand. "We did it!" He flung an arm over Kelly's shoulder.

"Next stop, law school…maybe?"

"Guess we'll find out any day now," Davis said. "I checked right before I came here, and still nothing."

Charles Wallace shook both Davis's and Kelly's hands. "I heard the results were to be released today, so keep checking."

"A toast to the graduates," I shouted out with a raised glass.

Everyone drank to their success, and in no time, the dinner was demolished. A big cake with a graduation hat was brought out and cut up. Knowing for the most part how awful nondairy cakes tasted, I wouldn't force everyone to suffer through it, and watched as they stuffed their faces with Davis's favorite cannoli cream.

"Poor baby." Davis gave me a creamy-sweet kiss on the lips. "No cake for you?"

I caught him around the waist and dived in for another kiss. "I'll get my own special Davis-slice later tonight." I nibbled on his lips.

Waving his phone, Kelly called out from across the room, "Davis, results are in."

The room grew quiet, and Davis appealed to me with his big beautiful eyes, I knew exactly what to do.

"Sorry, everyone." I took him by the hand and pulled him into the living room, where we sat on the couch.

"If you don't want to look at it now, you don't have to. They'll understand."

"It's silly, right? I mean…it's a test score. And if I didn't do well, I can always retake it."

"Absolutely. If at first you don't succeed…"

With a firm nod, he took his phone from his pocket and

opened the mail app. "It's slow logging in to the account. Must be all the traffic." He scrolled for a moment, stopped and hit the screen. Not a muscle moved on his face as he read the email.

"Tell me."

He blinked and handed it to me with a shrug.

Dammit.

I scanned past the standard nonsense, going straight to where I remembered the score would be from my own test results.

"Hot fucking damn. 174?" I grabbed him and kissed him full on the mouth until we were both gasping. "That's almost perfect. I knew you'd nail it. I knew it."

"I can't believe it. I never thought I'd be a lawyer."

I hugged him tight. "You can be anything you want to be."

"I appreciate the confidence, but I think heart or brain surgeon might be a stretch."

"More like waiter. You know, since we've been down that road already?" I smirked and held him at arm's length to gaze into the face I needed to see first thing in the morning and couldn't fall asleep without having next to me on the pillow every night. Loving Davis had become as natural as the next breath I took. And as necessary.

"A fact you never let me forget. You're going to tell that story for the next twenty years, aren't you?"

"Maybe longer. Like…forever?" I reached into my suit jacket pocket and pulled out a platinum band. "Marry me?"

"Marry you…Carson, what are you talking about? Are you serious?"

The overhead light caught the gleam of the ring in the palm of my hand. "Do I look like I'm joking?"

"But you said you didn't believe in marriage, that you weren't interested in it. That we're fine as we are."

I scowled but then noticed his lips twitching. I studied

the ring. "Maybe I made a mistake."

"You don't make mistakes."

"You mean I'm perfect? Thank you." Davis remained annoyingly, frustratingly serious.

"You are perfect. For me. But I don't want you to think you have to marry me to keep me with you." A warm, soft kiss to my lips followed those words, and I held him near, so near that I could feel his smile in the air between us and hear the beat of his heart if I listened hard enough. He kissed me again. "Every day I fall for you, over and over again. I'll stay with you forever, if that's what you want."

"I want you." I slipped the ring on his finger. "And I have a matching one for me."

"Where is it?"

I reached into my pocket and held it out. Davis took it from me, and I held his hand with the ring gleaming on his finger. "I never thought of having you wear the ring as keeping you with me forever. It was more to show that I was the lucky one to have found you."

"We're both lucky. You're mine, and I intend for everyone to know it." A beautiful glow radiated from his face. "So let's roll the dice together and win it all." I held out my hand, and he slipped the ring onto my finger.

Thank you so much for reading Carson and Davis's story! I hope if you enjoyed it, you'll consider leaving a review. Reviews are the lifeblood for independent authors. The more reviews, the more it helps our books get seen by the reading public.

If you're interested in reading more of my books, visit my **Payhip Store**, where I offer a wide selection of my books at a discount.

Did you enjoy this meet not-so-cute as much as I enjoyed writing it? **If you subscribe to my newsletter**, you get a FREE copy of my first self-published book, *Memories of the Heart*, where another not-so-meet cute takes place between the arrogant Dr. Micah Steinberg and sweet, down to earth Josh Rosen takes place.

FELICE STEVENS writes romance because what is better than people falling in love? Her favorite part of a romance novel is that first kiss…sigh. She loves creating stories of hopes and dreams and happily ever afters. Her stories are character-driven, rich with the sights, sounds and flavors of New York City and filled with men who are sometimes deeply flawed but always real.

Felice writes gay romance because she believes that everyone deserves a happily ever after. Having traveled all over the world, she can safely say that the universal language that unites people is love. Felice has written in a variety of sub-genres, including contemporary, paranormal, and she has a mystery series as well. You can find all her book listed on her website.

Felice is a two-time Lambda Literary Award nominee and the Lambda award-winner in Gay Romance for her book, *The Ghost and Charlie Muir*.

BOOKBUB
https://www.bookbub.com/profile/felice-stevens

NEWSLETTER
https://tinyurl.com/y85e69ab

READER GROUP
https://www.facebook.com/groups/FelicesBreakfastClub/

FACEBOOK AUTHOR PAGE
https://www.facebook.com/felicestevensauthor/

INSTAGRAM
https://www.instagram.com/felicestevens

GOODREADS
https://www.goodreads.com/author/show/8432880.Felice_Stevens

WEBSITE
felicestevens.com

PAYHIP STORE
https://payhip.com/FeliceStevensAuthor

9 7 9 8 8 8 9 4 9 0 1 0 4